BREAKING JESS

BREAKING JESS

H.B. MOORE

USA Today Bestselling Author

Mirror Press

Cover design by Rachael Anderson
Cover image: Deposit Photos #33834511
Interior design by Cora Johnson
Edited by Haley Swan and Lisa Russo Leigh

Published by Mirror Press, LLC

ISBN: 978-1-947152-47-2

Thrillers by H.B. Moore

1

LOGAN

THE MOMENT A patient walks through my office door, I can usually assess him right away. Does he make eye contact? Does he make the first move to shake my hand? Does he slouch in his chair?

My second patient of the day is Charles Harper. Immediately I know he's going to be a challenge. He makes eye contact, his expression closed, which tells me he's not here for counseling but to argue.

"Good morning," I greet Charles as I swing the office door wide to let him in. We shake hands, and not surprisingly, he has a firm grip.

He's not a tall man, perhaps five-nine max, and his hair is prematurely gray. Based on the birth date in his case file, I expected to see a man in his thirties. What I get instead is a man who's twenty-seven in age but whose appearance leans more toward his fifties.

His skin is sallow and pulls about his eyes—not from laugh lines but from squinting. He wears a dress shirt that was probably once pressed. His khakis are ill fitting, and I wonder if he's recently lost weight. It's hard to say, though. Some computer geeks could care less about appearance. Charles wears glasses, fitting the computer engineering stereotype to a T. He also carries a recording device. This should have been my first clue that Charles has some extreme personality traits, though I always try to stay open minded in first sessions.

I'm a firm believer that although a patient might not be facing or dealing with reality as most of us know it, their reality is real to *them*.

Charles's voice is low as he says, "Hello, Dr. Mayer."

"Call me Logan." I gesture to an overstuffed chair.

I find that a couch creates too much of a stigma, so I keep three overstuffed chairs in my office. My desk is positioned in the corner—unobtrusive and out of the way. And I have a view over the Pacific Ocean. Not too shabby.

There are definite perks to living in the beach town of La Jolla.

Charles's gaze is drawn to the churning surf beyond the large window. The morning is overcast, and the weather report predicts afternoon rain. Otherwise, the temperature is mild for mid-February.

"Where did you grow up, Charles?" I ask, using a proven icebreaker.

He takes his time in answering, and for a moment I wonder if he's heard me or perhaps gone into one of the trances that I read about in his medical file.

"Not far from here," he finally says.

"A local, then?" I say.

Charles turns to face me. His blue eyes are dull against the gray light from the window. Something in them shifts, and not for the first time, I wish that I could read minds—it would make my job so much easier.

Perhaps not in Charles's case, though. His engineering company has sent him here because he's had blackouts on the job. After going through various tests at the hospital, the medical professionals decided that the causes of his blackouts might be psychological.

Enter: *me.*

I know from his file that his parents are dead. He has a sister who's a full-time resident in a psychiatric ward—I plan to explore that avenue—and he has a great-uncle, who lives in a retirement community in Arizona.

No wife, no kids, and I'm assuming no girlfriend. Though I'm the last person to assume anything. Charles probably makes decent money, and there might be a girl out there somewhere for him.

When Charles meanders to the overstuffed chair and takes a seat. I sit as well. Charles holds the recorder loosely in one hand so that I'll see it—here I am, assuming again.

I sit across from him and settle a notebook on my lap. I take notes, but mostly it's to show the client that I'm paying attention. I have a surveillance camera in my office that will record the entire conversation. Later, the office receptionist will type it up. Sandra is one of those saucy, no-nonsense women and does secretary work for the three therapists in our office suite. I'm a psychiatrist, and the other two are psychologists. Sandra is the epitome of keeping confidences, a must-have attribute in our line of work.

"I've been in La Jolla for only a couple of years, but I love it," I say. When Charles doesn't respond, I continue, "Tell me about what's been going on with your blackouts, Charles." I poise my pen over the notebook.

He exhales, and I have a sense that our session together might be a bit slow going. I'm already dragging the simple responses from him.

"I've been having blackouts a couple of years," Charles

says after a moment. "In other words, I pass out and don't remember what happened."

I'm surprised since I distinctly remember reading that the blackouts started only a few weeks ago. I lean forward. "Tell me about the first one."

Another exhale, and his gaze strays to the window. "It was on my way home from visiting my sister. I started to feel extremely nauseated, and so I pulled my car over on the side of the road. I woke up with my head resting against the steering wheel and someone knocking on the window."

It's a miracle he didn't crash his car. "How long do you think you were unconscious?" I ask.

"A few minutes," he says. "I'm not sure, though. I mean, it could have been longer."

"When was the second episode?"

"The very next week on a Tuesday again." His voice grows hard, and his gaze flicks back to me. "It always happens on a Tuesday—that's the day I visit Jessie. Every week."

"Jessie's your sister, right?" I ask, and he nods. I'm trying to read his expression. His voice has changed when he speaks of his sister, as if he resents her for some reason. I won't connect the visit to his sister with his blackout episodes just yet. That would be too simple. There are many factors—time of day, temperature, hunger, dehydration . . . all could play a part. But the medical records I read through have already dismissed most of those reasons.

"Tell me about her," I continue.

He laughs.

Charles doesn't have a jovial laugh, one that might be contagious or make you feel like smiling or laughing too. No, his laugh is grating, almost staccato. I write down this observation even though it will be plain in the video recording when I listen to it.

"I'm not crazy like her, if that's what you're getting at," Charles says, rising to his feet.

I have no idea who his sister is, so I'm not getting *at* anything. I watch him walk to the window. There's no rule that says he has to sit down during our session, but it always puts me on edge when a patient starts to wander my office. I could easily overpower a man his size, if it came to that. And I'm quite proficient on the shooting range now—something I've prided myself in ever since getting my concealed weapon permit. I always hope I will never need to use it.

"Is your sister crazy?" I ask, knowing it could be opening a can of worms. But that's why we're here, right?

Charles turns from the window. "I'll let you determine that, Dr. Mayer. Go ahead and google her. I need to get back to work. In other words, I have things to do."

I think my mouth drops open as he strides out of my office. I hear Sandra say, "Have a good day, sir."

Charles doesn't answer her. I know he's not returning to his office since he's on work release.

I stand and walk into the reception area, where I see him climb into a car that's probably an Uber since Charles's driver's license has been suspended.

"That was quick," Sandra observes in a dry tone.

I nod and watch the car pull out of the parking lot as the first raindrops fall. I turn to look at Sandra. She's dressed in purple today. The thing about Sandra is that she goes all out in whatever her daily choice of color scheme happens to be. A matching top and necklace isn't enough. Her shoes will also match, as well as her earrings, bracelets, and most times, even her makeup. Her age is indeterminable. Between the other therapists in the office, we guess mid-forties. "Let me know when my ten o'clock is here."

Sandra lifts a single eyebrow. "Of course, Dr. Mayer."

I have nearly thirty minutes until my next client arrives,

and of course I allow curiosity to overtake me and I do a Google search on Jessica Harper.

An entire series of articles come up, one as recent as two years ago, which is titled "Where is Jessica Harper now?" I click on the link.

The San Diego Chronicle *recently attempted to contact Jessica Harper, who has been dubbed Jessica the Reaper. She currently resides in the San Diego Psychiatry Care Facility as a full-time resident. Her medical adviser reports that Jessica will not be doing any interviews as long as she is under their care.*

Jessica Harper was sentenced to full-time psychiatric care when, at the age of sixteen, she was accused of killing her parents, Richard and Lisa Harper. Jessica claimed to have no memory of the murders or any of the events leading up to the crime. She was diagnosed with a dissociative disorder during the trial proceedings and was then moved to the San Diego unit.

Richard and Lisa Harper were found in their bed with their throats slit on June 29. Their oldest son was at scout camp, and their daughter was the only other person in the home at the time. No sign of intrusion was discovered. Jessica claims she discovered her parents in their bed, already deceased, when she called 911.

Previous articles on the case state that Jessica was a troubled teenager and frequently fought with her parents over curfew and boys.

I skim the rest, my heart in my throat. It's a tragedy all the way around, and one that I probably had heard of at one point but hadn't fully processed. I think of the parents—sleeping—and wonder what their last thoughts were moments before they died. What did they see?

How was Charles told of the tragedy? Did a Boy Scout

counselor come to his tent and break the news? And then I think of Jessica, a teenaged girl who claimed to not remember killing her own parents. Whatever she did or didn't remember, her life was forever altered by her actions. And now it seems that the effects of that tragedy are still crippling her brother. The powers of mental health and mental illness absolutely affect the physical well-being, as Charles has so recently found out.

Chapter 2

I DON'T WANT my brother to come, but no matter how much I protest, Marlene forces me to dress, and I obey. Marlene is at least six inches taller than me, and her shoulders are as broad as any man's. There's also the fact that she has the power to order me into a straitjacket.

My stomach has been hurting since Monday morning, although this is nothing new. My brother visits each Tuesday afternoon. So from Tuesday evening through Sunday evening, I don't have to think about him. From the moment I awake on Monday, my body knows what's coming the next day. I can't keep food down. I can't sleep Monday nights. I want to do anything, and everything, to prevent the visit.

When I see my brother, I remember that my parents are gone, and they're never coming back. And I remember that it's my fault.

"Brush your hair," Marlene says, handing me the hairbrush.

It's a soft-handle brush, one that all the patients are given. I don't look in the mirror as I brush my hair. Nothing about me has changed in the nine years that I've lived here. Nothing about me ever changes. My hair is a dull blonde and hangs straight down my back. My eyes are blue like my brother's, and my mother's. If I'm ever released, I'll get colored contacts so that my eye color can be anything but blue.

I keep my nails cut short so that when I garden in the center's small vegetable plot I can wash easier. I inherited my dad's height, so I'm an inch taller than my brother. It used to vex him, but he never comments on it anymore.

In fact, he hardly ever talks to me on his visits. He speaks to the nurses, goes over my medication list, then sits across from me in the recreation room while he scrolls through his phone.

Once, I tried to take the phone from him when he was visiting in my room. Some of the patients here have phone privileges, but my brother has always made it clear that I cannot. He yelled for the nurse. When she came running, my brother told her I'd stolen his phone and tried to attack him.

My computer privileges were revoked for seven days. Some weeks, I think the only thing that is keeping me alive is the hour I can spend on the computer each day. It gives me something to look forward to in my life of routine, and I've enjoyed researching all kinds of things.

"Do you want to change your clothing?" Marlene asks.

"No," I say. I'm wearing my gardening shirt and pants. Dirt stains a few areas, but I plan to garden again after my brother leaves. Thankfully, Marlene doesn't argue with me. She always seems to get her way, although I usually put up a fight.

Someone knocks on my bedroom door, and I know it's time.

Marlene opens the door, and I follow her into the corridor. Patrick is there, waiting to take me to the recreation room where my brother will be waiting. I refuse to allow him into my room anymore, not after he accused me of attacking him.

I may not remember what happened the night my parents died, but I haven't forgotten a thing since then.

Patrick is a large, lumbering man, with skin the color of chocolate. He also laughs with his whole body. When he started working here a few years ago, we became instant friends. This is unusual for me, since I have only two friends: Patrick and Erin.

Erin is another patient, about ten years older than me, and she doesn't have visitors, ever. She won't talk about her family, and it's just as well, because if I ever met anyone in her family, I would go on the attack and lose privileges for much longer than a week. If the scars that crisscross all the way up her arms are any indication of her former trauma, I'm more than happy to stand up for her.

No one stands up for me. Not really. Patrick might—but even he leaves me alone with my brother.

"Jessie," my brother says as I step into the recreation room. There are about seven or eight other patients scattered about the room, in addition to two attendants. My brother is standing by the never-used fireplace, holding a gift bag. This makes me curious but in no way helps me relax.

"Hi, Charlie," I say in a dutiful voice, proving that I can be well behaved. My brother knows I hate the nickname Jessie, and he likewise hates the name Charlie. He says that Charles is more sophisticated, but I don't care.

Charlie crosses to me, holding out the gift bag, a bright smile on his face. I am probably the only one in the room not fooled by his fake smile. "Happy birthday, sis."

I am twenty-five today, which means that I've lived in this place for nearly ten years. I want to spit in my brother's face. I want to slam my fist into those yellowing teeth of his. I want to watch his eye swell with a bruise delivered by me.

I can feel Patrick watching me, closely, as he should.

Instead of following my instinct, I reach for the gift bag. Standing in the middle of the room, with the other patients watching, I pull out the white tissue paper. Beneath is a hardbound, white children's book. I read the title. "Put Me in the Zoo."

"Remember?" my brother says. "It was one of your favorite stories as a kid. I thought I'd give you something to bring back memories."

It's the cruelest gift I could imagine.

Memories . . . of my parents . . . who everyone thinks I murdered. The memories of reading the book with my mom at night crash around me and make me feel breathless.

I slip the book back into the bag and manage to mumble a thank-you.

Charles sighs with exasperation. "Well, aren't you at least going to look through it?"

I can't do this. He is mocking me. Just like he always has, just like he always did.

I cross to a chair to sit down, then look about the room, fighting a swell of tears. I am in a zoo right now. Erin is sitting at the puzzle table, intent on fitting tiny shapes with other tiny shapes. Mona, an older woman in her sixties, is sketching at the art table, drawing pictures of her hallucinations. One of the aides hovers over her so that Mona doesn't eat one of the crayons. She has a wax fixation. Nicole is younger than me, and she stands by the double-paned windows and watches the clouds skirt across the sky. Every conversation I've had with her has been about clouds and the weather.

I hold the gift bag on my lap, but once Charles leaves, I'll throw it away. He pulls a chair next to me. It seems he wants to speak with me today. I don't look at him, though. I don't want to see his blue eyes—the same blue eyes that I have. From my peripheral vision, I see him scratch the side of his head, as if he's at a loss for words. Which would be unusual for Charles, at least around me.

"I received a phone call from your nurse," he says in a low voice.

I've never liked the way my brother smells. He's been using the same soap for years, and it has a sharp antiseptic scent to it. One would think that because I live in a mental health facility I'd be used to that smell or wouldn't mind it. But in truth, this psychiatric center smells of Febreze, not like a sterile hospital.

"You know that your medications can't be adjusted," he continues.

I still don't look at him.

"You don't want the headaches to come back, Jessie."

I bristle at the use of his nickname. I shouldn't let it bother me—I am a grown woman, after all. I meet his gaze with my own blue eyes. "What if I can find the right medication that fixes my memory?"

We've discussed this before, and he seems to take a calming breath. "Do you want to go through a trial again? The hell of months and months of questions from lawyers and reporters and more doctor appointments?" He waves his hand about the recreation room. "At least here you have peace."

I exhale. Here, I am already in prison. "I want to remember," I say in a low voice. "My therapist thinks if I remember that I'll get better because remembering will start the healing process."

"Look at you," Charles says in a mocking voice. "You sound like one of those goons already. What happens when you remember? The courts won't believe in the mentally incompetent plea anymore. You'll be kicked out of here and have to stand trial all over again. In other words, you'll go to prison, Jessie. *Prison!*"

The last word is like a sharp jab to my stomach. My mouth goes dry as I watch my brother's eyes bulge with his anger.

He continues, despite the fact that my hands are shaking as I grip the gift bag handle. "What are you reading during your computer time?" he asks. "Maybe you should stay off that thing."

My stomach roils. "No," I whisper. Not the computer. But one word from my brother and my computer privileges could be revoked.

Charles's hand wraps around my wrist, his fingers strong and biting into my flesh.

A distant memory filters through my mind—something from long ago. The way his fingers are locked around my wrist is familiar. Before I can dwell on the memory, he says, "No medication changes. Understood?"

"I understand." I blink back the hot tears threatening to spill out. I will not tell him that I've begun to skip doses. I have become an expert at deceit. I am, after all, a murderer.

CHAPTER 3

LOGAN

CHARLES IS LATE to our appointment the following week. I don't comment on it since I usually wait until the client is late more than once. Frankly, I wasn't even entirely sure he'd show up.

Sandra texts me that he's arrived, and I text back: *Let him in.* Moments later, Charles enters my office.

I rise to shake his hand, but he waves me off and sits in one of the overstuffed chairs.

Well then.

I move to sit across from him, notebook and pen in hand.

"My sister killed our parents nine and a half years ago," Charles says, his eyes focused on me.

I must admit, his statement is a bit unnerving, even though I've already done the research.

"I'm assuming you googled the incident," Charles continues.

"Yes," I say, holding his gaze. "Do you want to talk about it?"

"It's been years," he says. "I've talked about it plenty to those pediatric shrinks. But you need to make some sort of diagnosis as to why I'm blacking out, right?"

I nod and say, "Yes." This man is on a mission today. For what, I'm not sure yet.

"I remembered yesterday that my sister used to have extreme migraines and blackouts." He steeples his fingers. "What if I'm having the same type of thing and it's genetic?"

"Possibly," I say. "From what you told me last week, your blackouts might be related to your visits to your sister. Are they stressful?"

He laughs. A laugh that sends shivers along my skin for some reason.

"I'll let you be the judge of that."

"What?" I ask, confused now.

"I'm firing her therapist," he says, leaning forward. "I've done some research on you, and I'd like you to be my sister's therapist."

I don't speak for a moment. It's not the first time I've been asked to consult with more than one member of the family, sometimes together, sometimes separately.

"What's wrong with the therapist she has now?" I ask, keeping my tone mellow.

"Dr. Linpinski is not helping her see reason," Charles says. "She's giving my sister ideas that are unrealistic and recommending experimental drugs."

I don't know Dr. Linpinski. "Is she a psychiatrist?" I ask.

"No, but she consults with Jessie's doctor," he says. "But you can bypass the doctor and prescribe medication yourself."

"Yes," I say. I make sure every exchange between us is verbal so that it can all be typed up later in Sandra's transcription of the session. "What type of medication are you worried about?"

Charles rubs the side of his face. "You'll see when you access her records. It's written in the recommendations section." He drops his hand. "I can't be to every session or appointment with my sister, so I need someone I can trust to be there."

I stare at him, dumbfounded that I'm on his short list of trusted people. "You do know about patient-doctor confidentiality clauses?"

"Of course," Charles says, his face growing pink. "Jessie tells me what she wants of her own free will. But I am still responsible for her. In other words, I make all the decisions for her. She signed away her rights; otherwise, she'd be a ward of the state."

Something feels off here, but I can't put my finger on it. "So you can change your sister's doctors at any time?"

"I can," he says. "Although I haven't needed to until now." He pulls his phone out of his pocket. "Right before I came, I emailed you the medical transfer and cc'd Jessie's current doctor. As of this moment, you are her psychiatrist."

Most of my patients have been private patients. I've never treated anyone at the local psychiatric care center, although I interned years ago up north at another care center. The work is less rewarding for residential patients because they are living in such a controlled environment, surrounded by caregivers, that there seems little room for patient independence. Not that I'd recommend releasing the long-term patients out into the world in the first place. They wouldn't survive more than a few days.

I set my notebook aside. "Mr. Harper," I say. "Some patients don't do well with switching doctors. I don't want to interfere with your sister's routine."

"I understand your concern," Charles says. "That isn't the case here. I'll explain things to Jessie, and she'll cooperate. This is better for her in the long run. I won't have my sister being used as a guinea pig in the mental health industry. As her legal guardian, I've already made the decision. By the time you meet with her, she'll be apprised of the change."

"All right," I say, wondering what I've gotten myself into. "Now, let's talk about you and figure out your blackouts."

"Sure thing," he says with a half smile as if he is looking forward to the session. "Let's start with the day that my neighbor picked me up from scout camp and told me that my parents were dead."

I pick the notebook back up, and while he talks, I imagine a young man whose life was turned upside down in an instant. His story is of a typical California kid—not a surfing beach bum but one who excelled in his classes, had a couple of friends in the computer science club, and was looking forward to his senior year in high school. He'd already applied to a few college engineering programs, which he eventually completed after a year-long delay.

By the time he went to college, funded by a full academic scholarship, his sister was a full-time resident of the psychiatric unit of the local hospital, soon to be moved to the care center.

"Tell me about your relationship with your sister growing up," I say when he breaks in his narrative.

Charles hesitates at this. "We were like most siblings," he finally says. "Had some arguments, but mostly ignored each other."

"Did your parents favor their only daughter over their only son?" I say it mostly in jest, but I know that sibling rivalry is a powerful connection, for better or for worse.

His face pinks again. "They thought Jessie was perfect. She was their princess, and when she got that boyfriend, you'd have thought someone in our house died."

I don't miss the irony of his analogy.

Charles plows ahead. "She was grounded the week I went to scout camp." He shrugs. "She might not have left the house, but she sure got into trouble."

I can't help but raise my brows as I make a couple of notes, mostly about the emotional distance that Charles seems to have with his sister ... yet, he's obviously internalizing something. "What do you talk about with your sister when you visit her on Tuesdays?"

"Ah," he hedges. "Not a lot. Sometimes she tells me about the other residents. Sometimes I talk about my job. Otherwise, the visits are short and generic."

"Would you say that there's tension between the two of you?" I ask.

Charles's eyes narrow. "Not as much now as there used to be," he says. "During the first few years she lived there, we got into several arguments. I mean, she did kill our parents. It's a hard thing to fathom, let alone to be related to a murderer."

I study his mannerisms as he speaks—the slight tremble of his hands, the tilt of his chin. as he speaks. "It's remarkable that you speak to her at all," I say. "That you have taken her care upon yourself. That you visit her each week."

He straightens in his chair a bit. "It hasn't been easy."

Things have become cordial between us, like we're starting to mutually respect each other. "What would happen if you skipped a visit?"

"I've skipped only once," he says. "When I was extremely sick." Then he shrugs. "The world wouldn't end if I don't visit her, if that's what you're asking. But I keep my commitments in all things. When I found out what my sister did, I didn't see her as 'Jessica the Reaper' like the media claimed. I knew she was a teenager, like me, and had done something horrible. In her case, she could never make it right."

Hm. Charles is more compassionate than I originally gave him credit for. "Would you go so far as to say you've forgiven her for her crimes?"

At this, he turns his head toward the window and the ocean view beyond. The sun is bright today, the ocean an unending blue.

"I could never forgive her," he says at last.

CHAPTER 4

JESS

MARLENE STANDS OVER me, a water bottle in her hand. "I'll pour this on you if you don't get up."

I don't doubt her; she's done it before. If there's one thing I hate, it's water poured on my face. Today I'm meeting with my new psychiatrist. Today, I wish I could be sick enough that I'll be allowed to stay in bed.

"You have five seconds, and then I'll start pouring," Marlene continues.

I look up into her wide face that might be pretty if she cared enough about makeup. She told me once that she'd been married for a couple of years, but there hadn't been any children.

I guess I'm her child now. Shoving the blanket off me, I climb out of bed and walk to the bathroom. There's no door on the bathroom, and Marlene watches me while I wash my face and brush my teeth. At least I have the decency to do that before my meeting with my new doctor. I scrub my hands, knowing that I'll never fully get the dirt out from beneath my nails. My favorite activity in this place is working in the communal garden. Any of the patients can plant and pull weeds, but most of them lose interest quickly. I'm the only one who has stuck with it. In the afternoons, before the dinner hour, I'm allowed time in the garden.

Next, I walk to my closet and change into a clean T-shirt and a baggy pair of jeans. Everything I wear is donated to the center. When my brother used to buy me clothes, I'd give them to another patient. If only to annoy him. There's something fascinating in wearing a stranger's clothing. I imagine all kinds of scenarios that this shirt must have seen.

The T-shirt I'm wearing is tighter than I normally like. The faded Roxy logo is what made me pick it out of the donation bag. I remember wearing name-brand clothing before . . . before my life changed. There's a pale stain on the sleeve, and sometimes I pretend it's from a date that the previous owner wore it on. She got into an ice cream fight. Or maybe she had a little kid who smeared something greasy on it. Or maybe she was running from a guy that was giving her a hard time and she tripped and rolled down a hillside.

The latter scenario is the more typical train of thought my mind entertains. I used to love watching suspense movies. In the center, we aren't allowed to watch anything above a PG rating. The patients here, including me, are extremely impressionable. Even some of the more violent cartoons are banned.

"You're wearing that again?" Marlene asks, her tone disapproving.

So what if I've worn this shirt three times this week? Does it really matter? I mean, I want to feel comfortable. And this T-shirt is comfortable.

"I like it." I start for the door.

"At least change your bra," Marlene says.

I look down. Sometimes the donation bags contain sports bras—the only type we're allowed to wear. I usually try to grab them before one of the attendants puts it in the discard pile. I wouldn't wear used panties of course, but bras are a different matter. Besides, I can get only white ones through the center. This one is navy blue. And the outline shows through the faded pink word *Roxy*.

"Your new psychiatrist is a man," Marlene says. "You might want to look less trashy."

"I know he's a man," I say. "He's probably ancient and wears bifocals. Besides, in order to be called a trashy woman, I'd have to be allowed to do trashy stuff. It's better than being called a freak."

Marlene flinches at the word but says nothing.

I put a hand on the doorknob and wait for Marlene to buzz it open. When she does, I step out into the hallway.

I am a patient, a *mental patient*. I'm crazy. I'm a freak. I killed my parents. I have memory loss. I have to take medication to function on the lowest level of society—in a psychiatric care center where there are aides everywhere I turn to boss me around. I'm also far from trashy. My parents found my journal the week before they . . . died . . . and read about how Trevor and I planned to sleep together for the first time on our three-month anniversary.

My mom flipped out. My dad threatened to call the cops. On what, and who? Nothing had happened.

I slow as we reach the end of the hallway where the consultation office is. I haven't decided if I'll miss Dr. Linpinski yet. She always smelled like hot dogs and mustard. And I think I spent more time watching her pick at her hangnails than I did listening to her. Lastly, she'd never take a stand against my brother's opinion. It was like she was almost afraid of him, which I thought was funny. She's a tall woman, at least five eleven, and towers over him. The only favor she did me was during our first session together when Charles came. She politely dismissed him. And that was that.

"Ready?" Marlene asks, but the question is completely rhetorical. She raps on the door twice.

A moment passes, then a tall man opens the door.

The first thing I notice is how young he is. He can't be more than thirty, and this surprises me. I've been picturing my new psychiatrist as a sixty-year-old man with plenty of gray in his hair. Perhaps some thinning on top. And definitely glasses.

But this man has dark hair; no sign of baldness either. His hair is disheveled on top, as if he'd run his fingers through it. He wears a pale-blue button-down shirt with the sleeves rolled up to his elbows. The pale-blue color sets off his tanned forearms. The thought of him spending plenty of time outdoors makes me envious.

His eyes draw the most attention. They're brown, but not a dull brown. They're a deep brown that's somehow warm as well. If I were to imagine a modern absentminded professor stereotype, Dr. Mayer would fit.

Once our gazes connect, I know there's nothing absentminded about this man. His gaze is intense, as if he's trying to figure me out in all of ten seconds.

He won't. If I can't figure out myself, how will a stranger? He might get some credit for making a valiant effort.

"Jessica?" Dr. Mayer says, holding out his hand to shake mine.

"Yes." I place my hand in his. I like how he gives me a firm handshake, as if he considers me an equal and someone worth knowing.

"I'm Logan Mayer," he says. No formal "doctor" precedes his greeting. "Nice to meet you."

Marlene shuts the door without so much as a word to the doctor.

The office contains a desk and a chair on one side for the doctor, and two chairs on the other side of the desk. I sit on the chair on the right. Instead of going around the desk and taking his place, Dr. Mayer sits in the chair near me. Both chairs are bolted to the floor. I guess the facility is worried about patients becoming distraught during therapy and trying to cause damage to property or themselves with a chair.

I expect Dr. Mayer to launch into questions about changing doctors and perhaps ask some questions about my previous treatment, but instead he says, "I can't be your doctor, but I'm happy to recommend one of my colleagues."

I stare at him. "I don't understand. My brother told me that you're in charge of my psychiatric treatment now."

Dr. Mayer gives a nod. "That's what your brother would like." He folds his arms.

I drag my eyes away from staring at his tanned forearms. It makes me think there is another world out there, one I like to pretend doesn't exist. "Is there a conflict of interest? Charles said that you're treating him as well for his . . . episodes."

"I've treated family members of patients before," he says. "It can sometimes be beneficial because you get a broader viewpoint." He seems to hesitate before continuing. "I don't play games."

My brows shoot up. "Games?" I think I know what he's saying, but I would never voice it aloud to anyone. I know that my brother can be manipulative, at least until he gets what he wants. I've looked up manipulative attributes in my online research and found that Charles meets several of the attributes under narcissism. Or maybe he's just plain selfish.

"Maybe 'games' isn't the right word," Dr. Mayer clarifies. "Your brother is making all of the decisions in your life. This means that he'll feel like he can dictate to me as well."

"Charles is my guardian," I say in a quiet voice.

"He's been assigned your guardian by the state, which enables you a measure of protection," Dr. Mayer says. "But when I treat clients, I need to be able to implement whatever treatment plan I see as the most beneficial."

I'm catching on. "And you don't want Charles to tell you how to treat me?"

"Correct," he says. His voice is firm, but his gaze is soft.

A doctor who won't be manipulated by my brother. "Dr. Mayer," I say. "Do you believe in patient-doctor confidentiality?"

"Of course," he says.

I give a small shrug. "So there shouldn't be a problem."

The doctor slides a hand through his hair, and I find that I'm staring at him. I quickly look away. He's hesitating and taking my suggestion seriously.

"Look," he says at last. "I read through your medical files, and I read through your court case." His brown eyes seem to see right into me. "I don't know if you're guilty or not of your parents' deaths, but I do know that suffering from memory repression doesn't mean you can't be a fully functioning member of society."

I try to process all that the doctor said. I feel as if ice is growing in my chest—the same feeling I have every time I think of the night that my parents died. I don't remember any details; all I know is that whenever I try to remember or even think about that night, my body trembles and I'm cold all over.

"Jessica?" the doctor's voice cuts through the cold.

I blink and realize that I've been closing my eyes. I blink again, trying to clear the darkness that's creeping through me. I try to hold his gaze and focus on the warm brown color of his eyes as if it's enough to keep me in the present.

When it's clear that I'm back on earth, he says, "Jessica, you're an intelligent grown woman. You may or may not have committed a crime nine years ago. Until there is evidence that you are a murderer, you should be able to live a normal life."

I can't look at him. The hope in his eyes is something that

I have never seen in my brother's. Charles looks at me with only pity, anger, or disgust.

Hope ended nine years ago.

"What if my memory does come back?" I ask. "Charles tells me it's better to be here—to avoid another trial, to avoid prison."

The doctor is silent for a while. I still can't look at him.

It's as if he's waiting for me to confess something. "I don't know what happened that night," I say. "I've tried to remember."

"Jessica," he says, his tone gentle. "Whatever happened that night, you've been through a tragedy. Your post-traumatic stress speaks to that. I need to tell you that there are thousands of people who live functioning lives with post-traumatic stress outside of the walls of an institution."

I exhale, but I can't speak.

"I'll let your brother know who I recommend treating you," he says. "And know that I wish you the very best. I think you can live a full and satisfying life."

I nod and clasp my hands in my lap.

He waits for me to respond, but when I don't, he says, "It was nice to meet you."

I glance up, quickly, then look back to my twisting hands.

He rises from the chair and picks up a notepad and pen from the desk—ones he must have brought to take notes. I wonder why he brought them at all if he was already planning on telling me he couldn't treat me.

I can't watch him walk away. I met this doctor only moments ago, yet he's told me something that I've long wondered but haven't dared to hope. I squeeze my eyes shut to prevent the tears from forming.

I hear him walk to the door. I hear the doorknob turn.

"Wait," I whisper.

Remarkably, he hears me.

"What is it?"

"I believe you," I say. "And I want you to help me." I force my eyes to open to focus on his inquisitive gaze. The words won't come, so I have to force those too. "I've stopped taking some of my medication, and I've begun to remember some things."

Chapter 5

Logan

HER MEMORY HAS returned, is all that I can think as Jessica Harper looks at me with those lake-blue eyes. At first, the shape of her eyes reminds me of her brother's, but then I realize that Jessica's are a clear blue, not the dull blue-gray of Charles's.

I'm not sure whether I can believe her. Her eyes have taken on a wildness, as if she's throwing out something for me to grasp on. Even though we've barely met, I could see that she was genuinely invested in our conversation. This doesn't always happen in initial meetings with clients. It can take several sessions to build up a rapport.

With Jessica, I am intrigued, which is unexpected. I had planned on shaking her hand, apologizing, then leaving the facility. Instead, I sat next to her and had a conversation.

"Do you need a lawyer?" I ask, still hovering by the door. Legal matters are out of my jurisdiction. But if she's remembered events from the night of her parents' murders, she probably needs legal counsel.

"I don't know," she says, looking away again.

She has a habit of that. Her words are clear and intelligent, but she has very little confidence in her opinions and ideas.

I watch her body language carefully. Her legs are crossed, and she sits with her shoulders erect. Her fingers are clenched together as if she's forcing herself to stay calmly in the chair. When she first came into the room, I was struck with her pale skin and delicate features. Her clothes practically hang off her, not as if she's too thin or malnourished but because she's not wearing clothing that fits her petite frame.

Her blonde hair is brushed and pulled back into a pony-tail, and from my position at the door, I can see that she has a sort of quiet elegance that's not found in many of my patients. Her neck is graceful, her cheekbones high, her lips full, her eyelashes long . . .

"Do you want to tell me what you remember?" I ask, knowing that offering to listen to her memories would mean that I'm acting as her doctor after all.

She glances at me. "Will you tell my brother?"

I step away from the door and sit down in the chair next to her again. "I always uphold doctor-patient confidentiality."

She focuses on her hands for a moment. "I remember that I was wearing a red shirt," she finally says.

I nod and wait for her to continue. When she doesn't, I prompt, "Is that all?"

"Yes," she says in almost a whisper.

Is the shirt significant? I doubt it. I think she's trying to coerce me into staying for whatever reason. I jot down the information on my notepad. "How long have you remem-bered this?"

"Eleven days."

I'm surprised at her detailed answer. Patients I've con-sulted with usually generalize or exaggerate. Something that happened a few days ago will turn into weeks, or even months.

"Is this the first time you've remembered something from that night?" I ask.

"No," she says. "I've remembered other things, too, but I haven't told anyone about them."

My pen is poised over my notepad. I won't press her. Mostly because I'm not sure I want to know things she should be telling her real doctor—whoever that might be.

She exhales and unclasps her hands. Then she turns toward me, blinking rapidly. I realize that tears have formed in her eyes.

I have the urge to take her hand or pat her shoulder. Her distress is real. I can't imagine what it would be like to remember something after nine years of suppression. Of course I don't touch her—she's my patient—or *a* patient.

She wipes at her cheeks, then sniffles. Her voice trembles when she speaks. "Look at my chart and you'll see a list of prescriptions. Two of them have side effects of memory loss."

I'm well familiar with her medications, although I'm not sure what she's claiming. One is an antianxiety medication. The other a mood stabilizer. She also takes a sleep aid. She makes her point in the next sentence.

"I've been on those medications for nine years," she says. "Since almost immediately after . . . my arrest."

I wait for her to continue, and when she doesn't, I ask, "Do you remember anything between the time your parents were found—and when you started the medication?"

She looks away now, and I realize I've been expecting her to break eye contact. It's what she does.

"I don't know," she says, linking her hands together. Her knuckles turn white, but at least the tears seem to have stopped.

She falls quiet again, and the only sound in the room is the faint ticking of a clock hanging on the wall. The black-and-white clock is too high for anyone to reach. It's probably bolted to the wall.

Jessica is silent for so long that I know the subject has been closed for now.

She doesn't seem to be crying anymore, and I think over our conversation so far. Jessica is like a fragile bird in a cage. She keeps trying to slip through the bars, but there's a chain about her foot holding her to the ground. I have no doubt that this short time with her has been a breakthrough. She hasn't told anyone about her returning memories—except for me.

I exhale silently, thinking of her brother and how over-protective he is about his sister. I don't exactly blame him. If it were my sister, I wonder what I might do.

"Look," I say after several moments pass. "What if we try meeting for a month? As a trial run?"

She lifts her chin, and even though she isn't looking at me, I sense a weight lifting from her shoulders. Not to pat myself on the back, but she seems to respond to me.

"Okay," she whispers.

I wait a little longer for her to say something else, but she's staring straight ahead, her hands clasped.

"I'll see you next week, then, Jessica."

She gives a slight nod. "You can call me Jess."

I rise from my chair and make my way to the door. My last glimpse of her before I leave the room is her staring straight ahead, a small smile curving her mouth.

Twenty minutes later, as I pull into the parking lot of my office, Charles calls. I pull off my motorcycle helmet and answer.

Apparently he has my private cell phone number. I'll have to ask Sandra if she knows how he got it.

"How's Jessie?" he asks, skipping over any greeting.

"We ended a little early, but that's typical for a first

session," I say. Normally I wouldn't offer up even that much information, but Charles is the brother and full guardian of a very ill woman.

"What did she say?"

I raise my eyebrows at his question. I suppose I shouldn't be entirely surprised. "You know I can't divulge our conversation."

"I understand," he says, although his voice is tight. "But ... were there any confidences? Did she tell you something that's not in her files?"

I want to laugh, but I keep my tone professional. "She's exactly how you described her. She was calm and sometimes distracted. I think her medications are doing what they're supposed to."

Charles breathes out audibly. "Anything else?"

"No," I say. "I've another call coming in."

"All right, I'll see you at our next session," he says.

I click END on my phone, wondering why I lied to Charles. More than once. I withheld information, sure, but lying is a different matter.

I don't have any more clients today, but I need to check on several things and possibly print them out to add to Jessica's file. First, I'm starting with her prescription medications.

Sandra looks up when I push through the double-glass doors. "Ah, you're back." She holds out a pink Post-it Note. Today, she's wearing turquoise, from her Navajo jewelry to her turquoise jumpsuit that reminds me of something from the eighties. Sandra will definitely attract attention when she steps out of this office tonight.

"Gwen Stevens called," Sandra says as I grasp the note.

I slow my step at the same time my gaze lands on Sandra's looped writing with Gwen's name and phone number.

"All right, thanks," I mumble, my thoughts splitting in several directions.

"Um-hm," she replies in a knowing tone.

Gwen and I used to date, and Gwen even met Sandra a time or two. But we broke up about a year ago, and there hadn't been any communication between us . . . until now.

I walk into my office and stop for a second, staring at the note. What does Gwen want? I don't want to quiz Sandra—she'll start to assume things I don't want her to.

A shot of anxiety spirals in my stomach, so I shut the office door and dial Gwen's number. It's still saved on my cell phone.

When she answers, her throaty voice takes me right back to where we left off—before our heated breakup, that is.

"Logan, you called," she says.

Humor laces her voice, and I find myself smiling, which I'm not sure is a good thing. "Did you doubt?"

"Well . . . ," she hedges. "It's been a while."

"Yep," I agree, perching on the edge of my desk. I can't quite relax. Hearing her voice is doing all sorts of things to my emotions. I don't know if my training as a psychiatrist is helping me or hurting me. Why is she calling? I don't want to be rude and ask outright. "How have you been?"

She gives a half laugh. "You're still the same, always asking how I'm doing in that sincere tone of yours."

I wait for the punch line, but there is none. I picture her shoulder-length cropped red hair and the slim cut of one of her power suits. "So . . . how *are* you doing?"

"Great," she says, although the confidence she's probably trying to convey isn't coming through her voice.

Still I wait for her to tell me the reason she's called.

"Rex died," she says.

Rex is her dog, or *was* her dog. A rambunctious Golden-doodle that you couldn't help but love. "What happened?"

"Oh, he was old, you know," she hedges. "I guess it was his time."

When she pauses, I say, "How long ago?"

"About a month."

So she's not calling about her dog, although I'm glad she told me. Rex and I spent many a time walking the beach.

"My neighbor tells me I need to get a puppy," she continues. "I don't know, though. No one can replace Rex."

"I agree," I say. "But you're a dog lover and would give another dog a great home."

"Yeah," she says, her voice soft.

"Work going all right?" Gwen's a detective, and well, we met when she had a warrant for some information about one of my clients. Apparently we're chitchatting. She still hasn't told me why she called.

"That's the thing," she says. "I've been assigned some cold cases."

Another client of mine is connected? "Anything interesting?"

"It's all interesting until the trail goes cold." She laughs.

I laugh, too, at her pun, although I'm feeling on edge now. My ex-girlfriend, a San Diego detective, is calling me out of the blue.

"I've gone through about five or six of them in the past couple of weeks," she says, "and they've all dead-ended. Except for one."

This is why she's calling, although I'm not sure how it involves me.

"I found a few things that don't line up in the initial reports," she continues, talking rapidly now, and I don't know if I'll be able to entirely follow her. In the past, whenever she's talked about cases, I've felt a bit lost. But she taught me a lot, which I believe enables me to be a better doctor to mentally ill criminals.

"Then I found out you're treating the brother of a famous teenage criminal who's basically incarcerated in a psychiatric unit—"

A knot forms in my stomach. "Jessica Harper."

"Yes, have you met her?" she asks.

The question is odd, and I know that she can't know—yet—that I'm her new doctor. "Her brother is my client," I say, withholding the additional information, for now. I don't know why I'm suddenly protective of Jessica. It's not like she hasn't been protected for nine years by her brother.

"Yes, Charles Harper," Gwen continues. "He's the one I'm interested in."

"Charles?" This surprises me. But I can't ask more questions or go into more detail unless Gwen has a warrant for information. Ex-girlfriend notwithstanding.

She lowers her voice, which makes it even more sexy. "Can we meet, Logan? Talk off the record?"

The knot in my stomach turns into a rock.

"Gwen . . ." Oddly, I do want to see her, but I really don't want to get caught up in something that could be a breach of confidentiality.

"Please," she says in that same sexy tone. "It will take only few minutes, and you, of course, can refuse to answer."

There's more to this than a couple of questions about Charles. And, I'll admit, I'm curious about seeing Gwen after all this time. Even though our breakup was completely final, she still has a pull on me. I'm not sure I want to explore the reasons why, but I end up agreeing. "All right. Name the time and place, and I'll see what I can do."

CHAPTER 6

JESS

THE SOIL IS cool and damp as I dig out the errant weed with my bare hands. I'm not allowed a shovel or a trowel. Too sharp, too dangerous. But I love the dark, rich earth of the garden box. It's only about six-by-six feet, but it's perfect for me to work by myself.

Of course I'm not entirely alone. An aide is sitting on a nearby bench, watching me as if he's watching grass grow. I don't bother to get to know the names of the aides other than Marlene and Patrick. Patrick's the only one I really talk to. Marlene I just obey.

The weed comes out, roots and all. I take a minute to run my fingers over the root, knocking off some of the dirt that came up with the weed. I set it on the side of the redwood two-by-four that encases the garden plot. There aren't many weeds because I'm out here almost every day, even in the rain.

I sit back on my feet as the breeze filters through the young plants. Their pale-green leaves and maturing stems make me feel like I can be more like them. I can keep learning and growing. I can keep living.

"Jessica." Marlene's voice interrupts my thin serenity. "It's time to clean up."

It's visiting day again with my brother.

I sigh and brush off my hands, then stand.

The nameless aide stands as well. His job is done for now.

Marlene doesn't have to ask me twice. I know that delaying or protesting will do no good with her. I walk with her into the building, through the locked double doors that she triggers open. Inside my room, I scrub my hands, change my T-shirt, redo my ponytail, and then I'm ready. Marlene doesn't comment on my compliance. The aides know that even a compliment can provoke a patient in a negative manner.

I follow her down the hallway and into the recreation room. Charles is early, and I'm not surprised. He waits by the fireplace, but I won't join him there. I have shared something with Dr. Mayer as a test to see if he'll pass it along to my brother. The red shirt—yes, it's a memory, but not a significant memory, not compared to the other ones I've had. Those, I'm not ready to share.

My brother's gaze is immediately riveted on me, but I continue at my normal pace. I glance at him, then sit in my usual chair. A week might have passed, but the other patients look as if they haven't moved. The puzzle is out, and Erin is bent over it. Mona sits on the other side of the table, coloring what looks to be an intricate graphic of a peacock. Nicole is pacing by the windows, mumbling something too soft to hear.

Patrick nods as I look at him. I nod back. It's all the acknowledgment I'll give him as long as my brother's in the room. Sometimes, after Charles leaves, Patrick will sit by me, and we'll talk about whatever I've looked up on the computer. Surprisingly, Patrick is willing to answer all my questions.

Now, Charles approaches me and pulls a chair close.

"Hello, Jessie," he says.

I don't look at him.

But this doesn't deter him. "How did you like Dr. Mayer?"

"Fine," I say, keeping a slight pout in my voice. I don't want him to know that I am counting down hours until my next session with the doctor.

My brother leans closer. He smells like spicy food, and I wonder if he ate Mexican for lunch. "What did you talk about?"

I look at him finally. His blue eyes are murky today, tinged with storminess, although he's keeping it out of his voice.

For the first years I was in this facility, I told my brother everything. He would listen, and he would offer advice sometimes. Then, once I told him I remembered something from the night I killed my parents. I had remembered voices shouting, but it wasn't an argument between my two parents. My dad was yelling at another man.

My brother told me that he thinks that my boyfriend Trevor came over that night and my dad kicked him out. But if I told anyone about my memory, then Trevor would be questioned too. At the time, I didn't want Trevor to face the cops. At the time, I also didn't know that I'd be tried for murdering my own parents.

Soon, I started taking the medication, and even the memory of the argument faded until I couldn't remember it anymore. Just that I had remembered it at one point.

Trevor found another girlfriend, of course. Charles told me about it. What did I expect? For Trevor to be devoted to a murderer? Was he going to visit me at the psych center?

During those first few years in this facility, I was happy to let my mind go numb. I couldn't remember anything, and I decided to be grateful for that. Who wants to remember such a despicable act? If the memories returned, I knew that I would truly go crazy.

But something happened over the past few months. On

the internet, I read about how the brain protects itself and will block out traumatic events. Perhaps that's what my brain did. But after a while the events will resurface. There are artificial ways to make this happen, of course, such as hypnosis. Typically, it would eventually happen on its own unless the patient was taking medications in a certain drug family.

I read through the list of medications. I was taking two on the list.

Now my brother shifts closer. "Jessie?"

"We went over my medical history," I say to appease him. We didn't go over it much, but it sounds like something that might have happened. And it's true that I did tell Dr. Mayer about the two medications that caused memory loss. I want to stop taking them completely, to see what happens, but I'm afraid. Afraid of what I might remember. What if Trevor really had come over to my house and argued with my dad? What if Trevor was the one who killed my parents?

Or what if I remember what I did?

I think of the picture I found of Trevor and his wife online. They have two little girls—both blonde. I don't know the woman he married, and I have no idea where he met her. I could pull up only so much on Facebook without being a member.

"Have you remembered anything more?" he asks. A standard question from my brother, but today it bothers me more than usual.

"No," I say. He doesn't push me, which makes me think that Dr. Mayer truly did keep his word.

"How are you sleeping?" he asks. Another standard question.

"Fine."

Charles sits back in his chair and pulls out his phone from his pocket. He scrolls through some things, and I look away again, as if I'm bored. In truth, I'm counting the minutes until he leaves.

When the obligatory hour is up, I nod as Charles says goodbye. Some weeks he doesn't even say that much.

"Why don't you like your brother?" Erin asks when he's barely out of the room. Her voice is childlike today—sounding like she's ten years old instead of thirty-five.

I look over at her, surprised at her question. Erin's head it still bent over her puzzle.

"I like him," I say.

"No you don't," Erin insists. She snaps a puzzle piece into place, then looks up at me, shoving her blunt-cut black hair out of her eyes. "I can hear you arguing."

"We weren't arguing," I say. Erin's annoying me.

She touches her forehead, and the scars all up and down her arm seem to flash in the light of the room. "In here. I hear you in my head."

I sigh. Erin is schizophrenic, and there's no use debating with the voices that she hears.

"I don't like him either," she continues, then gives an exaggerated shudder.

"Erin?" I say, testing to see if she'll answer to the name.

"Melanie."

Ah, she's *Melanie* today. It frequently changes.

"I wasn't arguing with my brother, Melanie," I say. "And we like each other fine. He's my brother, you know."

She wrinkles her nose. "I *heard* you."

From her pacing by the window, Nicole stops and turns to face us. "They weren't arguing, Erin."

I cringe. Nicole and Erin have never gotten along. Nicole is waiting for her family to come and visit—which they rarely do because they live up north. But she's convinced if she watches out the window, they'll come sooner. Erin likes to tell her that no one is coming. This often sends Nicole into a crying fit. But now Nicole is turning the tables against Erin.

"Don't call me Erin," Erin says. "And they *were* arguing! I heard them in my head!"

"Your name *is* Erin," Nicole spits out, her freckled face growing red. "Look at your birth certificate!"

Patrick starts to cross the room, walking toward Nicole. She notices him right away, and before he can interfere, she yells at Erin, "You're so dumb that you don't even know your own name!"

Watching grown women fight like little kids on a playground is a typical event here. No one ever wins, though. Everyone loses.

Patrick grasps Nicole's arm with a firm grip and leads her out of the room. All the while she's yelling about Erin being dumb.

I look over at Erin, whose head is bent, her dark hair hanging in her face again. She's staring at the puzzle pieces, not moving.

Marlene has moved closer to Erin, and everyone in the room is watching her.

"You're right, Melanie," I say. "My brother and I were arguing. And I don't like him."

She sniffles, and a tear drops onto the table, making a tiny puddle. Then she lifts her hand and slowly picks up a puzzle piece. A few seconds pass, and she snaps it into place along the border.

I watch her putting together puzzle pieces for several moments until the familiar rattle of the medicine tray comes into the room. I don't need to turn my head to know that Nurse Rollings has arrived. It's almost dinnertime, and we are to take our medicine and then eat. Behind her another tray is wheeled in by one of the aides.

When Nurse Rollings stops by my chair, she sets down a water cup and a smaller cup with three pills. Red, blue, blue. I take the blue ones, swallow them down with the water, then pop the red one in my mouth. I don't swallow the red pill, though.

Nurse Rollings continues to Erin/Melanie and watches her take her medication. Next, a food tray is set in front of me. I pick up the bottle of juice and open it to drink, but instead I slide the red pill into the juice. It will slowly dissolve in there, and no one will be the wiser. Satisfied that no one has noticed what I've done, I pick up the limp turkey sandwich and take a bite. Food is only a Band-Aid to prevent the headache that will come in about an hour. I found out when stopping the red pill that the withdrawals amounted to headaches. They usually go away in a few hours, but I can't let anyone know about the pain or I'll be given more medication.

Erin picks at her food like a bird. Normally she's a healthy eater, but if she's in Melanie's personality, it makes sense that she eats like a small child. She spills her juice, and Patrick is quick to clean it up.

"I'm finished," I tell Patrick.

"Great," he says, his rich voice always calming. "Are you ready for your computer time?"

I nod, and he gives a chuckle. He knows how much I covet the chance to look at the outside world.

He picks up my tray since patients aren't allowed to carry their own trays. Utensils—albeit plastic ones—go missing, and the trays themselves have been used against other patients. I walk to the corner of the room where the computer desk sits. The monitor faces out so that an aide can see which website I'm on at all times.

This doesn't bother me because they don't pay attention 100 percent of the time. I sit at the desk and wake up the monitor. The sound is on mute, and although sometimes I'd like to listen to videos that accompany articles that I read, I make do.

Today, I'm going to look up Dr. Logan Mayer. The first link that comes up is a website that lists two other doctors. The address is not listed, which doesn't surprise me. In all my research, I've found that psychiatrists often don't make their addresses public. You need to be a client before you get the privileged office address.

I find a phone number, and I read through it several times until I have it firmly memorized. It's the only way I can keep track of information. I could write it down in my journal, but those are transcribed and added to my file every six months, so it's not a place where I can write anything confidential.

The picture of Dr. Mayer is at least a few years old, and I gaze at it for a moment. His brown eyes seem to look through the screen right at me. It's unwise for me to assume, but somehow he seems trustworthy. At least he didn't tell my brother about the red shirt memory.

I scroll through his bio. Nothing is mentioned about him being married. I click over to the other psychologists' profiles listed on the website. One mentions being married, the other one isn't. I'm not sure why I'm fixated on that small fact. Dr. Mayer is a good-looking man, but he's also my doctor, and I'm institutionalized for life.

Moving on, I click on another link that came up in the search and discover that Dr. Mayer has testified at some trials. It's not unusual in and of itself for a psychiatrist to be brought in as an expert witness, but it also tells me that if something were ever to happen to me, a warrant could be issued for the information that I share in our sessions.

I don't bother to read through any of the news articles

about the trials, and I instead click on his Facebook profile. I can access a page only if it's been marked public since I'm not allowed to join Facebook. But I'm always surprised at how much information I can still find.

For example, it looks like Dr. Mayer has posted only once in the past year. It's a tagged picture with a couple of buddies—they're on a fishing boat in the ocean somewhere. Mayer's dark hair is windblown, and he's grinning at whoever is taking the picture. His arms are slung around two other men. All the men look to be in their thirties, tanned, fit, wearing tank shirts and board shorts. Brothers? Friends?

I scan the tagged names. They don't share a last name, so they must be friends.

I scroll to the next picture. It's of Dr. Mayer sitting at a table with a group of people. A red-haired woman sits close to him, her hand wrapped around his upper arm, as if to state "we're together." She's smiling broadly at the camera, and Dr. Mayer looks like he was just laughing at something. I check the date: eighteen months ago.

Is the woman his girlfriend? Wife? Are they still together? I'm staring at the picture, and I have to force my gaze away from it. I close the site, and then with what seems little self-control, I type Trevor's name into the search engine. His Facebook profile comes up, and I look through a couple of recent pictures that he's tagged in by his wife. "Fun afternoon at the beach. Lilly ate her first sand. LOL." The picture is of Trevor's wife and a little girl who can't be much older than one. The next picture is of Trevor again, with his older daughter on his shoulders, holding a lopsided cone of pink cotton candy. They're both grinning. The little girl has her daddy's green eyes.

Trevor still has his dirty-blond hair and his tanned skin, and his shoulders have broadened with age. He's become a good-looking man. He was a good-looking teenager.

"Jessica," Patrick's voice cuts into my thoughts. "Time's up."

I close the browsers, then delete the search history while Patrick watches me. He says nothing, and I say nothing back. I rise to my feet and face him. "I'm ready to go back to my room now."

"Are you all right?" he asks.

Patrick is the only one in this place who asks me that with sincerity.

"Old memories," I say.

He searches my gaze for a moment. Patrick knows that one of the reasons I'm not incarcerated is because I don't have memories—at least the important ones. His eyes are black as he gazes at me, his skin dark and warm. I guess him to be about forty years old, although I've never asked his age. Sometimes I want to hug him, but I never do. It's not that we aren't allowed to hug in this facility, but I don't want to touch anyone, and I don't want anyone to touch me. The only time I allow my mind to wander in the direction of human affection is right before I fall asleep.

I move toward the doors and motion to Marlene. She crosses to me and walks me back to my room. I can have an hour of quiet time per day in my room by myself. Otherwise, I have to be involved in an activity, which can be as simple as sitting in the rec room, doing nothing.

Marlene unlocks my bedroom door, and as I step inside, she asks, "Do you need anything?"

"No," I say as the first pains in my head begin. I am expecting them, so I don't even wince. At least not until Marlene shuts and locks my door. I cross to my bed and lie down. Then I start to rub my temples, the only thing I find that will help that doesn't involve medication.

I hope that I've made the right decision about not taking my pills as prescribed. I want the memories to return. Or at least I think I do.

CHAPTER 7

LOGAN

GWEN SITS ON the empty bench at the edge of La Jolla beach. I turn off the engine of my motorcycle, then unclip my helmet.

Gwen doesn't move, even though I'm sure she heard my engine. Our relationship has been like that—we're *aware* of each other. Her long, slim legs are crossed as she taps something into her phone. With her red hair blowing in the wind, I see that she hasn't changed much. She's still beautiful and lithe.

Echoes of our last argument have long since faded, but in seeing her I'm reminded that I'd been the one to instigate our breakup. She'd increasingly asked me to cross the line in my profession when she wanted information about a psych patient. More and more over the months that we dated, she'd ask me to look up files—on patients who weren't mine.

Yes, I had access to the national databases and could ask for favors. But after the first favor I did for her, I just couldn't do any more. It was borderline unethical. Not that I'm as straitlaced as one might think, but I could see a pattern, and I didn't want to be involved.

"Find another contact if you insist on breaking the law," I'd told her that last day together in her condo.

She'd smirked and set down her half-full wine glass on her granite countertop. "I'm a detective. It's my job to find out secrets."

"There's a distinction between confidential and secret," I shot back.

Her eyes went dark with anger, her face flushed red. "What is it?"

I didn't have an answer. When she realized I wouldn't budge, she threatened our relationship.

I snapped. "It's over, then. I don't want a girlfriend who's dishonest in her profession and wants to drag me down with her."

Her eyes had widened, then narrowed. "Get out, you bastard."

Looking back, I agree that I'd been a bastard. The Dr. Mayer of a year ago was different than the Dr. Mayer of today. Not that I've gone back on my ethics, but I've seen more and more cases where the lines are gray. Nothing is black and white.

The fact that Gwen has called me again tells me that she's run out of whatever resources she'd been using since our breakup. The question is, what does she want from me? And what does she think I could give her?

I jog across the street to the sidewalk edging the beach.

Gwen turns her head as I step onto the sidewalk. She ends her call as she rises to her feet. The wind tugs at her pale-green blouse and black pencil skirt. Her curves have always been in all the right places.

I close the last few feet that separate us, and she raises her arms. In an instant we are hugging. Her scent has changed. It's more spicy than floral now. I pull back, trying to keep the contact brief while not being rude. Yet touching her, holding her, even for a brief moment, is doing all kinds of twisty things to my heart.

"You look great," Gwen says, stepping away and reaching up to tuck a blowing strand of hair behind her ear.

"You do too." And I mean it. I know it's something people say to each other in greeting all the time—which includes ex-boyfriends and ex-girlfriends. But, Gwen is . . . beautiful.

Her gaze gives me a quick once-over, and I'm now wondering if my shirt is tucked in, if I'm wearing my scuffed shoes or my newer ones. I don't want to look down to check. Did I overdo it on the cologne this morning?

For a moment, we just look at each other. Her, with a slight smile on her face, as if she approves. Me? Probably with a hound dog look on my face.

"Have a seat, Logan," Gwen says, breaking the electric moment between us.

I haven't forgotten her take-charge tendencies. One of the many things that makes her a great detective.

I follow her to the bench and loosen my tie as I sit down. I don't often wear ties to the office, but today I had an administrators' meeting at the local hospital. It wasn't because I was meeting with Gwen.

Gwen turns halfway toward me, casually draping her arm on the back of the bench. "Tell me about Charles Harper."

I blink, and I know that I'm stalling. "Did you bring a warrant?"

"Oh hell, Logan," Gwen shoots out. "Pretend we're friends, talking about another friend."

I swallow against the sudden dryness in my throat. Despite my misgivings, I'm more than curious. Besides, the way that Gwen greeted me has me believing she might invite me back to her place for a glass of wine, and more. Not that I would go. Maybe. It's just been a long time.

"Charles is a recluse as far as I can surmise," I begin. "He works, he sleeps, then goes to work. The only deviation from his routine are his Tuesday visits to his sister."

Gwen is nodding, as if nothing I'm saying is new information to her.

"But that makes his routine even more solid," I say.

"And you're treating him for blackouts?" she asks.

I hesitate. "Yes. As of now, we've connected the stress that he experiences in being his sister's protector and guardian to creating his blackouts."

She leans a bit closer, and I catch her scent again. "So, what's your diagnosis, doc? Stop the visits to his sister?"

"No," I say immediately. "She depends on them. And *he* depends on them as well."

Gwen tilts her head. "Sounds like the ideal brother, don't you think?"

I nod. Charles has stuck with his sister through a horrific crime. He certainly deserves a medal in the forgiveness department.

She continues, "Is Charles her only support system? Does Jessica have anyone else outside of her environment to interact with?"

Now that her questioning has turned to Jessica, I'm feeling the first inklings of doubt. "Charles is it."

"No relatives, no cousins? Grandparents? Friends?" she presses.

"I don't know," I say honestly. "What about this case has you so interested? Are you reopening it?"

"Not yet," she says. The wind dies down, and it's like we're in a small cocoon of warmth and calm on the beach. A couple of seagulls hop close to us but find nothing interesting.

She holds up her phone, and on the screen I see a PDF icon.

"What's this?" I ask, my senses going on alert.

"The interview with one of their neighbors a few days after the murders," Gwen says. She hands me the phone. "It's relatively short, but you should read it. Tell me if there's anything that stands out to you."

Gwen is nothing if not thorough. Her idea of a fun weekend consists of curling up on her couch, wine glass filled, dog at her feet, while she reads report after report. For her, it's fun to analyze data from all angles. Which is why she's a detective, of course.

I take the phone, open the PDF, and tilt it so that the lettering enlarges on the document. It's a handwritten report, which doesn't surprise me. Gwen always goes directly to the core source, not even relying on a typed-up report. She wants to see the actual first-hand account.

The neighbor, Kendall Belcher, first talks about how quiet the neighborhood is and how great of a family the Harpers are.

Lisa Harper is one of those ladies who will help you with anything. When I had my hysterectomy, she brought dinner over for a week. I think I gained ten pounds. She was also fun to talk to. Really seemed to care about things. Offered to get my mail whenever we went out of town. Fed our dog. That sort of thing.

I skim through some of the details that don't relate to the night of the incident. Kendall describes the father as being a quiet man but someone who frequently took in her garbage can after pickup.

He just did things. Never took any credit. His kids were great too. Charles was a quiet kid, but more than once he helped me carry groceries into my house. One strange thing happened once, and it's probably nothing. When I came home from an extended trip helping my mom in Colorado, I found Charles in my house. I'd given his mom a key in the event of an emergency. Charles said he was checking to make sure there weren't any gas leaks or other issues going on. He was kind of a techie kid—super smart. I think he was working on his associate's the same time he was in high school—that sort of thing.

The interview continues, with some random comments about other neighbors and a story of when Lisa Harper helped Kendall make funeral arrangements when her mom in Colorado died. I slow my skimming when I reach the comments about Jessica.

Boy, Jessica was trouble this last year. I saw her sneak out of her house more than once. I'm a light sleeper, you see. And sometimes I'd sit by my front window and watch the trees blow in the wind. Jessica was smart, though. She'd hurry down the street—always dressed in dark colors—then meet her boyfriend at the end of the street. His name was Trent, or something. Trevor, maybe. I found out because I reported Jessica's actions to her mom, of course. I would want to know if my daughter was doing that. Not that I have any kids at home right now. All I can say is that I'm in shock. The night of the . . . murders . . . her boyfriend was over. This caught my attention because I knew she'd been grounded from seeing him. I think she was grounded from leaving the house. But I saw that boy's car drive past my house, then park down the street. Moments later, he hurried around the side of their house where Jessica's room was. I don't think her parents knew—at least at first—because I saw him arrive really late, after midnight at least. His car was gone when I woke up the next morning. I didn't think much about it until I found out what happened to poor Lisa and her husband.

I reread the paragraph, then looked up at Gwen. She was watching me, waiting patiently for my reaction. "So, the boyfriend?" I say. "Surely he was questioned."

"He never was," Gwen states.

"How can that be?" I ask, handing back her phone. "This report is pretty clear that Jessica wasn't the only one at the house that night. I mean, he could have left before . . . but still, he was there and might have more insight."

She shrugs. "He was a minor, and he was pretty protected as far as I can tell."

I'm in shock. Jessica can't remember what happened for whatever psychological reason. But her boyfriend—he might know what happened. How can Gwen seem so unaffected by this? She called me for a reason—wasn't this it?

She pulls up another PDF on her phone and hands it over to me. I expand the PDF, seeing immediately that it's a medical record. One for Trevor Mills, age 17. Birth date October 10. Caucasian. 6'3". 175 pounds. Surgery scheduled for a broken ankle. Date of surgery is the day before the murders took place.

"You don't think he drove over there," I deadpan.

"He couldn't drive," Gwen says. "He broke his right ankle, and if you read further in the medical records, Trevor was supposed to stay off his ankle for four weeks. *If* he was there—and *if* that was his car like Kendall Belcher says—he wasn't the driver."

My gaze snaps to her face. "Who was driving his car?"

She gives a half smile. "I don't know about you, but in my high school days, we swapped cars sometimes. If I didn't feel like driving, I'd ask a friend. Or I'd tell a friend to take my car and pick me up later."

I've never done that, but to each their own.

"You think Jessica had his car?" I ask. "She's already been placed at the crime scene. What does this prove?" I tap the medical report I'd read.

"What if . . . ," Gwen begins, lowering her voice as if she's about to tell me a great secret. "What if Jessica was driving his car—he let her borrow it since he wouldn't need it for a while. She was grounded, apparently, and so this gave her a way to sneak back and forth and see him."

I think about it for a moment. "So she was coming back home, and her parents caught her? They argued, and she killed them?"

Gwen looks thoughtful. "It might have been the instigator of the argument, but I think there's more to it."

"More? Was her boyfriend with her, hobbling along on crutches?"

Gwen smiles. "Teenagers are stubborn."

I exhale. "I don't buy it. Your theory about the car might be right, but if her boyfriend had surgery the day before, chances are that he was home, drugged up."

She arches a single brow.

"You think a teenager high on painkillers from his surgery would drive over to his girlfriend's house and kill her parents?" I laugh. Then I sober. Gwen isn't laughing with me.

"All I know is that it thickens the plot," she says in a quiet voice.

I know that look in her eyes—it's a bit wild and a bit devious. Two things I'm familiar with. It's as if I'm psychic, because I say, "You want to question the boyfriend, don't you?"

This time she smiles. "You're a smart man, Logan. Always have been." Then she leans forward, her scent coming closer. She moves her lips next to my ear. "And I want you to come with me."

I draw back. "I'm not a cop."

"No, you're better than a cop," Gwen says, still crowding my space.

Not that I entirely mind, but she's messing with my head with those fiery eyes of hers.

"You're a head doctor," she says. "You can read people, Logan. I need your help."

CHAPTER 8

I RARELY SLEEP through the night, so when I wake up in the morning in the near darkness, I'm not bothered. I used to take sleeping pills because it took me forever to fall asleep. And if I did wake up, I could rarely get back to sleep before the 7:30 a.m. breakfast time. Dr. Linpinski was sure to prescribe me sleeping pills every thirty days, which I've faithfully taken.

Marlene hands me a pill each night, and for the past few days, I've put it in my mouth and pretended to swallow. When she leaves, I take it out and smash the moist pill in my fingers, then run the bits through my hair.

Tonight, I follow my routine. I know I won't sleep well, but my research online tells me that the longer I'm off my medication, the sooner I'll remember. But I also read that self-hypnosis will help too.

I close my eyes and even out my breathing, focusing on inhaling, then exhaling, trying to fully relax. First, I think about my feet and how they are heavy. Next, I think about my calves and completely relax them. Then my knees. My thighs. My hips. My back. My hands. My arms. Shoulders. Neck. Head. Eyes.

I am completely relaxed, and I wonder if I'll fall asleep before I can remember anything.

I think about Trevor. His green eyes are what first attracted me to him. We were in health class together—he was new to the school. I had heard about him before I actually saw him. My girlfriends had already checked him out, sent a bunch of texts out about the "hot new guy."

∿

When he walked into health class, I knew immediately he was the new guy my friends were ogling. Mr. Wright put him in the empty desk next to mine. There was always an empty desk next to me since I sat in the front row. It was my penance for being late to class every day. Well, almost every day.

A 7:45 a.m. start time wasn't easy for a sixteen-year-old girl who was a night owl. Once Trevor started coming, I arrived on time.

"Hey," Trevor had said, glancing over at me with a half smile.

I stared at him in surprise. The "new kid" wasn't supposed to be friendly. I was the one who should be welcoming *him* to our school.

"I'm Trevor," he said, extending his hand.

Who was this guy? I shook his hand, becoming curious and infatuated at once.

Mr. Wright continued his lesson as if the entire earth hadn't just shifted on its axis, and I couldn't help but steal glances over at the green-eyed hottie next to me. He stole glances as well, smiling each time. I could barely keep my heart from banging out of my chest.

Class ended, and as the kids around us gathered up their stuff, I stayed in my seat.

Trevor stood and crossed to where I sat—which was only

a couple of feet away. "Are you going to lunch?"

I looked up at him. He was really tall when he stood over me like that. "I'm on lunch detention."

"What does that mean?" he asked, his green eyes full of humor.

"It means that for the next two weeks, I have to sit here during the lunch hour and do my homework."

"What did you do? Cheat on a test?"

"I got in a fight," I said. The interest in his eyes made me feel flattered.

"With who? Another girl?"

"Ha," I say. "With my brother."

His brows furrowed. "At school?"

"Not exactly," I hedged. "It was . . . we fought at home, but then I spray-painted the inside of his school locker."

Trevor blinked a couple of times, then he laughed.

"Mr. Mills," Mr. Wright said, coming back into the classroom after talking to a student in the hall. "You need to make your way to the lunchroom now."

Trevor gave me a wink that seemed to shoot straight to my heart. I was glad he turned away before he could see my blush.

When I told my girlfriends about my conversation with the "hot new guy," they predicted that he'd ask me to prom.

Trevor entering my life was like a whirlwind, or more accurately a hurricane. I didn't know I had the capability to become so obsessed with another person. We went to school activities and games together. He tried out for the basketball team and made it. I used to wait for him after practice every day, and he'd drive me home.

My parents thought I was at a girlfriend's doing homework.

When my report card came back less than stellar, my

brother Charles ratted me out. He was only a grade older than me, having barely missed the cutoff to be two grades ahead. It was annoying having a 4.0 student as a brother. And apparently, he was a snitch as well.

I couldn't threaten him with anything because he was my parents' perfect child. Perfect grades, perfect manners, always did his chores without asking, and then some. He didn't even sleep in on the weekends.

My mom sat me down in my room and gave me a horrible 1800s version of why I shouldn't have a boyfriend. Then she narrowed her eyes at me and asked me if I'd already slept with Trevor.

"No, Mom!" I yelled at her. I couldn't believe she'd think so low of me. I was only sixteen, and I hadn't even been kissed. Besides, some of the things my friends had talked about doing with boys sounded kind of gross.

My mom started leaving work early to pick me up from school since Charles was always staying after for one high-achieving project or another. She couldn't even trust me to ride home with my own brother.

Eventually my mom started to calm down, like most parents do, and she told me that as long as I came home right after school, I could ride the bus or get a ride with a friend.

Trevor first kissed me in our kitchen. He was the one bringing me home right after school. He'd have to turn around and get back to practice, but we'd have a precious fifteen or twenty minutes to hang out together. No students, no teachers, no brothers, no parents around.

Our first kiss was strange. Awkward for me because I didn't know what I was doing, and I was afraid that Trevor would be turned off by my inexperience. By our second kiss, I was feeling more confident, and I ran my fingers through his hair, tugging him close as he pressed me against the kitchen counter. When he groaned against my lips and hiked my legs around him, a sense of power and pride flooded through me. I could make him want me.

I suddenly understood my mom's warnings. Up until Trevor and I started spending so much time together, I had been innocent and oblivious. I didn't even need to be with Trevor to think of him. His green eyes, the set of his shoulders, the way he pressed me against the counter to kiss me, the heat of his hands on me . . . I loved him in the color red.

❧

My eyes shoot open, and my mind goes on alert. My room is quiet. The light coming from the hallway through the crack under my door is dim. *Red.* Trevor was wearing a red shirt the night of my parents' murders. I squeeze my eyes shut again as my chest tightens in panic. I don't want to remember. I don't want to know if Trevor was at my house that night. In my parents' bedroom with me.

I had told Dr. Mayer that I remembered a red shirt. Had it been my subconscious knowing? Or had I tricked my mind into believing it, and now it was creating a memory?

I breathe out, trying to fight the gripping panic building in my chest. But the panic comes anyway, and I want to push the emergency call button and demand my red pill.

No. No pills. I command myself. *Remember the red shirt. Where was Trevor when he was wearing it? My bedroom? The kitchen? Where?*

I squeeze my eyes shut, trying to will the memory to fully form. Trevor, his messy hair after we kissed, his bare shoulders and chest and stomach that I ran my hands down. The memory returns. This time it's stronger and lasts longer.

Trevor pulls back on his shirt—his red shirt—and climbs off my bed. He opens my bedroom door.

"No," I whisper. "Go out the window. My parents will hear you."

He turns to look at me. "I need to pee."

I roll my eyes. "Can't you wait until you get home?"

He flashes a smile. "It's either the bathroom or the yard."

"Fine," I say. "But don't flush the toilet. I swear my mom has hearing like a dog."

He's gone for only a minute, and then I hear the rush of water through pipes.

"Trevor," I grumble, climbing off the bed. I open the door as he's coming down the hall back to my room.

"I forgot," he says with a shrug. "Habit."

"Get in here," I whisper, grabbing him and pulling him into my room again.

He wraps his arms around me and laughs against my neck. I hush him.

"Jessica?" a voice rings out from the stairway down the hall from my room.

"Shit," Trevor says.

My mom's awake. Why isn't she asleep? It's after midnight. The stairs creak as she comes down them.

"Get in the closet," I tell Trevor, motioning for him to get away.

But my mom is too quick. She opens the bedroom door—a door she told me to leave open at night to keep the air circulating, even though I know it's her way to check up on me.

The memory cuts off before I can see my mom come into my room. I open my eyes to see only darkness filtered by the white blinds in my room. My skin is damp from perspiration, my breathing shallow. "No," I whisper to myself. Closing my eyes again, I try to force my mind to remember what happened next. "Come back," I demand of the memory. I wasn't sure if Trevor made it into the closet or if my mom saw him too.

Was this where it started? The fight? Did I go find a knife and use it on my mom and then seek out my dad?

I don't know the answers, but my pulse is beating like mad, and I feel every bit of the emotion of a teenage girl who's in trouble. Yet somehow, I know that my mom was wearing her white bathrobe. Was the red I remembered Trevor's shirt or my mom's robe soaked with her own blood?

I turn over and reach for the journal in the bottom drawer of my bedside table. It's one of the ones that's already been transcribed. But no one knows that I've been writing other things on the back pages—things that I don't want to tell anyone. Not yet.

There's enough moonlight coming through that I can make out the lined paper. From a thin rip on the side of my mattress, I pull out a pen that I've kept hidden. Pens can be used as weapons or to self-harm, so I'm allowed to use one only under supervision.

I begin to write what I remember of the dream. Of Trevor and his red shirt. Of the toilet flushing. Of my mom coming down the stairs. After I've written every detail I can possibly remember, I turn the page and start writing about Trevor's new life. His life of freedom, with a wife, two little girls, trips to the beach. Smiles, laughter, and love.

I hate him. I hate that he didn't have to pay for what he did that night.

CHAPTER 9

LOGAN

"WE NEED TO catch him before work," Gwen told me the night before we plan to talk to Trevor Mills. She's staked out his favorite coffee shop and even knows what he orders each morning. I don't know how she does that all so quickly.

So we meet up on the corner the following morning, down the street from the coffee shop. Gwen is dressed to the nines, wearing one of her power suits. Her high heels make her almost as tall as me. She's wearing a lot more makeup than she was the other day, and her lips are painted a dark red.

I tear my gaze from her as we start to walk together. The street is bustling with morning commuters, and smells of baked goods and coffee waft around us, coming from various cafés and bakeries.

"How have you been doing?" Gwen asks, looking up at me as if I'm the most interesting man she knows.

"Oh no, you want to make small talk?" I say.

She laughs—her low and throaty laugh—and it stirs my blood.

I look away from her and focus on walking. I decide to answer honestly. "I've been pretty buried with work, but that's not unusual, I guess. You?"

"Great," she says in a breezy way. I can feel her gaze on me. "Girlfriend?"

I miss a step. "Nope."

She laughs. "I'm not seeing anyone either."

I'm not quite sure why this makes my pulse escalate. Gwen and I have been over for a long time. When we broke up, I had no desire to get back together with her. Yet, despite the scent of coffee in the air, I can smell her spice and hint of something sweeter.

"Here we are," she says, and I look up at the coffee shop sign. She checks her phone. "He should be here in a few minutes."

I swallow, my throat feeling dry.

"Don't worry," she says, seeming to read my every thought. "We're going to scare him a little. I want you to pay close attention to his eye contact and body language. I don't have a warrant, so everything will be off record anyway."

I pull open the door and hold it for Gwen. She passes by me, and I find myself watching her hips sway as she enters the shop. I lift my gaze, pulling my thoughts back to center.

"Are we ordering?" I ask, eyeing the line in front of us.

"When he gets here, we'll get in line behind him."

I nod.

She looks down at her phone and fiddles with it, keeping up the pretense of looking busy.

Not five minutes later, Trevor Mills walks in. I recognize him right away from the pictures that Gwen showed me. He holds the door open for a couple of people coming in right behind him. Then he gets in line after them. I'm impressed with his appearance. He's wearing a sky-blue shirt that looks perfectly pressed and a decent tie.

He pulls out his phone and scrolls through it as he stands in line. Gwen and I file in right behind him.

After about thirty seconds, Gwen says, "Trevor Mills?"

He turns around quickly and sees her, but there's no recognition in his eyes. "Yes?"

"I thought that was you," she says, sticking out her hand and giving him a brilliant smile. "Remember high school?"

"Yeah, that feels like two lifetimes ago." He smiles at Gwen, but his eyes still haven't registered who she is. Of course they haven't, and they won't, because he doesn't know her.

"Remember Mr. Wright's class?" She continues. "He was such a control freak."

Trevor gives a sort of half laugh as he looks Gwen up and down. He might be a married man with kids, but he isn't dead. He definitely appreciates Gwen's looks, and this, of course, makes me want to insert my own claim on her. But I'm not a caveman.

"You don't remember me, do you?" Gwen continues. "I'm Gwen . . . it's been forever. Did you go to the last reunion?"

"No," Trevor says. "My wife was nine months pregnant."

"Oh," Gwen says, lifting her brows. "You're married, then?"

"Wife and two kids," Trevor says, and his face flushes a little.

Interesting reaction on his part.

"Wow," she says. "You're like the whole package."

This comment makes his face grow even redder.

"Sorry, I'm being incredibly rude," Gwen says. "This is my friend, Logan. Logan, this is Trevor Mills. We went to high school together." As if I hadn't heard the entire conversation.

Still, I shake Trevor's hand, and he gives me a brief smile accompanied with an appraising look. I wonder if this guy is a player.

"I don't think I've seen you since graduation," Gwen continues, her smile bright. "And now look at you—do you work around here?"

"At Lund's Financial one street over," he says.

"Nice," Gwen purrs, placing a hand on his arm. "I love a man who can manage his money."

I smile and shake my head as if I'm used to Gwen's flirty ways. I slip one hand in my pocket, keeping my stance casual.

The line moves forward a couple of people, and we all shuffle ahead.

"My senior year was kind of a whirlwind," Trevor says. "We moved to that school in the middle of the first semester, and I didn't get to know a ton of people."

"Except for your basketball teammates and the cheer-leaders," Gwen says with a wink.

I can practically see Trevor wondering if Gwen was a cheerleader.

"But you had a steady girlfriend," Gwen continues as the line moves up another notch. "I mean, Jessica Harper was such sweet girl. Who would have thought—" She cuts herself off and covers her mouth with her hand. "I'm really sorry. Didn't mean to bring that up."

The line shifts forward.

It's Trevor's turn to order. "Don't worry about it," he says, then steps up to the counter and places his order.

His shoulders are stiff, and his voice sounds a bit stilted as he talks to the cashier. Signs of distress? Signs of buried guilt?

He moves to the pickup counter, and Gwen orders for the both of us. I watch Trevor out of the corner of my eye. He shifts his weight a couple of times. Checks his phone. Just as his order is called out, Gwen turns to him. "Care to sit with us for a few minutes? I'd love to talk to you about my investment portfolio—off the record, of course. I'm not super happy with my financial planner right now, and I've heard nothing but good about Lund's Financial from a couple of friends."

Trevor's demeanor brightens. "Yeah, uh, of course." His gaze once again travels the length of Gwen. She's well dressed, and it's anyone guess what her profession is, but she's obviously successful.

We settle at a small table that really seats two, so it's a bit of a crowd with the three of us. The café noise bustles about us, but we seem to be in our own little world.

Gwen asks a couple of questions about Trevor's investment philosophies, and I have to admit that I like his answers. Maybe I'll hire him myself.

Then Gwen abruptly changes subjects. Placing a hand on Trevor's, she says, "I know I wasn't able to tell you at the time, but I'm so sorry about what happened with Jessica."

His mouth opens, then closes.

"I mean, I couldn't believe what she did to her parents," she says in a conspiratorial voice. "No one could." Gwen gives a dramatic shudder. "It must have been horrifying for you and your parents."

Trevor sits very stiffly, his eyes on his coffee cup.

I'd love to hear what he's thinking right now. He seems very uncomfortable with the turn in conversation, and I know that Gwen is highly aware of this too.

"Jessica was always kind of different, if you don't mind me saying so," Gwen continues. "I mean, we were in PE class together, and she wouldn't even change in front of the other girls. She was so . . . modest."

"Shy," Trevor interrupts. "She was shy. Or what we call *introverted* in today's psychobabble."

I try not to take offense at his description of my field of expertise. He lifts his gaze and holds Gwen's, and I begin to feel uncomfortable.

It seems that after all this time, and all that happened, Trevor is staying loyal to Jessica. This concept fascinates me, and I wonder if Gwen has picked up on it as well.

"Well, I mean that she was different from most girls," Gwen says in a breezy voice. "But maybe that's what you liked about her?" She lets the sentence hang.

"Jessica was an amazing girl," Trevor says.

I take a sip of my coffee, trying to keep my attitude nonchalant because I sense that he's finally opening up. Sure enough, Trevor glances at me.

"Logan will keep our conversation private," Gwen prompts.

He looks back to her, and I'm relieved he's buying into Gwen's story.

"I couldn't say the same thing about her family, though," Trevor says. "I mean, not that I'd ever want her parents to be killed." He clears his throat, and I make a mental note of his actions. "Her parents were like jailers. You wouldn't believe how strict they were."

Gwen nods and rolls her eyes. "Oh, I heard stories," she lies. "That time when we went to a birthday sleepover and her mom wouldn't let her stay past ten o'clock. And that was our freshman year, so I'm sure it only got worse after that."

Trevor scoffs. "That's nothing. She found a security camera in her room."

Even my eyes widen at this.

A half smile crosses his face. "We found a way to loop it, though, so that her mom thought there was nothing to see."

"Wow, that sounds really techie," Gwen says.

Trevor shrugs. "It was actually Charles that adjusted it for us. Probably the only nice thing he did for his sister."

"Yeah," Gwen says, playing along. "Charles was a really strange duck, though. He was always mean to her. Makes me feel sorry for Jessica. So, who could really blame her for what she did? Her home life was a nightmare."

I'm watching Trevor closely while pretending not to stare at him.

Trevor's eyes shift, and I'm almost 100 percent sure he's about to lie to us.

"She's better off where she is now," he says in a quiet voice.

I stiffen. What does he mean? She's better off at a residential psych unit than a prison? Or she's better off with her controlling parents dead?

Gwen is thinking along the same lines. "I know what you mean, a psychiatric care center has got to be better than prison."

Trevor leans closer to Gwen, completely ignoring me. "Better than living with her brother."

I exhale. I'm dying to ask him questions, but I'm not playing the role of pretending we went to high school together.

Gwen shakes her head slowly, and I see by the look in her eyes that she's scrambling for something to say—something to keep this conversation going. "Did I tell you that Charles asked me to Homecoming?" she says, glancing at me.

I can tell she's desperate.

She's giving me a segue to help her. My mind spins, and I jump into the conversation. "*That's* the Charles you told me about? Jessica's *brother*?" I push out a breath of air. "Wow. Now I see more of the picture. No wonder you turned him down."

Trevor looks interested. We've taken over the conversation—fake as it is.

I continue. "Yeah, I mean you were smart to see the warning signs right away." I make eye contact with Trevor. "This Charles dude put a crate of live chickens on Gwen's front porch. And the note read: *Don't be chicken to go to Homecoming with me.*"

Gwen's shudder is my reward. "It was so weird. I mean, I suppose Charles thought it was funny and clever, but it wasn't my sense of humor. I didn't know what to do with the chickens."

Trevor nods, his gaze moving between the both of us now. "What *did* you do?"

"That's the creepy part," I jump in. I'm having fun with this. "Gwen didn't want to go, so she made up some excuse and returned the chicken crate to his house. Later, she heard Jessica tell a friend that one morning she found three dead chickens in their backyard. No one in the family knew where they'd come from."

Trevor leans back in his chair and rubs his neck. "No wonder Jessica never got along with her brother." He shifts again and leans forward this time. "She absolutely hated him."

CHAPTER 10

JESS

AGAIN, I'M READY before Marlene comes into my room to fetch me for my therapy appointment. I've done my gardening already, and even though my fingers are stained with dirt that I can't quite get out, I'm presentable. I'm looking forward to my second appointment with Dr. Mayer, especially after experiencing such a vivid memory. I haven't decided how much I'll tell him yet, if anything, but for the first time in nine years, I feel like I'm making progress in my life. Instead of going backward or staying stagnant, I'm moving forward.

"Well, you must like Dr. Mayer," Marlene deadpans. Her tone isn't exactly approving. But I don't care what she thinks.

Today I'm wearing a silky blouse that I pulled from the donation bags, matched with a pair of really worn black leggings that have been washed so much they're more of a dull brown than black. I'm not so concerned about the color because I know that they look good on me. And they're a far cry from my usually baggy, sloppy clothing.

It's been a long time since I wished I had makeup to wear. But even I won't let my wishes spiral that far out of control. My hair is pulled back into its usual ponytail. Nothing special there.

Dr. Mayer is already waiting when Marlene knocks on the door. I'm a few minutes late, and I'm impressed that he's cognizant of time as much as I am.

"Hello." The doctor holds out his hand to shake mine as I enter.

Before shaking his hand, I turn to look at Marlene, effectively dismissing her. She pulls the door shut, leaving Dr. Mayer and me alone.

I stretch out my hand and grip his in what I hope to be a confident shake. I read online that in order to impress someone you meet, your handshake should be firm.

Dr. Mayer's hand is warm and firm, just as I expected it to be. When he releases my hand, I wish he didn't have to release it quite so soon. With what little affection I receive in here, I appreciate the smaller bits of contact.

He's asking me something, but I've let my mind wander. When he smiles and waits for my reply, I'm caught up in the way his lips curve up and his even teeth peek out.

"What did you say?" I ask, because really, my inattentiveness won't surprise him. He's read my chart after all.

"I asked how you're feeling today," he says. "It looks like you've been gardening."

His smile remains. It's a nice smile, not a condescending one.

"Yes, it's a nice day to be outside," I say, not adding much more. My headache pinches, although I'm pretty much used to the constant head pain now. It's the price I'm paying for adjusting my medication. I step past him, surprised that he hasn't already moved back and taken his seat. Like last time, I sit in the right chair, and he sits in the left. He doesn't seem to want the desk separating us.

I cross my legs and fold my hands together, as if I'm determined to be perfectly mannered, which I am. Then I meet his gaze. His dark-brown eyes seem lighter today, but still they're warm brown. This is my favorite part about him—his eye color. Trevor's were green, my brother's blue, my parents both blue . . . the brown is a nice change.

"The report that Marlene gave me a little while ago says that you've been a peacemaker this week," he says.

I shrug. "I'm always the peacemaker around here. The other women get pretty hotheaded over childish stuff."

He nods but doesn't seem to let Marlene's report go. "You've grown close to some of the patients, haven't you?"

"I suppose," I say. "I mean we've become friends, although I'm more like a mom to them sometimes."

Dr. Logan writes something on his notepad. "Were you the peacemaker at your home while growing up?"

I exhale. Here we go. He wants to talk about my childhood. I decide to humor him for now. "Since I only had one brother, I didn't have anyone else to try to keep the peace with."

"Did the two of you get along, or did you experience the typical sibling rivalry?" he asks.

What is he getting at? Why all this interest in the relationship with my brother? "He teased me a lot," I say. "Sometimes I tried to give him a hard time, too, but it usually backfired."

He chuckles, like we're old friends ratting out our siblings. "He was your older brother, so he probably had the upper hand most of the time."

"If that's what you want to call it," I say before I can stop myself.

His expression doesn't change much, but the air between us shifts. "What's something you did to get back at him for what he did?"

A memory flashes into my mind, unbidden and sudden. It's of when I was probably about twelve, and I suppose I never really forgave my brother for what he did. It seems harmless enough to tell Dr. Mayer—something that I can tell him even if I'm not sure how much I can trust him.

"Ever since I was little, I collected Barbies," I start out. "By the time I was twelve, I had a good collection. I didn't keep them in their boxes or anything, but I took good care of them. I was probably too old to keep playing with them, but sometimes I'd pull them out and play for a couple of hours. Maybe it was nostalgic." I link my fingers together, trying to keep my voice steady. It's been a long time since I thought about this.

"One weekend, when my parents were out Christmas shopping for us," I continue, "Charles came into my room. He laughed at me when he saw me playing with Barbies. He grabbed one and stripped off the clothing. Then he said some disgusting stuff about the Barbie. I tried to grab it from him, but it only made him meaner. He picked up most of the Barbies, at least the ones I wasn't holding hostage, and he took them in the backyard and lit their hair on fire."

Dr. Mayer isn't writing anything down as I speak. He watches me and listens. I appreciate this.

I can still see the silhouette of my brother in the early evening light as he knelt on the ground and used a lighter to destroy my Barbies. "I was too afraid and upset to go outside. So I stood at the window and watched. When he looked up to make sure I was watching, I ran back to my room and locked the door."

"What did your parents say?" Dr. Mayer asks.

"I never told them," I say in a quiet voice. "I don't know what Charles did with the melted Barbies. It wasn't until a week later that I finally got my revenge."

Dr. Mayer lifts a brow. "I hope it was good."

"It was bittersweet, since I got in trouble for it." I almost smile, although a knot has formed in my stomach. "My brother always kept his bedroom locked up, but one night when he was gone, I broke in and looked around for something to take and destroy. My brother was really into computer and electronics."

"No surprise," Dr. Mayer observes.

"Yeah, so I knew that if I took something he valued, I'd have my revenge," I say. "It was all a jumbled mess and finally I took a couple of cords and one of his tablets. I meant to toss them into a garbage, but instead, I stuck them under my mattress. A dumb hiding spot, I know."

Dr. Mayer just watches me.

"Charles raised hell as soon as he came home," I say, looking down at my hands. "Under my mattress was one of the first places he looked, and he'd dragged my parents into the room as witnesses."

"Did you tell them about the Barbies?" he asks.

"I never did, and I don't know why," I say, holding up my hand. "Believe me, I've asked myself more than once. I think I was afraid my parents wouldn't believe me, and that would make me feel so much worse."

"Were you grounded, or what?"

"For a week, and I lost TV privileges." I look away from the doctor. The compassion in his eyes makes the memory sting. "After that, Charles used to hiss at me when he walked by."

"Hiss?"

"Yeah, like he was mimicking the sound of fire—and how he'd burned the Barbies." I blink because my eyes start to water.

Of course Dr. Mayer notices, and he shifts forward in his chair. "You know, sibling rivalry has been going on forever."

"I know," I say. "Back to Cain and Abel."

Dr. Mayer seems surprised at the reference; then he

smiles. "Yeah, you could say that." Then he sobers. "It's just that I've heard a lot of sibling rivalry stories, and I even have some myself. Everyone goes through stuff as a kid. But . . ." He taps his notebook. "Sometimes sibling rivalry crosses the line."

"What? I'm abused now? Neglected? Bullied?" I raise my hands in mock surrender. "Add that to my crazy diagnosis."

Dr. Mayer doesn't crack a smile. "You were *all* of those things, Jessica."

I fold my arms. "Like you said, everyone goes through crap. Mine just led me here." I'm blinking my eyes again.

"What's one of your good memories with your brother?" he asks after a moment of silence.

I'm surprised at the question. It's one I haven't been asked before. "I suppose . . ." I think back to the moments I shared with Charles. Family meals, holidays, going on errands with my mom when we were younger. But nothing surfaces. Charles was always in some sort of competition with me. He always dominated whatever situation we were in. It wasn't until I had my own circle of friends that I started feeling like I was a separate entity from my brother and parents.

"Jessica?" Dr. Mayer says in a gentle voice.

"I don't know," I finally say.

"You don't know, or you don't have any good memories of your brother?"

I meet his gaze, and I'm glad his eyes are brown. "I don't know."

Dr. Mayer seems to be looking past my eyes, deep inside somewhere. It makes me feel vulnerable, a feeling that I usually hate, but with Dr. Mayer, I want him to see. I want him to see my pain. I want him to hear my pain. To feel it. To understand.

My hands are trembling, and I fold my arms to stop the shaking. My eyes slip closed, and I know even if I sit here another hour thinking of my childhood, I'll not be able to come up with one good memory of my brother.

Dr. Mayer places a hand on my shoulder. The touch startles me, and I open my eyes.

He quickly lifts his hand.

But I won't forget the weight and warmth of his touch. It feels like safety.

CHAPTER 11

LOGAN

"WHAT'S SHE LIKE?" Gwen asks me as soon as the waitress at this hole-in-the-wall Mexican restaurant leaves with our orders scratched out on her notepad.

I don't have to ask who Gwen is referring to. After our meeting with Trevor, Gwen's interest in the cold case has only grown hotter. When Trevor talked about Jessica hating her brother and then Jessica shared the Barbie story in our session, I knew the Harper murders might not be so cut and dried.

Whatever happened that night, I don't think Jessica was alone. And perhaps she didn't act alone. Despite the medical records that Gwen produced about Trevor, I wonder if they were forged. I'd met desperate parents before, and desperate people will go above and beyond the law to protect their own.

Regardless of any theories I might have, I'm starting to believe that things have been covered up in the case. By whom and about what, I don't know yet. But I do know that if Gwen and I work together, we have a better chance of finding out. We have to get enough leads in order for Gwen to reopen the case.

"Jessica's really smart," I say in response to Gwen's

question. "She reminds me of a baby bird that's fallen out of a nest and doesn't know she can fly."

Gwen tilts her head. "How so? You think she knows more than she admits?"

"I think she's truly blocked out her memories of that night. She doesn't remember because her mind is in protective mode. But I don't think it will last forever." I take a sip of the ice water the waitress has set on our table.

"Like . . . her psyche will kick it all out one day?"

"It will be gradual," I say. "The emotions will be torturous, and her mind and body will continue to protect her. So it could take months, or even a year, for her memories to fully return once they start."

"Hmm." Gwen keeps her gaze on me.

"People who go through terrible tragedies will find a way to protect their minds from comprehending the whole of it," I continue. "They lock away certain things, certain images. And when a memory returns, it can be physically crippling."

"Like what a military veteran goes through with PTSD," she surmises.

I pause. It's a good analogy. "Exactly."

The waitress bustles over and places a large bowl of fresh tortilla chips and a smaller bowl of salsa in front of us.

Gwen picks up a chip and dunks it. "Does she have triggers?"

I smile. Gwen has become more intuitive than when we were last dating. "That's what I'm working on. She has some major issues with her brother—ones that go all the way back as far as she can remember."

"Sibling rivalry?" Gwen asks, then pops a chip in her mouth.

I scoop up salsa with a chip of my own. The stuff is fresh. "It goes beyond that." I tell her the Barbie story. I've already sworn Gwen to secrecy, and if she wants to use any of what I say to reopen the case, she'll have to get a warrant and we'll have to go through the official process. But for now, two heads are better than my own.

By the time I've finished telling Gwen the Barbie story, she's forgotten the delicious salsa and is staring at me.

"So . . . ," she says in a slow voice, "What are you thinking?"

"I don't think she was the only one at home that night, besides her parents, that is."

She gives a brief nod. "How do you explain her brother at scout camp and her boyfriend fresh out of surgery?"

"That's your job, ma'am."

Her eyebrows lift. "Oh really?"

"You're the detective," I tease.

"Okay," she says. "You said that Jessica is delicate like a bird . . . one who hasn't even spread her wings yet. I'm assuming you've read the statements in court about how she single-handedly slit the throats of two grown adults."

I nod. I've put off eating salsa for a bit.

"Have you seen the pictures of her as a teen?"

"I have."

"Impression?"

"She's a couple of inches taller now but still petite in bone structure and frame." I take a sip of my water. "If you read the full report, you'll remember that both of her parents had taken sleeping pills that night."

"Sleeping pills that were prescribed only to the mom," Gwen points out, "although the prescription was over a year old."

"Which means that she didn't normally take them," I say. "That doesn't explain why both parents would take them on the same night, especially if they were having issues with a daughter who had a history of sneaking out at night or sneaking her boyfriend inside."

"Yep," Gwen says, picking up another chip and dunking it. She eats it with satisfaction, then reaches across the table and grasps my hand. "We still make a pretty good team."

Her touch is warm, soft, inviting. In this single gesture, I know what she is saying. The question is whether I want to rekindle anything. Short-term or long-term.

I turn my palm up and link our fingers. "What's the next step, detective?"

She grins, tightening her hold on me, and my heart rate decides to speed up. "You need to find out what Jessica's triggers are—get those memories coming back. And I ... I have another visit to pay to Trevor, and this time I'll tell him what my profession is."

"I'm coming with you," I say.

Gwen lifts her brows just as the waitress appears with our meals. Gwen releases my hand. I've ordered the chicken enchilada plate, Gwen the vegetarian burrito. I thank the waitress and start to cut into the steaming dish.

"If Trevor is guilty, even by association, I don't want you alone with him."

"You're sweet," Gwen says with a grimace. "I'm not meeting him in private—yet. Besides, I'm a detective."

I exhale. "Then tell me the time and place and I'll stay incognito."

"So protective," she murmurs, cutting into her own food. But her smile is there, and I know she's liking my protectiveness.

"When are you thinking of meeting him?" I ask, not letting this drop.

"Tonight." She takes a bite of her food. "There's a company barbecue on the beach. Thought I'd happen to stroll by."

I raise my brows. "Won't he be with his family?"

"All the better—get his wife's reaction."

"I think you need to be strolling with a date," I say.

"And you're offering?" She flashes an innocent smile.

"I'm offering." I know she's going to say yes, but my pulse is still drumming.

"Does your motorcycle still hold two?" she asked, her eyes gleaming at me.

The deal is sealed. We finish eating, and she insists on paying half of the bill. I let her because I know it's useless to argue about it. At this point.

When I walk her to her car, she turns to me, lifts up on her toes, and kisses my cheek. "Pick me up at eight thirty. I'll be ready."

"All right." I watch her get into her car and pull away from the curb before I realize I'm standing on the sidewalk, staring after her.

Am I really thinking about dating her again? I try to picture a scenario where I'm asking her out—and she says yes. Then what? We go back to how we were? Pick up where we left off? Does my supposed high moral ground count for nothing now? I guess it's true when they say that people can change.

I shake my thoughts away and walk the half block to where I parked my motorcycle. I have more appointments this afternoon, and I hope the ride back to the office will clear my head of thoughts of Gwen and what her touch used to do to me—still does to me.

By the time I reach the office, I'm still foggy minded. Not even Sandra's yellow dress, earrings, necklace, and bracelets shock my mind.

"You're back early," Sandra says. "Good. Because one of your clients stopped in to see if you had even ten minutes to give him."

I pause by her desk. "Who?"

"Charles Harper."

I'm suddenly very focused.

"Is he . . . distressed?" I ask in a hushed voice, glancing at my office door. It's shut, and this is the protocol that I've given Sandra if I'm ever late for an appointment. Patients don't like to see other patients in a waiting room. Some psychiatrists have private entrances to their offices.

She lowers her voice as well. "He's flustered—but not at risk."

At risk could mean more than one thing. It could mean he might self-harm, or it could mean that he might try to harm me or someone in our office.

"Thanks," I say to Sandra and cross to my office door.

Pushing the door open, I expect to see Charles standing by the window, or at least sitting in a chair. Instead, he's lying flat on the ground, his eyes closed.

Panic jolts through me, until I realize he's breathing.

He cracks open an eye as I approach. "Was feeling dizzy, so I laid down. Hope you don't mind."

Very carefully, I exhale. "I don't mind." I snatch a blank notebook from my desk and sit in a chair. "Did you have a blackout episode?" I ask.

He doesn't answer for a moment. "Not exactly. It's more of an epiphany."

Again, he stops. So I say, "What about?"

"About my episodes, of course." His tone is mocking. "My sister is the cause of them."

The way he says this raises the hairs on my arms. We've already talked about connecting his episodes with his weekly visits with his sister. This isn't what I'd call an epiphany.

"Do you think blaming your sister is going to help or hurt you more?" I ask in a casual tone.

"Everything about my sister hurts me." He still hasn't opened his eyes.

"Have you thought about taking a break? For your own mental health?"

Now his eyes pop open. "Ha. If I don't stay on top of her medical condition, she'd crumble."

I lean forward, holding his gaze. "How? She's surrounded by caretakers. Do you really think that your one hour a week is what keeps it all going?" I'm being bold, but his arrogance is astounding, especially after hearing from Jessica about their childhood.

"One hour a week? Is that what you think it is?" Charles's eyes slide shut again. "I emailed you my chart for the last two weeks. One glance and you'll know that I invest much more than an hour a week on my sister."

"You emailed me?"

"Just a few minutes ago. Before you came into the office. Go ahead, pull it up."

I'm normally not on my phone or laptop when I'm with a client, but with his invitation, I take my phone out of my pocket. I scroll through a couple of new emails to find one sent about ten minutes ago. I open it and click on the attachment.

A spreadsheet loads. I keep my mouth shut, although it wants to fall open. The first row is a chronology of time, by half hour. The column has a list of medications, activities, and miscellaneous information. I scan one row that's labeled: "Interactions with other patients." I stop on the name "Jessica" and see there's a link embedded.

I click on the link, and a text document opens with a transcribed conversation. I skim through the text—it's an ordinary conversation between the two women, talking about another patient that Erin doesn't seem to like. I'm not sure where or how Charles got this information. I'm assuming there are security cameras throughout the facility, but how does Charles have that access?

I look at Charles on the floor. His eyes are closed.

"You put this spreadsheet together yourself?" I ask, almost afraid to hear the answer.

His lips stretch into a smile, and he slits his eyes to look at me. "Impressive, huh? I am a data analyst, though, so it's second nature."

"Do you have access to your sister's conversations?" I ask.

"I do," he says, then chuckles. "In case you think I'm invading her privacy, I'm her legal guardian, and she's being cared for in a separate location, so it's the only way I can make sure she's being taken care of."

Without asking the obvious questions of whether what he was doing was legal, I say, "Does she know about your monitoring?"

Charles pushes himself up on onto his elbows, looking as relaxed as a cat sitting in the sun. "I don't want to make her paranoid. If she has nothing to hide, then she shouldn't worry about anything else."

This is a turning point in our conversation, and since Charles introduced it, I pursue. "Do you think she's hiding something?"

"Always," he says. "I can see it in her eyes. She won't even meet my gaze half of the time. She's defensive when I ask her questions about her routine or therapy."

"Can you clarify for me?" I ask. "Do you think she's hiding things about the tragedy of your parents' deaths, or hiding things that are happening in her residence?"

Charles climbs to his feet, now standing over me since I'm still sitting down. "She doesn't remember that night. We've been doing therapy for nine years." His laugh is low and dry. "I mean, if she hasn't remembered by now, what are the chances she'll remember anytime soon?"

He pauses, and I realize that he's asking me a question and not just stating his opinion.

"There's always a chance," I say, and I know it's not what he wants to know.

His nostrils flare slightly, the only indicator that he isn't happy with what I'm saying. "What has she told you?" He is controlling his voice. "Has she remembered something?"

I don't hesitate. "No," I say. "She hasn't remembered the events from that night." She told me about the red shirt, but I don't know if that's a memory. And I won't tell anything to Charles about his sister. I have to keep some principles regarding these two siblings, knowing that I'm breaking others.

He leans down, and I catch a whiff of something spicy he must have eaten. "As soon as she tells you, I need to know. I need to be there for her."

I don't agree or disagree. "I think you'll be the first to know." It's a joke, but I don't say it like one.

He doesn't laugh.

My office intercom buzzes just in time. "Look, I'm glad I was able to see you for a short time; my two o'clock is here."

CHAPTER 12

JESS

NICOLE HAS GIVEN me a precious gift, one more valuable than anything I've ever owned. This morning at breakfast she said something about Facebook. I asked her if she used to be on it, and she said it was her favorite thing before she was admitted. But her family made her stay off the computer because she was looking up her old boyfriends and asking them lots of questions.

I can only imagine what those questions were. "Do you still have the account?" I asked Nicole.

She looked around the room before answering in a whisper, "Yes, do you want to know my email and password? My mom told me to never tell anyone."

"Your mom was right." The idea took only a few seconds to form. "But you and your mom can trust me."

Nicole smiled at me, really smiled, her freckled face beaming. She leaned over and whispered the information.

Now, lunch is over, my red pill dissolved in my untouched juice, and it's my computer time.

I open the browser on the computer, then look behind me to see how carefully I'm being monitored. Patrick gives me a slight nod. His attention is drawn to Erin, who stands up from her table and sweeps her arm across her half-finished puzzle. Pieces scatter everywhere.

"I hate horses!" she screeches. As if on cue.

Patrick hurries to her side.

Erin's temper tantrum is the distraction I need. I love Erin. Even though I don't know if her fit is intentional, this will give me at least a few minutes of time on my own.

I quickly open Facebook. Because of my memory a few nights ago, I'm convinced that Trevor was in my house the night of my parents' deaths. I've remembered it, so it must be true. My mom was coming downstairs because she thought I was up late. I hadn't turned in my phone that night because they had forgotten to ask.

She remembered when she heard the toilet flush. Which probably meant she'd been awake. Charles told me that the coroner's report had said both my parents had taken sleeping pills. But that didn't make sense. My memory clearly showed that my mom had been awake.

Or was the memory faulty? Of a different night?

I've tried the past three nights to get the memory to return. But there is nothing.

So I'm going to message Trevor on Facebook.

I know it's a risk.

I could get caught and lose all computer privileges. Nicole could get in trouble too.

Exhaling, I log in to Facebook under Nicole's name.

I click on the message icon and stare at the white square for a moment. *Just write something,* I tell myself. I don't have time to waste. Erin's now screaming at Patrick, but his deep, calm voice is overriding her hysterical one.

I start to type: *Trevor, it's Jessica. I'm using a friend's account because I can't access Facebook on my own. It's been a long time, I know. Please reply as soon as you can because if*

I'm found out, this account will be deleted. Did you come over to my house that night?

My heart hammers at those few sentences I've typed, and I quickly log out as Erin is restrained and led from the room by two aides.

Patrick's attention is back on me, and he goes back to his usual place, standing against the wall and generally observing. I'm browsing a local news website.

I don't think I'll have a chance to check Facebook again today. It will have to wait until tomorrow, and I don't know if I can count on Erin having another meltdown. My adrenaline is in a hyper state, and I'm tempted to tell Dr. Mayer about my memory of Trevor. I know I can request to see him earlier than our next scheduled appointment. But Charles would find out and he would question why.

"Time's up," Patrick's voice cuts into my thoughts. I've been staring at the same article on the computer about the rise in opioid use throughout the country despite the legalization of marijuana. I've wasted my computer time when I could have been researching hypnosis. Not that Charles would ever allow me to do hypnosis. When the court brought it up, he had the lawyer shoot it down, citing unreliable science and traumatic consequences. I agreed with him at the time; at least I think I did.

The next twenty-three and a half hours crawl by until it's my turn at the computer again. Lunch ends, and all is peaceful. Erin is back at her puzzle table, and Nicole paces in front of the window. I walk to Nicole and say, "Do you want me to check your Facebook account for you today? Maybe there's a comment from one of your boyfriends."

Her eyes widen. "Yes," she whispers, and I'm grateful she's excited. I hope that she won't give me away. "See if Brandon or Matt have posted on my page." She clasps her hands together and looks upward as if the thought of it brings her happiness.

"I will," I whisper back. "You need to talk to Patrick for a few minutes so that I can check."

She giggles, then winks at me.

I turn to look out the window as she continues to pace. When Patrick announces that I can go to the computer, I walk over there, trying not to act like I'm up to something.

First, I pull up the news website. The top report is a homicide in San Diego. I skip past that story. I purposely avoid any articles about other murders. Maybe someday I'll be able to read them. I scroll past a series of articles.

"Look!" Nicole calls out, while pointing at the window. "It's a lost bird."

No one pays her attention until she starts to speak again. "There's a cat trying to get the bird!"

The patients in the room shuffle to the window, Erin included. Patrick looks over, keeping his eye on everyone.

"I don't see a cat," Erin declares.

"You're not looking in the right place," Nicole says. "Look where I'm pointing."

"I am looking!" Erin insists.

Mona rests her head on the window, squinting against the brightness. "I see that cat! It's brown and white!"

Patrick takes a couple of steps closer to the window.

I log in to Facebook. My heart hammers as the website pulls up and I type in the memorized username and password. My breath stalls as I wait for the password to go through.

There's a red circle on the messenger icon, indicating a message. From Trevor?

I glance again over at Patrick, whose gaze is focused on the patients looking out the window. Erin is still arguing with Nicole over the existence of the cat.

I click on the messenger icon.

I'm sorry for everything, Jessica. Believe me. I can't respond through something that's not secure. I'll think about this and I might try to visit you.

Hope surges, and I blink back sudden hot tears. He's not blowing me off. He's not refuting what I asked either. Although he's not admitting that he was at my house that night, I'm feeling more and more sure of the memory. If I can rely on that memory, then I can rely on others that might come.

Regretfully, I reply: *Thank you. You don't know how much it would mean to me to see you again.*

I click out of messenger and log out before I can change my mind about such a vulnerable message. Then I delete the browsing history and type in "Hypnosis." Dozens of links pop up, and I haphazardly click on one just as Patrick moves back to his position.

Erin returns to her puzzle, still arguing with Nicole, but all the fuss has seemed to die down.

Although I'm scrolling through the website, my mind is far away from the rectangular computer screen. Trevor said that he would contact me, that he would visit me. I look up at Nicole and Mona still standing by the window. I see the room with new eyes. I see the female patients who are living in their own worlds, far from reality, although reality is only on the other side of the gardens.

I see the aides and the nurses who are putting in their time before going home to their normal lives. What will Trevor think of all of this? How will he see me? It's been nine years.

I look down at my hands. Hands that have killed the two people I love most in the world. It's time for me to remember. It's time for me to stop living in this bubble of medication and therapy and control. It's time for me to face my past. And my future.

CHAPTER 13

LOGAN

I PULL UP to Gwen's house on my motorcycle, and she's out the door before I can climb off. She practically floats toward me, wearing a flowery sundress and strappy sandals. Her hair is scooped off her neck and pinned up. Long earrings dangle against her neck, and I know before she even gets close that she's going to smell great.

I'm right.

Her smile goes straight to my heart. "You're on time?" she says in a teasing tone.

"I'm a changed man," I say with a wink. I hand her my second helmet, and she steps close to me to strap it on.

She smells of coconut and some sort of flower. Her scent wafts around me as she slides onto the bike behind me. Her arms wrap around my waist, and it feels as if my heart has shot into my throat.

Well then.

"Ready?" I ask, pulling away from the curb.

"Always," she says with a laugh.

The laugh works its way through me, and I'm smiling like a fool. Eventually I close my mouth, because the sun is setting, and bugs are plentiful.

We don't try to talk as we coast along the road toward the beach. Orange and red splash the sky, blending one color into another. The line of cars makes the barbecue location easy to pick out. I find a place across the street in the empty parking lot of a nail salon.

Gwen climbs off first, hands over the helmet, then fusses with her hair. I remove my own helmet, then stand.

"So . . . ," Gwen starts. "We need to put on a good show. We don't want to scare off the wife." She extends her hand, and I take it.

We cross the street, our fingers linked, and warmth shoots through me from our touch.

A couple of canopies are set up, and beneath one sits a row of grills. Beneath another are tables and chairs. Down the beach a little way is a bonfire where a group of people stand around, holding drinks in their hands. Spicy barbecue smells drift on the wind that's blowing toward us. I estimate about sixty people milling about. Not a large crowd, but one that will give us enough anonymity, I hope.

Gwen squeezes my hand. "There he is."

I look over where her chin is pointing. Trevor is wearing khaki pants and a button-down Hawaiian-style shirt. A blonde woman is standing by him, her arm linked with his. She's pretty in an all-American way, and she looks like she spends plenty of time at the gym and salon.

"Wife?" I ask.

"Yep," Gwen says. "Let's mingle."

We walk through the crowd, and we each pick up a drink before heading over to Trevor and his wife.

No one really pays us attention. Each person is probably thinking we're connected with someone else.

"Trevor!" Gwen says in a bright voice as we near him.

He turns his head, and there's a small moment of hesitation, before he says, "Gwen . . . and Logan, right?"

"Right," I say, and stick out my hand to shake his.

Trevor gives me a hearty shake, and his smile is a little too wide. "This is my wife, Aimee," he says.

She sticks out her hand and gives me a semi-limp handshake. It's more of a polite gesture than any real interest. Her gaze moves away a second after it connects with mine. I know that will probably change as soon as Gwen starts talking.

"You're right, Trevor," Gwen says in a peppy voice. "Your firm is impressive, and I'm interested in switching some of my investments over. I mean, I've always been impressed with you personally, so it's not really a stretch for that to reflect in your good work."

"Oh really? That sounds great," Trevor says, that smile still plastered on his face.

Aimee looks at Gwen, then to her husband.

I can't help noticing a slight narrowing of her eyes. "Do you two work together?" his wife says.

"Not at all," Gwen says with a laugh. "I knew your husband in high school. It's Aimee, right?"

The blonde nods, her gaze wary.

I smile like I'm engaged in every aspect of the conversation.

"Wow." Aimee glances at her husband.

"Gwen and I had some classes together," Trevor says with confidence I know he doesn't have.

"We weren't really all that close, though," Gwen assures his wife.

I try not to laugh.

"I mean, he was pretty much tied up with Jessica all the time," she says with a wink. "Plenty of us were jealous of *her*."

I couldn't have predicted it any better. Trevor's wife's face drains of color.

I surmise it's because Jessica is a sore subject between husband and wife.

Gwen reaches out and lightly touches Aimee's arm. "None of us could believe what happened, and I'm sure Trevor was equally shocked."

Trevor's gone pale too.

I want to tug Gwen away from this couple and kiss her soundly on that sassy mouth of hers.

"Yes," Aimee says in a firm voice. "We don't really—I mean, Trevor has put that all behind him." She leans forward a tad. "We have kids now, and we're trying to make a good life for them. We don't really want to keep the negative past at the forefront. Trevor had to go through some counseling, along with his parents, after the incident with his ex-girlfriend. So, basically, we're not open to this sort of conversation at a company barbecue of all places. We'd appreciate your cooperation."

Wow. I'm impressed with Trevor's wife. The buck definitely stops with her.

Trevor's face flushes. He's caught between talking to an interesting and dynamic woman that he doesn't quite remember and his very assertive wife. A hard place to be.

"It's been a long time since I've seen anyone from high school," Trevor says, apology in his voice.

"I completely understand," Gwen soothes, leaning against me and tilting her head. "Logan has gone through some hard stuff as a teen, and he'd rather forget all of it."

Wait. *What?* I roll with it, because what else can I do. "Yeah, life's not easy for anyone."

Gwen trills a laugh. "Tell me about it. All day, every day, I deal with other people's tragedies." She holds up her glass. "Unwinding at the end of a long day is definitely a priority." She takes a well-timed sip of her drink.

Aimee is laser-focused on Gwen now more than ever.

"What is it you do . . . Gwen?"

Here it comes. I shift my gaze to Trevor.

"I'm a detective," she says. "San Diego Police Department."

The various conversations around us seem to hush, and I swear that everyone within fifty feet of us heard Gwen. Trevor's mouth opens, and he sways back as if he were just shoved in the chest.

Gwen takes another sip. "So, I totally get the whole 'leave the past in the past' thing . . . unless new evidence comes to light." She looks up at me. "Ready, hon?"

"Yeah," I say. "We should really get going. It's my mom's birthday." When did lying become so second nature to me?

Gwen reaches out her hand to Trevor, who shakes it like he's a robot. Then she shakes Aimee's hand as well. "Great to see you again, and great to meet you, Aimee." Her gaze shifts back to Trevor. "I'll call your office tomorrow, and we can set up a time to go over my current portfolio."

"All right," Trevor barely chokes out.

"Have a nice evening, everyone," I throw in. Then I turn with Gwen, our hands linked together, and we walk casually away.

It's not until we reach the motorcycle in the parking lot across from the beach that Gwen releases my hand and turns to me. "What did you think?" she asks.

Her eyes are sparkling with triumph.

"He's as scared as a cat with its tail on fire," I say.

She grins and throws her arms around me. I nearly lose my balance. She laughs against my neck, her breath warm and soft. I slide my arms around her, pulling her into a tight hug.

"You're the perfect partner," she says.

And then we're kissing. I don't exactly know how it happens, but with her body pressed against mine, the electric charge that's been between us all night has ignited. Her fingers slide through my hair, and her mouth moves hot and urgent against mine.

I kiss her back, sliding my hands over her hips, tugging her even closer. Gwen has always been a good kisser—it was probably one of the things I missed most about her. Our past comes rushing back, and it seems I've forgotten all the negative stuff. My mind isn't processing any of the implications of what we are doing in the middle of a dark parking lot. I can only feel her soft warmth pressing against me and her mouth on mine, making heat flash through my body.

When she finally pulls back, we're both breathless. "Take me home?"

My reply is only one word. "Definitely."

CHAPTER 14

JESS

TREVOR DIDN'T COME today, or yesterday. It's been two days since he told me he would speak to me in person. Am I a fool to believe him?

The moonless night outside my window gives me no opportunity to write on the back pages of my journal. Still, I try to read the words I recorded about my memory with Trevor in my house. After I've read through it in the dimness, I hold the journal against my chest and lie on my back, squeezing my eyes shut.

I think through each part of the memory, but nothing new comes to my mind. What happened after my mom opened my bedroom door? Did Trevor make it in time to hide in the closet? Did I pretend to be asleep? Did I block my mom's entrance and act as if it had been me in the bathroom?

Keeping my eyes shut, I review the details a second time. What had I been wearing? I think through what I typically wore to bed—something clicks. I was wearing a fitted tank, loose sweats, feet bare. I remember this now because when the police arrived, they made me put on shoes and one of them put a jacket over my shoulders.

I think of Trevor's picture on Facebook. He's aged, but

he's still good-looking. His green eyes haven't changed. I'd told him many times how much I loved his eyes.

"You're trying to butter me up," Trevor would say.

The memory is so subtle that I almost don't realize that I've started to remember more of that night.

"Mom, I just went to the bathroom," I tell her as she swings my door open. I'm halfway through climbing into bed.

She looks about the room, her sharp gaze missing nothing. Thankfully Trevor is inside the closet, and although the door is ajar, I can't see his body at all.

Then my mom sniffs. Actually sniffs the air.

"Do you smell something?" I say, and I can't help my acid tone. It's like she can't trust me even in the middle of the night . . . of course, she really can't, but she doesn't have to know that.

"It smells like cologne," she says.

"It's probably the bathroom spray I used," I say. "It lingers."

Her eyes snap to mine and start to narrow.

I exaggerate a yawn and pull the covers up and over me. "Goodnight." It's civil, yet hopefully gets the point across.

My mom hesitates. She doesn't seem to want to argue at midnight any more than I do.

I close my eyes, as if there's nothing strange about my mom standing in the middle of the room, staring me down while I'm trying to fall asleep.

Moments later, I hear the door click, and moments after that, her footsteps going up the stairs.

"Finally," Trevor whispers, opening the closet door.

I sit up. "Shhh." I wouldn't be surprised if my mom was still listening at the top of the stairs.

Trevor joins me on the bed. His arms snake about me, and he tugs me against his chest. I stifle a laugh and burrow against his warmth. Goosebumps cover my body, and I'm not sure if they're from the adrenaline of almost getting caught or because Trevor's arms are around me in the middle of my bed.

My heart hammers as his hands slide from my waist to my hips.

"You're so beautiful," he whispers against my neck. He kisses me right beneath my ear, where he knows it makes me crazy.

Something thumps against my window, and we both freeze.

"What the hell was that?" Trevor hisses, his arms tightening around me.

I can't move. "I don't know." My mind races. Have my parents found us out? My nosy neighbor? My blinds are pulled up from when I let Trevor inside. But the window is shut.

Trevor climbs off the bed and crosses to the window. I want to tell him to hide in my closet again, but I can't seem to say a word.

He leans forward, pressing his forehead against the window, peering out into the night.

"Maybe it was a bird," he finally says, turning to me.

I don't like the look in his eyes—suspicion mixed with fear. Maybe anger.

I'm freaked out.

"You should go," I say. What if my mom really didn't go upstairs?

"Out the window?" Trevor says. "What if your dad is waiting?"

My breathing hasn't calmed down at all.

"Let's wait, then," I say.

Trevor locks my bedroom door, and I'm not sure that's a good thing. But I say nothing. He crosses to the window again and looks around, then shakes his head.

I scoot back on my bed and lean against the wall. Trevor sits on the corner of the bed, glancing over at me. "I'm tired of hiding from your parents."

"Me too," I whisper.

"I'm tired of all parents," he continues. "I'm almost eighteen, but I'm treated as if I'm a kid."

I'm nearly seventeen, but between my brother and my parents, I might as well live in a prison. I reach out and touch Trevor's arm, sliding my fingers along the warmth of his skin.

He grabs my hand and pulls me toward him until our bodies are flush.

"Let's get out of here," he says.

"Where? It's the middle of the night." Even if we didn't have to worry about parents, where would we go? A park? A gas station?

He tugs me off the bed and steers me toward the door, then unlocks it. I don't know what his intentions are, but I walk with him. Silently, we walk down the hall, past the base of the stairs. We enter the family room, and at first I think that Trevor wants to hang out there—maybe easier to hear my parents if they wake up. Instead, he says, "Let's check out your brother's room."

"No," I say, automatically. Charles has banned me from his room. Not that his ban stopped me from sneaking in—I can pick a lock like any teenager. But the last time I snooped around over a year ago, I found his entire closet was papered in porn.

It made me sick to my stomach. It's one thing to hide it on your phone or computer, but anyone could open his closet door and see it. Was he flaunting it? Was it a dare to my parents? Of course, they never went in his room either. That day I left his room not wanting to ever go back in or consider what else he did in the closet.

Trevor jimmies the lock and opens the door. "We won't be bothered in here."

A chill spreads through me. Charles's room is dark, of course. Pretty much everything he owns is black, and that's also reflected in his choice of bedspread and sheets and rug and curtains.

Trevor stops in the middle of the room, still holding my hand. He turns to me, and I can barely see his face in the dim light. Not much of the moonlight comes through the black curtains.

"We need to stand up for ourselves against our parents," he grumbles. "We deserve more respect." His arms wrap around me, and I instinctively wrap my arms about his neck. But his hold on me is hard, his fingers digging into my waist.

Then, something thumps against Charles's window.

∾

I open my eyes. I am trembling. It takes me a minute to realize where I am and that the wind outside is forcing a tree branch to thump against the window.

The memory of Trevor and the way he was holding me in my brother's room is still fresh. Was the thump on the window a memory or the present? I close my eyes, trying to will my mind to return to the memory—to Trevor telling me that we needed to stand up to our parents. To the anger that I felt coming from him. It both scares me and relieves me at the same time.

I wasn't alone. I wasn't alone. I wasn't alone.

What does this mean?

The branch thumps against the window again, sending my heart racing. I pick up my journal and with shaky hands begin to write the memory on the backs of the pages in the light of my glowing alarm clock. It's slipping away fast, and I need to write down as much as I can.

After I finish, I don't fall asleep for a long time, and when I do, it seems that morning arrives too quickly.

But I hurry to get ready this morning because today Trevor might come. Today, I might be able to finally question him in person.

The morning passes, and Trevor doesn't come.

I log on to the computer during my time, but Patrick's attention never strays and I'm not able to look up Facebook. I type in searches, but I don't read anything. I can't concentrate.

Trevor doesn't come after lunch.

He doesn't come at all.

CHAPTER 15

LOGAN

When Jessica comes into the room, I immediately know something is different. But I also know that I can't jump on it, because I don't want to scare her off.

Her hair is pulled into a messy bun, and her cheeks are a soft pink as if she's excited about something. She tucks her feet beneath her on the chair and sits up straight. But her hands tremble as she folds them in her lap.

"How has your week gone?" I ask. This is not a generic question because my patients know that I truly want to know and that I'll truly listen.

She looks at me, right at me. Her blue eyes are clear, direct, and not like most of my patients—whose gazes are often furtive and confused.

Her body language is skittish, but I realize something else right away. Her clear-eyed gaze tells me she's not taking her medication. Or at least all of it. This fact hits me right in the chest.

"I've remembered something," she says.

My mouth almost falls open. After nine years . . . she's remembered something *this* week?

The doubt creeps in. If she's stopped some of her medications, there's a good possibility that she could hallucinate.

Perhaps not strong hallucinations, but ones that might seem like memories.

"Dr. Mayer," she says, her voice soft in the quiet room. "I wasn't alone that night."

I wait for her to continue because I don't feel like I can be the judge or the jury. Then she proceeds to tell me about her memory, about Trevor being in her room at midnight, about her mom coming down the stairs, about the thud against her window.

"Well, I'm not sure about the thump on the window. When I woke up, a branch was hitting my current window. So maybe that wasn't a memory."

I am staring at her, my attention so fully on what she is telling me that it takes a moment for my mind to catch up and to process everything she's said.

"Was Trevor in a cast?" I say.

Her brows knit together. "A cast? For what?"

"For ankle surgery." I know I shouldn't be giving her any information or leading her on. I need to stop. "He wasn't injured just before that night?"

"No." Her gaze is wary. "Is that what his excuse was?" She untucks her feet and stands.

I'm immediately on alert. I haven't seen her this agitated, not yet.

"He promised to come," she says, turning from me and wrapping her arms around her torso. "He said he wanted to talk to me in person."

"Who? Trevor?" I'm on my feet too. She's pacing in a small space, and her breathing is growing erratic. I might have a panic attack on my hands.

She stops, and at first I'm relieved, then she turns toward the wall and knocks her head against it.

I'm across the room in an instant, folding her into my

arms and pulling her away from the wall. She seems to sink against me, and I'm glad that she's not resisting. Her legs sag, and I hold her up.

"Jessica," I say in a quiet but firm voice. "Did Trevor contact you recently?"

She nods, and I feel sick.

"Tell me what happened."

She doesn't speak for a moment, and I keep my arms around her. She feels weightless against me, and her hair smells of cherries. I don't know why I notice her scent; maybe it's because many of my patients are not always hygienic.

When her breathing regulates, I relax my hold on her, testing.

She puts more weight on her feet, and I keep a hold of her arm and lead her back to the chair. When she sits down, relief washes through me.

I sit down too. And wait.

"I messaged Trevor on Facebook." Her face reddens.

I may not know every single rule in this psychiatric center, but I'm 100 percent sure that patients aren't allowed on any social media. "Do you have an account?"

Her gaze flickers to mine, then back down. "I used an old account of one of the patients." She exhales. "I can't tell you who."

"What did you say?" I feel like a lawyer instead of a psychiatrist.

"I asked him if he was at my house that night." She brings her hand up and smooths back a bit of hair from her face. "He told me he'd come talk to me in person."

This is impossible, but will it make her upset again if I tell her this? Charles has made sure that no one is allowed to visit his sister without his permission. And I don't see Charles ever allowing Trevor to visit Jessica.

She's staring at me, and I know I'm not going to like what she has to say. Especially when she reaches over and grasps my arm. This is why all of my sessions are videotaped in my office. The sessions with Jessica are only audio-recorded.

"Can you log in to the account?" she whispers. "Right now? Just to see if he said why he didn't come."

"Did he give you a day?" I know I'm stalling. I should not even be leading her down this line of questioning.

"It's been three days." Her eyes go from desperate to hopeful. "Maybe he messaged me."

It takes me three seconds to make a decision. If I hadn't met Trevor already and seen his reactions to Gwen's questions, I might have told Jessica no. Instead, I put my finger to my lips, then say, "I can't do that. I'm sorry."

I turn off the voice recorder. Then I pull up Facebook on my phone, log out of the app, and say, "What's the username and password?"

She tells me in a trembling voice, and as I type, she sniffles. She's that grateful, and for a moment, I feel the weight of her nine years of institutionalization.

The messenger icon has a red symbol by it. "There's a message." I tilt the phone so that she can read the message with me. I've already broken the rule this far.

I stare at the words, then quickly read them again. Next I screenshot the entire message strand. It takes three screenshots to get the entirety of the reply from Trevor.

Jessica covers her mouth with her hand, and tears drip down her face as she silently cries.

I log out of the Facebook page.

I can't look at Jessica for a moment. Maybe I'm in shock.

Did Charles really think he could get away with this?

Jessica might believe that the reply is from Trevor's wife, but from the first sentence, I knew that the blonde trophy wife I met at the beach wouldn't speak like this.

If that's not all, Charles inadvertently gave himself away. I don't know if Jessica will eventually realize that her brother somehow has control of Trevor's account or was able to hack into it.

More questions arise. How did Charles know to check Trevor's Facebook account on this exact week? Did he always monitor it?

With Jessica crying next to me, I read through the screenshots on my phone.

Jessica, this is Trevor's wife. He showed me your message, and we told our lawyer. We have kept a copy of the messages you've sent Trevor, and they are harassment. In other words, it's against the law for you to contact him in any way. Trevor won't be seeing you ever, meaning the rest of your life. Even if you were about to die and your last wish was to talk to Trevor, it would be denied. I would never allow it. In other words, it would never happen. If you ever try to contact Trevor again, you will regret it. You need to stop now. You need to forget you ever knew my husband.

Charles's favorite phrase seems to be "in other words," and if I'm not mistaken, he's given himself away.

I exhale, trying to understand the implications of this.

Charles closely monitors his sister—and this is proof that he's gone to quite an extreme. But who is he really protecting? Trevor? And if so, why? Or is he protecting Jessica from truly remembering the events of that night?

I place a hand on Jessica's back as her body trembles and her shoulders shake. I can't tell her that I suspect the message is from her brother. That would make this all worse.

She calms beneath my touch, and I know that our time is nearly up. It's been a hell of a session.

"Jessica," I say. "Can you keep a secret?" I should shut up now. But my mouth keeps moving when she lifts her head and I see her tear-stained cheeks.

"Yes." Her voice is a cracked whisper.

"I will find a way to talk to Trevor." It's only a white lie, in the myriad that I seem to be telling all the time now. "I'll find out if he was there that night."

Her eyes widen, and the next thing I know is that she throws her arms about my neck.

I've lost track of how many rules I've broken over the past hour.

Moments later, I have to peel her arms from around my neck. I may be almost-seeing Gwen again, but I am still a red-blooded man. Jessica is an attractive woman in a tragic wide-eyed waif sort of way. Not a woman that I'd normally approach. If she had a little more confidence, she'd fit right in on the high fashion runways. Thin, lithe, fairylike.

"Please, don't say anything," I say. "To *anyone.*"

"I won't." She's still touching me, her fingers wrapped around my hand.

The room is too warm, and our time is up.

"Can you write down your memories if you have any more?" I ask.

Her smile is secret, furthering her comparison to a fairylike creature. "I already have."

And then I remember. The medication.

Someone knocks on the door.

"It's Marlene," Jessica says, her expression turning sober.

"Our time's up," I say. "I'll see you next week." I glance at the door. "What medication have you stopped taking?"

Another secret smile, and before I can stop her, she's opened the door, greeted Marlene, and left.

I stare at the half-open door, trying to organize my thoughts.

Jessica is hiding meds. She's had a substantial memory.

And her brother has hacked her ex-boyfriend's account, pretending to be Trevor's wife.

I leave the psychiatric center, nodding to a couple of aides on my way out. For once, I wish I had a car, so I could call Gwen right away.

There is a weird triangle here. And I'm not sure the right person is in a mental institution, or if Jessica should be the only person here.

When I get back to my office building, I hurry inside. I've about ten minutes before my next appointment. I'm intending to call Gwen and hopefully reach her. But Sandra stops me.

"There's been an emergency," she says, waving her purple-nailed hand toward the hallway that leads to the other offices. "The ambulance just left."

"What happened?" I ask, coming to a stop and trying to reign in my thoughts.

"Dr. Hinrichsen's patient went haywire," she says. "Tried to choke her."

I blow out a breath. "Is she okay?"

"She will be, I hope," Sandra says. "Her husband came to pick her up."

"And the patient?"

"The patient scratched his own arms pretty good," she says. "The ambulance took him away. He'll probably be admitted."

I think of my most recent session with Jessica. It sounds tame compared to what happened down the hallway.

"Thanks for letting me know," I tell Sandra. "I'll call Dr. Hinrichsen in a little bit. Let me know when my two o'clock is here."

Stepping into my office, I cross to the window and gaze out over the horizon. The sun is washed out in a sky of pale blue. The ocean undulates with its ever-steady motions.

I call Gwen's number, but it goes straight into voice mail. I hang up without leaving a message. I know she's working on multiple cases, yet I need to make sense out of what's happening with Jessica and her brother and Trevor.

CHAPTER 16

JESS

I CAN'T FORGET the words that Trevor's wife wrote to me—his beautiful wife who is everything that I'm not.

It will be a long night.

Yet I refuse to take my sleeping pill and crush the soggy pill into my hair after Marlene leaves my room and turns off the light.

I am ashamed. I am angry. I am . . . filled with remorse, confusion, and distrust.

What did Dr. Mayer mean by Trevor wearing a cast that night? What did it mean that I remembered Trevor being at my house the night my parents died? He was angry. I was stressed and scared.

Did we kill them together?

If so, then why am I the one in here?

Why isn't Trevor in prison?

And then my thoughts turn to Dr. Mayer. Logan. He helps me more than he realizes. I told him about my memories, and he took it in stride. He comforted me. He listened to me. He pulled up Facebook on his phone for me.

And when his arms surrounded me, I felt . . . safe. Normal. Like a regular woman.

I turn on my side and curl my arms about my pillow, knowing that I can't ever have a boyfriend again. Living in here negates anything like that. I've heard stories of patients sometimes getting involved with an aide. But that is short lived, and there are severe repercussions.

I almost laugh to myself when I think of Patrick, the only male aide who I feel is a friend. Nothing would ever happen between us—even if we were stuck on a desert island. We're just not like that.

Logan.

I like that name. He's not much older than me. Maybe about five years. And even though it's his job to listen to me, to care about my feelings and thoughts, I know he's genuine.

My thoughts continue to turn over, and I cannot sleep. I don't regret destroying my sleeping pills. It makes me feel stronger and more in control, because in my life, I have very little control in what I do each day.

I can't even leave my locked room without permission.

Turning over, I face the door. Light from the hallway creeps underneath. The edges of the door are completely black—there is no space there. The door is double locked at night, and windows are made of thick glass that's impenetrable. I might as well be in prison. Not that I'm not grateful for all my brother did to ensure that I could come here instead of prison, but sometimes I wonder why he is still so worried about me.

As I lay in the dark, staring at the sliver of light coming in through my bedroom door, I think of what would happen if I tried to kick the door open. The first kick would probably go unheeded, but by the second or third kick, an aide would alert security. I'd be restrained, perhaps even put into a straitjacket.

That used to happen once or twice a week when I was first brought here. But I've been a good girl for a long time.

I exhale, thinking of what Dr. Mayer would say if I told him that all I want to do is get out of this room and reply to Trevor's wife. I want to tell her that I know he was in my bedroom that night. I want to tell her that I know he was angry at my parents, so angry that he might have been the one to kill them.

My gaze doesn't waver from the sliver of light.

What if I tried to pick the lock? I have nothing long and narrow. The aides make sure of that. There isn't even a shower curtain ring that I could bend into a lock pick.

Trevor, ironically, showed me how to pick a lock. He knew that my parents had locked me into my room more than once. They'd even had the lock changed to a key lock, and they frequently took away my own key so that I couldn't get out of my bedroom when I was severely grounded.

I, of course, climbed out of my window.

A memory returns—suddenly and unexpected—like a flash. Charles was watching a movie in the basement, and I walked past the family room. I paused to watch a scene where a man was using a credit card to open a locked door. It worked, and I remember thinking how dumb it was—not believing it would work.

Charles paused the movie and told me to get the hell out. He liked to watch movies by himself, and his favorites, he watched over and over. Oftentimes he'd watch the same scene multiple times.

The only time I could watch TV was when Charles wasn't home, *and* I wasn't grounded, *and* my homework was finished, *and* my chores were done, *and* my parents weren't angry about something else.

I didn't have a credit card. I didn't even have plastic, except for the cover on my journals. They were hard plastic, but much larger than a credit card.

I stilled. I only needed a square edge. Rolling over, I grabbed one of my older journals out of my drawer. Then I climbed out of bed and walked toward the sliver of light. The carpet was rough on my feet, and every step made my breath grow shallower.

If it didn't work, no one would know.

But if it did . . . could I make it to the computer without being detected? There were cameras in the hallway, but how closely was someone monitoring them? How much time would I have?

I slide the journal cover into the crack between the door and the doorframe. It stops dead when it reaches the bolt. I try to remember the movie scene, and I think the actor wiggled the door knob. So I try it, too, keeping as quiet as possible, while I shove the plastic cover against the bolt. Still nothing.

I pull out the cover and sit with my back against the door.

Closing my eyes, I exhale. I've been living in this room for nine years, and I haven't been able to get out before, even when I was throwing fits during the first year.

The words of Trevor's wife hurt. She's protecting him, and it's wrong.

What if . . . what if it was Trevor who committed the crime? I haven't allowed myself to believe that he could be responsible for killing my parents. I was there that night too. Yet the fact that he was there as well must mean that I didn't act alone, right?

A few months ago, I read about a case in Utah where a teenager was sentenced to prison because she was with her boyfriend who killed a cop. I can't remember if she was driving or if she was a passenger. Her boyfriend was shot and killed by another cop as they tried to escape.

So, even if I didn't actually kill my parents, according to the law, I was still guilty by associating with Trevor.

He was free.

He'd been free for nine years while I lived in this psych center, medicated around the clock and forced to sleep in a locked room.

I turn, more determined now, and jam the journal cover against the bolt as I twist the door knob. The only thing I accomplish is bending the journal cover. I drop the journal.

Trevor's wife is a criminal if she's protecting her husband's secrets.

We have kept a copy of the messages you've sent Trevor, and they are harassment. In other words, it's against the law for you to contact him in any way.

I hate her words; I hate that she knows and is trying to keep me from communicating with Trevor. I just want a simple conversation. I want my questions answered. I rub my head. She reminds me of my brother ... "in other words" ... it drives me batty when he overexplains things. Telling me the same thing, over and over again, in different ways. As if I were a three-year-old kid.

My stomach feels hollow at being talked down to, again.

My brother, now Trevor's wife ... maybe even Trevor. Maybe it was Trevor who wrote the message and pretended to be his wife. It was his account, after all. Or maybe it was my brother who hacked into Trevor's account.

A shiver runs along the back of my neck.

But there's no sound of the AC kicking on.

The shiver travels through my body.

I want to push away the idea of my brother hacking into Trevor's account and reading his private messages.

Charles used to do that to my Facebook account. He'd find out my password and then log in and post a stupid video. At first, they were dumb videos, but then he started posting graphic things.

I'd try to delete them as fast as possible, then I'd change my password. He always seemed to guess my password right. At least that's what I thought when I was a teenager. Now, I realize, he must have found a different way to access my account. Which meant he could easily access Trevor's account.

My skin is clammy, and my stomach roils. I make it to the bathroom in time to throw up in the toilet. My throat burns as my stomach clenches again and again. I am left sweaty and weak. The cold bathroom floor feels like heaven as I curl up on it.

What is Charles doing? What is he hiding? What is Trevor hiding?

CHAPTER 17

LOGAN

"TELL ME EVERYTHING," Gwen says, grasping my hand and pulling me inside of her condo. The place is bright with yellow walls, red couches, and white pillows, a contrast to the grittiness of Gwen's job. She has a birdcage in the corner, so the air is punctuated with occasional twitters.

Gwen is a plant lover, which is in evidence by the sheer number of plants on almost every surface. It's remarkable that she keeps up the watering and fertilizing of them all.

"Coffee?" she asks.

"No thanks."

I sit on the edge of her couch, resting my elbows on my knees. I'm still trying to piece everything together.

"Spill it, Logan," Gwen says, settling across from me so that our gazes meet.

I don't hesitate. I'm into this completely, and knowing that Charles is hijacking Trevor's Facebook to reply to his sister, has taken this to a new level. I show Gwen the screenshots on my phone.

She reads through them. "Forward those to me." She tilts her head. "So his wife knows some things, too, and is protecting him."

"That's one theory."

She doesn't miss my insinuation. "What's yours?"

I tell her about Charles's way of speaking and how the message from Trevor's wife matches his pattern of speech.

She nods yet doesn't look too nonplussed. "The plot thickens. We already know that Charles is a computer expert. Do you think it's part of his protection to monitor anything that has to do with either his sister or her ex-boyfriend?"

"Do you?" I ask, hardly believing that she would side with Charles.

Her mouth lifts, the mouth that I kissed quite thoroughly the other night. "No. What else?" she presses.

I tell her that Jessica is cutting back on her meds—unknown to the medical staff or her brother. The reduction of medication might be the cause of her returning memories. But it also might have contributed to her near panic attack. "I'm worried that these memories will trigger a mental breakdown of another kind. There's no way to predict how her PTSD will manifest itself."

"She has *you*, Logan," Gwen soothes. "You're a great psychiatrist. She couldn't be in better hands."

"I don't know about that—I mean, I've been breaking some rules with her," I say. I don't mention our hug or the other touching that's gone on. It was all innocent anyway. I hope that Jessica sees it that way as well.

"You know that rules are for the benefit of the general population," Gwen says. "Jessica is a unique case. Until she can remember what truly happened and be confident in her memories, we have to go through some back doors to get the full story."

"I know." And I've known it for a while. It's why I'm here, now, with Gwen, breaking more rules.

"So, are we still in this together?" she asks.

It's a fair question. I take her hand and slide my fingers

between hers, linking our hands together. "What's our next step, brilliant detective?"

"I'm going to reopen the case."

I'm surprised at this. I was expecting more sleuthing. Sneaking around corners. Following Trevor to the coffee shops. Maybe calling his wife. Asking some leading questions in my next session with Charles.

"How does that work?" I ask Gwen. "What basis of evidence are you going to reopen the case on?"

"On the basis that the accused murderer has remembered some of the events leading up to her parents' deaths," Gwen says matter-of-factly, but her eyes are gleaming with triumph. Her fingers tighten around mine. "I'll bring in Trevor for questioning. Charles too. And your patient will need a lawyer."

"What about her brother's guardianship rights?" I ask. I'm wondering about the emotional ramifications of this on Jessica. Is she strong enough to handle a new investigation? More questions?

Gwen shrugs. "Her lawyer will file to transfer her guardianship to the state, or prove that she's competent."

I frown. "How long will that all take?"

"It can be pushed through in a couple of weeks," Gwen says.

I release her hand and rise to my feet. I cross her wood floor and stop at the window that overlooks a shared green space in the condo complex. "I need to think about this."

Gwen rises too. "Think about what? That your client might have a partner in crime? That someone is free who should be incarcerated?"

"It's not that simple," I say, turning to face Gwen. She's still wearing one of her power suits, but her shoes are off. "Jessica's been institutionalized for nine years. She's been on medication for that long as well."

Gwen touches my arm and leans close. "Logan, we need to take this next step."

I don't pull away, but I don't exactly welcome the pressure either. "All right. Give me a few days, though. I need to talk to Jessica. I need to somehow prepare her."

Gwen smiles and lifts up on her toes. She kisses my cheek. The kiss turns into a kiss on the lips, and then we tumble onto the couch. Gwen is persistent in her attentions, and I find myself giving in, at least for now. We haven't had "the talk" about what's happening between us. There's no mistake that there is still a strong attraction between us, but I very well know that attraction alone can't be the foundation of a long-term relationship.

Even after I leave Gwen's place, Jessica is on my mind. I can't forget the gratitude in her blue eyes and the absolute joy she had when she hugged me so enthusiastically. Compared to Gwen, Jessica is so unadulterated, innocent and naive. Which is saying something of a woman convicted of her parents' murders.

I climb onto my motorcycle and pull on my helmet. Before I start the engine, I check my cell phone.

A missed call from the office. I didn't leave until after my last client, so this surprises me. I open the voice mail and listen to Sandra's message.

"Dr. Mayer, your client Charles Harper has been calling over and over, desperate to meet with you." She lowers her voice. "He says he's coming to the office to wait for you. I have to leave by six at the latest. Please call me back as soon as possible."

It's 7:15 now. I call Sandra's cell phone, but she doesn't pick up. I leave a quick message for her, then check the other missed calls on the phone.

Both are from an unlisted number.

Sitting in the parking lot of Gwen's condo, I can't deny

the chill creeping through me. I call my cell phone company's customer service and ask for the number that was listed as unknown. They text me the number, and I dial, not knowing what to expect.

The phone rings three times, then clicks over to a voice mail. A computerized woman's voice comes on, repeating the number and advising the caller to leave a message after the tone.

"This is Dr. Mayer, and I'm returning your call." I hang up, then wait.

Two minutes pass before my phone rings.

"Dr. Mayer," I answer.

"Well, well," Charles's voice comes through loud and clear.

Even though I suspected he was the caller—on my cell phone no less—his voice sends a hard jolt through me. I feel like a kid caught stealing a candy bar from the grocery store.

"Charles—" I begin.

"You didn't think you could get away with this shit, did you?" His voice is high pitched, and if I didn't know any better, I'd think he was high on something.

Well, I don't know any better. He could very well be.

I search for whatever calm I have inside of me. "What can I help you with, Charles?" I deliberately use his name because it should make him feel more valued, more heard.

"You've broken your promise to me," Charles says. "When I hired you, I made it clear that my sister needs to be protected at all times. That her medication cannot be altered without my permission."

"You sister is still protected," I say in my most soothing tone.

"How long have you known about her medication changes?" he asks, his voice bordering on hysteria.

"There haven't been medication changes," I say. "I suspect ... and it's a suspicion only, mind you, that she's stopped one or two of her pills."

Charles groans. "And you didn't tell me?"

"Take a deep breath and hear me out," I say. "I met with her today, just a few hours ago in fact. There hasn't been time to follow up with the medical staff yet."

"Jessica should be your priority! In other words, you should be informing me of any changes the minute you know about them!" Charles shouts into the phone.

"I understand you feel that way," I say. My mind is racing. Charles doesn't know about her returning memories. He's not admitting to messaging on Trevor's Facebook account. I change tactics. "How did you find out so quickly about the medications?"

"The aide found one of her pills dissolving in her drink at lunch and notified me," Charles says, his voice still seething.

I exhale. "What did Jessica say about it?"

"She refuses to talk," Charles says. "I got her on the phone, but she won't tell me anything. She stayed silent the whole time, then hung up. If I must, I'll order an IV."

"Whoa," I say. "You can't force her to take medication."

"I can, and I will," Charles spits out.

I want to confront him about the Facebook message, but that would open a whole other can of worms. It's better that he doesn't know what else I'm not telling him.

"Can you meet tomorrow?" I ask, if only to placate him. "We can go over what your responsibilities are toward your sister. You need to keep your own sanity, you know." Making him into the victim seems to work.

"I'm meeting with the aides in the morning," Charles says. His voice is much calmer now, and I start to breathe easier.

"Right after that, then?" I say. "I can shuffle around my schedule."

This seems to mollify Charles. We agree on a time. I hang up and text Sandra about the new appointment.

The sky has darkened, so I start my motorcycle and turn on the headlight. But instead of heading out of Gwen's parking lot and back home, I turn the other direction. I need to try to talk to Jessica tonight. I need to find a way to protect her from her own brother.

CHAPTER 18

MARLENE ESCORTS ME into my bedroom and waits as I change for bed. It's too early for bed, but I've told her I'm done for the day. I can still hear the other patients down the hallway. There's a rousing game of Ping-Pong, although I know it will be short lived. Someone will get upset. Someone will quit playing. Above the sound of the pit-patter of the ball hitting the table, the low tones of the evening music reach me.

Music is supposed to soothe the soul, we've been told. There are no lyrics to the music they pipe in; it's only instrumental. I pace my room, thinking of what Charles said to me on the phone.

I didn't want to answer it when Marlene told me that my brother was on the phone. When Patrick noticed the pill fizzing in my juice at lunch, he immediately took me to a private room where he and Marlene asked me questions about why I didn't take the red pill and how long I'd been doing it. I told them this was only the second time, but I don't think either of them believed me.

I wondered how long it would take for them to report to Charles. Less than an hour later, my brother called me.

Not able to plug my ears, I had to listen to him ranting at

me, telling me that I could become very agitated if I didn't take my pills regularly. I didn't say a word, when I wanted to yell at him to leave me alone. I was tired of being crazy. I wanted to know what it felt like to be a normal person.

It was like he read my thoughts. "Do you want to be like Erin?" he said through the phone. "Freaking out about everything and thinking you're an entirely different person?"

I love Erin, but I still said nothing.

"Do you want to be delusional like Nicole?" he said.

I wished he would shut up, but both Marlene and Patrick were watching me.

"Do you want to hallucinate like Mona?" he continued. "You don't even know how bad crazy can get."

Yes I do. My brother's words are making me crazy. Even though it's been hours since he called, I can't get his voice out of my head. Maybe I'm a new kind of schizophrenic.

Now, Marlene hands me my sleeping pill and stands over me as she watches me swallow. I do swallow it. When she finally leaves and shuts the door three minutes later, I rush to the toilet and stick my finger down my throat until I gag.

I close the toilet seat and rest my head on the cool plastic.

Someone knocks on my bedroom door, and I jerk upright. Did Marlene hear me throw up? I hear the key in the door, and the door opens. I stay in my place on the floor of the bathroom. The bedroom lights flip on.

"Jessica?"

It's Marlene.

"I'm here," I say. Where else would I be? The bed or the bathroom.

She peers at me. "Are you sick?"

"No," I say. "But I thought I might be. I'm feeling better now."

She stares at me for a moment; we both know that I threw up the sleeping pill.

"Dr. Mayer is here to meet with you," Marlene says.

I'm not sure if I've heard her right. "What?"

"He says that he has some exercises for you to work on before the next appointment." Marlene's voice sounds odd, as if she's not telling me everything.

Is this a setup? To get me out of my room without any incident so they can put me in a straitjacket and force medication down my throat? Or even worse, through a needle?

"I'm tired," I say. "I'm already changed for bed."

Marlene simply watches me, her expression unreadable. "You can put on a robe and come to the office."

It might sound like she's making a suggestion or request, but I know it's nonnegotiable. The robe will do very little to hide that I'm in my pajamas. There's not even a tie on the robe to hold it together—since that would be a hanging temptation.

I rise and say, "I'll just wear this."

Marlene gives me a quick once-over. "At least put on your bra."

"I don't sleep in my bra." Our bras are sports bras—again, we can't wear bras with narrow straps that might be used for strangulation.

I pass Marlene and walk to the door, which is ajar. I step into the hallway, and surprisingly, Marlene follows me, saying nothing.

We walk to the office. The door is wide open, and I see Dr. Mayer before he sees me. He's leaning against the desk, scrolling through his cell phone.

"Here she is," Marlene states, then shuts the door without any other conversation.

Dr. Mayer looks up.

For some reason, I feel a lot barer than I am. Maybe I should have worn my bra. Dr. Mayer isn't checking me out or anything, but I suddenly remember the way that he held me when I was panicking. And the way his body was solid against mine when I hugged him after he pulled up Facebook for me.

I'm not infatuated with my own doctor, or anything. But I like him. In another world, one in which my parents were still alive, and I wasn't living in a psychiatric center, maybe someone like Dr. Logan Mayer might look at another version of me with interest.

Still, my face feels warm.

"They told me you might be asleep," Dr. Mayer says. Then his eyes do stray from my face.

I'm definitely warm. I fold my arms, partially concealing my chest, at least I hope.

"I was throwing up, actually," I say. I'm sure I look terrible, but I'm also sure he's seen worse.

To his credit, he doesn't flinch. "The sleeping pill?"

I think my mouth drops open. "How did you know?"

One side of his mouth quirks. "I'm a doctor, remember." His gaze strays again, and I decide to take a seat. He does as well, then clears his throat.

Why is it that he seems nervous?

"Your brother called me," he says.

I tamp down a surge of anger. "I'm not surprised. He's livid."

Dr. Mayer chuckles. How can he laugh right now? "Sorry," he says. "Your brother is beyond livid, I'd say." He leans toward me, and I like that he's not afraid to share my space. "What have you stopped taking?"

I could lie; I've been lying. It would be easier. Because even if Dr. Mayer doesn't tell Charles exactly what I say, I might still be in trouble. Dr. Mayer is a doctor after all.

"The sleeping pill," I begin. "And the red pill."

His eyebrows lift, and I like that he's surprised, or perhaps impressed. I've been bolder than even he expected. "How long?" he asks.

I realize for the first time that he doesn't have a notepad and pencil. He's holding his silent phone in his hand.

"A couple of months for the red pill," I say.

"You've been dissolving that in your juice?" he clarifies.

I nod, and he continues, "What about the sleep aid?"

"A few weeks." I lean back in my chair and pull my knees up to hug them against my chest. "It's why I'm starting to remember."

He says nothing for a moment, just watches me. Then he drops his gaze.

I wonder what's going through his educated mind. Does he see me as a pathetic murderer? A woman whose only rebellion is to throw up a pitiful sleeping pill and think she can have some control in her life?

"In our first session, your eyes were not as clear as they are now," he finally says.

I stare at him.

"I've noticed that improvement over the past few weeks," he continues. "Your speech is clear, your thoughts rational, the color in your skin better, and you look . . . healthy."

Healthy. I haven't been diagnosed as healthy for more than nine years. I remind myself that he's only talking about my physical appearance. I unfold my arms and stare at my hands in my lap.

"What I mean, Jessica, is that I approve on reducing your medication."

I'm not sure I'm believing what he's saying.

He places a hand on top of mine, and I welcome the heavy, warm weight. *Safe. Secure. Comfort.* This man was born to be a psychiatrist. If touch could heal, he could have wrought miracles.

"We have to be smart about it," he says.

"How do we do that?" I ask, and my voice trembles without my permission. "I mean, my brother—"

He's gazing into my eyes. I love his brown eyes. "I'll worry about your brother. You worry about becoming the strong woman I know you are."

My eyes burn with tears, and I can't look at him. I pull my hand from underneath his and fold my arms again as if I could hold myself together.

"Do you believe you can become a stronger Jessica?" he asks.

The words are one you might hear a parent say to a small child, but the sincerity is what delves into my heart. My parents thought I was weak. They treated me as if I were weak. They never listened, they never trusted, which made me believe they didn't care. In my guilt over my part in their deaths, I've learned that they probably loved me, as most parents do their children, but they were afraid.

Charles was the son who obeyed. I was the daughter who rebelled. And they didn't know how to handle it, so they did what they thought would protect me.

I went from a teenaged girl living under her parents' thumb to a criminal living under her brother's.

"I'm afraid," I tell Dr. Mayer.

"I know."

His words are simple, direct.

I look at him again, taking the risk of looking into those brown eyes of his, those eyes that I am starting to trust. Something I never thought would happen to me. "How?"

"We start with reduced dosages on your medications," he says. "One at a time, of course. You record all your symptoms, good or bad, and any changes. We will do a blood draw and urine sample once a week."

I feel understood and free. Dr. Mayer is on my side. I lick my dry lips. "What about my brother? What will he say?"

"I will handle your brother." Dr. Mayer shifts in his seat.

"I'm going to put in a request to the facility that the visits from your brother stop for a few weeks."

This is unexpected. Charles won't like that. He's rarely missed a week. "He'll still come," I say.

Dr. Mayer turns so that he's more fully facing me and so I can't escape his gaze. "Listen to me, Jessica. This is very important, and I can't tell you every reason why. You need to get a lawyer to protect your rights."

I can't breathe. I want to look away, to process what he is saying, but his brown eyes hold mine. "Is this because of Trevor? Did you talk to him?"

"That Facebook message—"

"Was written by my brother, right?" By the look in Dr. Mayer's eyes, I know it to be true. I expect to crumple. My suspicions have been confirmed. "Are you sure?" I whisper.

"I am ninety-nine percent sure," he says. "I don't know what happened that night. But I don't think you were solely responsible. Trevor was involved somehow, and your brother might be possibly covering for him."

"Why?" I ask, my eyes burning. "Why would Charles lie for Trevor? Can they hate me that much?" Tears fall onto my cheeks.

"I don't have the answers," Dr. Mayer says in a soft voice. "Until we do, you need to hire a lawyer to protect your rights." He pauses. "This will be a custody battle over yourself. You need a lawyer to file a restraining order against your brother until you find out the truth."

I shake my head. "Charles will go ballistic. Even if I remember everything—whatever it is—they can say I'm lying."

"They can say whatever they like," he says. "You need to decide if you're willing to find out the truth. I think you're strong enough."

His words mean everything. But I still need to decide if I

am strong enough. My hands tremble as I clutch them together in my lap. I think of the phone call from my brother and how upset he was. I think of how he impersonated Trevor's wife on Facebook, warning and threatening me.

"What if . . . what if you didn't kill your parents?" Dr. Mayer asks.

"I've wanted to believe that for nine years." I can no longer hold back my emotions, and my sobs break through.

Dr. Mayer's arms come around me as I continue to cry.

I don't know how much time passes before I can breathe normally and speak again and can finally say, "All right, I'll do it. I'll get a lawyer."

CHAPTER 19

LOGAN

CHARLES HAS BEEN calling my phone nonstop, but I refuse to answer until the morning. Not that I'm sleeping, but I need the light of day to find some clarity in this situation.

I've advised Jessica to get a lawyer, and she broke down over it, but when she left the office, she seemed resolved and determined. I'm proud of her. She's a lonely woman in a place where it's hard to gain a lot of perspective and hope for the future.

I drive to my office as soon as dawn cracks the sky, and I forward the files that Charles sent over to Gwen.

I call her number, and not surprisingly, she answers. Her voice is low with early-morning sleep.

"What's wrong?" she asks, skipping over any greeting.

I suppose a call at six a.m. is unusual from me. I quickly fill her in on the events of the night before, of Charles's phone calls and of how Jessica is getting a lawyer and filing a restraining order against her brother. I might have to file one against him as well.

"Call the cops, Logan," Gwen says. "Tell them you have a disgruntled patient and they need to watch your place, both office and home for a few days."

"Do you think it will get that bad?"

"I think that Charles is hiding something big. I don't know if he's protecting Trevor, or himself—"

"*Himself?* Do you think Charles was a part of it?"

"Look," she says, the sleepiness disappearing from her voice. "Charles was older, he's extremely smart, he did some very cruel things to his sister . . . bizarre things as well. Burning her Barbies? Spying on his neighbor? Hacking into Jessica's account and bullying her? Come on, Logan, you're the psychiatrist. How many red flags do you need?"

I might as well hand over my PhD to Gwen. "He's a psychopath."

Gwen is silent. I know it gives her no joy to point these things out to me.

"Dammit," I say. "Jessica doesn't need a lawyer. She needs security."

"She needs both," Gwen says. "In fact, I'll put in a call to the department and get them to watch your place. You get to the psychiatric center and arrange for Jessica to be transferred to a new facility as soon as possible. One where her brother hasn't already bribed everyone to do his bidding."

"I don't have power of attorney to do that," I say.

"That's your next phone call," she says. "Get a lawyer to meet you over there. Call Allen."

"I'm on it," I say.

"Good. Meanwhile, I'm sending officers to both Charles's and Trevor's homes today to bring them in for questioning."

"This is all happening at once."

I can almost see Gwen's smile. "That's the best way. Talk to you soon." She clicks off.

Pulling up Allen Barlow's number, I hit SEND. It's 6:10 a.m., and I hope he'll answer. I've testified on two of Allen Barlow's cases over the years, and it's time I call in a favor.

"Tell me it's good news," Allen answers on the third ring.

"Meet me at the San Diego Psychiatry Care Facility," I say. "I'll fill you in when you get there."

"This better be worth my time," he says, then yawns.

"Oh, I think it will be," I say. "Better put your secretary on alert. We've got a bunch of paperwork to expedite."

After I hang up with Allen, I take my work laptop out of its locked drawer, then slide it into a backpack and sling it over my shoulder. I leave a note for Sandra, then lock my office and walk into the parking lot. My motorcycle is still the only vehicle in the parking lot. Sandra won't be here for another ninety minutes.

I pull out of the parking lot, helmet on, when a dark sedan comes down the street the opposite way. Wow, Gwen is fast, and her police connections even faster. I look over at the driver as we pass each other, and my blood chills.

It's not a cop, or even an undercover cop.

It's Charles.

He, of course, has seen me too.

I speed up while watching the car through my side mirror. The car's brake lights come on, and I take the next corner a little too fast. But I remain upright.

Refocusing on the road, my heart thumping hard, I look for my escape. Charles could easily follow me if I don't get out of sight fast. I take the next turn, then another. He's still not showing up in the side view mirror. If only I took note of the license plate, I could call it in.

I can't go home either. And Charles could easily guess that I might go to the psychiatric facility. But I have little choice. Allen is meeting me there.

I pull out my phone and dictate a sloppy text message to Gwen, one hand keeping my motorcycle upright. I hope she gets it before something more happens with Charles.

My heartbeats count out the minutes as I zigzag my way to the care center. When I arrive, I park in the employee parking lot in the back, hoping I won't be erroneously towed while I try to work everything out.

Then I call Allen. "How close are you?"

"Almost there," he says. "I even skipped my coffee."

"Good," I say. "Park behind the building. I'll brief you there. And hurry."

I hang up. Gwen hasn't texted back yet.

I text Sandra and tell her to cancel all my appointments for the day and inform her that Charles might be stalking me. I caution her about going into the office herself and ask her to inform the other doctors in the building.

Allen's red sports car pulls up as I click SEND. Of course he's driving a red sports car. Allen might be flashy, but he's also at the top of his profession. He climbs out of the car and strides toward me. He's a couple of inches shorter than me, but his height is quickly put on the back burner when he talks. He's loud, opinionated, and fights like hell for his clients. It doesn't hurt his persona that his idea of decompression is lifting weights. His head looks newly shaved, and he's sporting his signature goatee.

"What's up, Logan?" he says in his direct way, his nearly black eyes boring into mine.

We both skip a handshake and any pleasantries. He's holding a briefcase in one hand, and I'm hoping that he's carrying representation papers for Jessica to sign.

"I have a patient who's possibly been framed for the murder of her parents nine years ago." I point to the building next to us. "She's been ordered to live as a resident here. Her brother oversees everything from her medications to her sleeping schedule." I can practically see Allen's mind working as he weighs what I'm saying.

I tell him about the Facebook hacking by Charles, about Trevor and how Gwen and I chatted with him a couple of times, about Jessica's memories returning.

"Gwen's involved?" Allen's forehead crinkles. "You two back together?"

"Not exactly," I hedge. "Gwen's reopening the case."

"Nine years, you say?" Allen's eyes widen. "Are we dealing with 'Jessica the Reaper'?"

"Yep."

Allen blinks. "I think I read every article that was ever written about the case, and I always thought that case stunk worse than rotten eggs. Did you know that one of the lawyers involved has since been disbarred?" He continues before I can answer, "The pictures of her in the newspapers looked like she could be knocked over by a feather. What's she like now?"

"Physically, she hasn't changed much," I say. I've seen the old newspaper pictures. "She's codependent on her brother in an unhealthy way. But she's got guts. She's started to cut back on meds—hiding the fact from everyone—and she's started to remember some things from the night of the murder."

"Primarily . . . ?" Allen prompts.

"That Trevor Mills, the ex-boyfriend, was at her house until late."

Allen pulls out his phone and makes a call. It's apparent he's talking to a clerk for a judge when he puts in requests for two restraining orders on behalf of Jessica Harper, one for Charles Harper and one for Trevor Mills.

"Let's go meet her," Allen says, pocketing his phone.

I can only hope that Jessica will accept Allen as her lawyer.

The front desk attendant could pass as a security guard herself. Her nametag reads *Eliza*. A woman in her mid-thirties, she eyes Allen quite closely. She recognizes me, but she still asks questions.

"The residents awake in half an hour, then go to breakfast," Eliza announces. "I will talk to Jessica's aide to see if you can meet with her after that."

Allen steps up to the counter. "Ma'am, we have every reason to believe that Jessica Harper is in danger. We need to meet with her as soon as possible. I can call the judge and get an order sent over right now, or you could talk to Jessica's aide right now."

Eliza's gaze doesn't waver from Allen's.

I'm impressed.

She picks up her phone and pushes a single number. "Marlene? Dr. Mayer is here to meet with Jessica. He says it's urgent. He has a lawyer with him, Allen Barlow." She pauses and eyes me again. "Yes, I'll tell them. Thank you." Eliza hangs up.

"You know where the office is, Dr. Mayer." She lifts her chin, her gaze still distrustful. "Jessica will be there soon."

We stride down the hall to a set of locked double doors. Eliza buzzes us through, and I lead Allen to the therapy office.

While we wait, I pull up the spreadsheets on my phone that Charles had sent over to brag about how organized he was.

Allen's phone rings, and he answers. He listens for a moment, then says, "Then file for a reversion of power of attorney. She's a twenty-five-year-old woman. I have a report here from her psychiatrist that states she's competent to make her own care decisions. The only thing keeping her in the psychiatric center is the murder charge of an unsolved case." He hangs up.

"Send me a report stating that Jessica Harper is competent to represent herself." Allen sets his briefcase on the desk and opens it, pulling out representation papers.

I unzip my backpack and power on my laptop. Within

minutes, I've filled out a form, electronically signed, and email it to Allen, cc'ing myself and Sandra.

Just then, the door opens and Jessica walks in.

Marlene is right behind her, and she stops inside the door and folds her arms, eyeing both of us. Maybe Jessica does have someone on her side in this place.

Jessica looks a bit wild eyed but otherwise alert. "You can leave, Marlene."

The woman doesn't say a word, but her message is clear. She's not happy about this early-morning visit. Marlene shuts the door with a firm click.

"Is this the lawyer?" Jessica says, swinging her gaze to Allen. Her hair is hanging loosely around her shoulders, making her look even younger than she is. She's wearing more than she was last night, when she was in what must have been her pajamas. Now, she has a faded red T-shirt on that looks about ten years old and is probably a kid's size. It's too short for her and shows a couple of inches of her flat belly. Her sweats are also worn and hang low on her hips.

I don't miss Allen's quick scan of her.

But we are both professionals. I know that Allen is assessing her in order to determine her potential in reopening a nine-year-old case.

"Miss Harper," Allen says, extending his hand. "I'm Attorney Allen Barlow. I've handled cases for psychiatric patients for many years. I can tell you I'm an advocate for men and women in your situation who find themselves accused of crimes."

Jessica steps toward him and extends her hand to shake Allen's.

She's trembling slightly—I'm not sure if Allen will even notice. But I've learned to pay attention to her body language. Thankfully, her gaze is direct, and her mouth is set in a determined line. My hope rises.

"First of all," he begins, "I have called in restraining orders against your brother and Trevor Mills. This is a formality to protect you as you're going through the process of medication reduction and possibly recovering your memories."

Jessica exhales, and I wonder if she'll need to sit down. But she remains standing straight. "Do I need to sign something for you to represent me?"

Allen smiles. "I have the papers right here, whenever you're ready."

I watch Jessica exhale. "I'm ready." She crosses to the desk and Allen hands her a pen. She bends to sign her name.

It's started. We are on our way.

Allen takes a picture of the documents, then emails them to the clerk.

"Have a seat, Miss Harper," he says. Allen sits in the chair behind the desk, and I take my usual chair next to Jessica's.

"Call me Jessica," she says.

Allen nods. "Jessica. And you can call me Allen, of course. Are you all right with having Dr. Mayer in the room?"

"Yes," she says. Her voice is clear and confident.

"Have you remembered anything since you last met with Dr. Mayer?" he asks.

Jessica looks at me, her blue eyes bright. I love that they are bright. It's like she's starting to truly live.

"Yes, I have," she says. "I had another memory last night when I was trying to fall asleep."

Allen and I both lean forward.

"It's a strange memory, though," she says. "It may not be a memory at all. I mean, maybe I'm having hallucinations now. I've read about the power of suggestion, and that's a real thing too."

"It is," I say. "But tell us anyway, and maybe we can figure it out together."

She's looking at me now. "Remember when I told you that something thumped against my window that night, and how it scared Trevor and me? He got even more mad after that and started talking about how much he hated both of our parents."

"I remember," I say.

Allen is scribbling down something on his notepad, listening intently.

"I don't remember exactly what happened after that," she says. "Last night, when I couldn't sleep after your visit, I kept wondering what that thump could be. And then suddenly a conversation popped into my mind. A conversation between Charles and Trevor."

I'm staring at her.

"They were arguing, but I couldn't see them," she says. "I think I was trying to listen from inside the closet."

"Your bedroom closet?" I ask.

"Yes."

I look over at Allen. He's stopped writing and has a thoughtful look on his face. "We will subpoena the witnesses that reported on both your brother's and your ex-boyfriend's whereabouts that night. They were obviously false statements."

"What were they arguing about?" I ask Jessica.

She looks down at her hands. "They were arguing about me."

Chapter 20

Jess

I AM BEING transferred to another facility. My lawyer tells me it's for the best. I need to be in a place where my brother doesn't have influence. Dr. Mayer agrees.

I know they're right, but standing in the middle of the room I've existed in for all of my adult life brings me mixed emotions.

The room is plain. I'll be taking few things, my journals and select clothing. Toiletries will be provided at the new facility.

In the soothing way of his, Dr. Mayer assured me that they have a garden at the new place on the other side of the city. But I will miss my plants. I cross to the window where I can see the edge of the boxed-in garden. The tops of the plants are visible, and I imagine their earthy smell. My hands are still stained with evidence of my care. Who will weed the plants and water them when I leave?

"The van is here," Marlene says as she opens the door and comes into my room. "Is that everything?"

I look at my bed. I've stacked three shirts, two pair of sweats, and my underwear. Next to the stack are my journals. Inside one of the journals is a picture that Mona drew for me when she found out that I was leaving. Erin didn't even look at me when the announcement was made. Nicole started crying, though, thinking that I was going back to my family, and wondering where her family was.

"That's everything," I tell Marlene. I won't take any of the birthday gifts from my brother or any of the art projects that litter the corner of my room. I've never put anything up or displayed anything. I'd rather be working in the garden.

"Erin said to give this to you," Marlene says, holding out her hand.

On her palm is a single puzzle piece. Erin did understand that I was leaving. That single puzzle piece tells me that she's willing to say goodbye through giving me something that's very important to her. No one wants to be around Erin when she can't find a puzzle piece.

I take the piece from Marlene and slide it into one of the journals, where it will stay safe. Then Marlene loads my belongings into a plastic garbage bag. She carries the bag herself because plastic bags are suffocation hazards for small children and mentally ill patients.

I follow her out, and my step falters when I see Patrick at the end of the hallway, waiting to say goodbye.

Him, I will miss.

As I near, he steps toward me and opens his arms. I fall into a hug, and my eyes start to burn. I won't cry. I won't cry.

I won't cry.

When I pull away, I'm dry eyed, but my heart has been wrenched.

Patrick nods, and I nod back, neither of us saying anything. Neither of us needing to.

Marlene steers me through the double doors, and we cross the lobby. Through the glass exterior doors, I see a dark-blue van waiting. My heart trips. Marlene, who has rarely touched me before, places her hand on my shoulder. "It will be all right," she says. "When it's all over, you can come back."

I swallow against my tightening throat.

Leaving behind Patrick, Erin, Nicole, Mona, and even Marlene makes me feel more alone than I normally feel. I close my eyes as we walk outside, not wanting to see the van. But I must open my eyes to see where I'm walking.

A door opens and a man in a gray shirt—obviously a uniform of some sort—climbs out. His face is impossibly round, and the shirt is too tight at the collar, making his wide neck seem to spill over its edge. I think he must be glad to get out of his uniform shirt each day. He definitely needs a larger size. His thick whiskers stand out on his face, and I'm surprised he doesn't have to be clean shaven for his job. Maybe the place I'm going to has a more relaxed atmosphere. The aide grins at me.

Maybe this won't be so bad. He has a friendly smile, and there's no pity behind his eyes. His grin remains as he opens the sliding door of the van. "Is this okay?" he asks.

He wants my opinion? This is new.

"Yes," I say, and my voice sounds hoarse.

"We'll see you soon," Marlene says.

I turn to look at her. She gives me a quick hug, so quick that I barely have time to respond. Then she takes a step back. "Go on," she says, her voice strangely thick.

So I do. I'm obedient to the end. I climb into the van and sit in the captain chair.

"Buckle up," the gray-shirted aide says in a jovial tone.

I look around. I can't remember the last time I've been in a moving vehicle. I've been on a few field trips with the other patients, but Charles put a stop to my participation a couple of years ago.

"Here you are," the aide says, extending the seat belt toward me. I clip it in.

"Great job," he continues.

I can still buckle a seat belt, thank you.

He slides the door shut, and the doors automatically lock. I'm not surprised. A van, transporting psychiatric patients shouldn't have an easy way out.

As the aide walks around the front of the van, I look out the darkened windows. Marlene is standing a few feet away, waiting for us to pull away. It's unexpected, and my throat seems to grow tight again. Maybe she has been my taskmaster, but I can see now that she truly cares in her own way.

I don't want to watch her any longer, though. I don't want to cry in the van on the way over to my new home. I don't want this new aide to pity me. He climbs into the driver's seat.

"Here we go," he says in a pleasant voice, a little too loud considering I'm just a couple of feet away from him.

He doesn't latch his seat belt, which means that the van starts up a beeping sound when we pull out of the front parking lot.

I have no idea how far we are going, but I lean forward and peer out the window to take in our surroundings. It might be months, or longer, before I get a chance to see part of the surrounding city again. Not even the time I spend in my garden can compare to the feeling of actually leaving the property of the center.

"Did you eat something today?" the aide asks.

I'm surprised that a driver would bother with that sort of question. "I had breakfast," I say. Although I ate very little, at least I ate something.

"That's good news," the aide continues in his cheerful tone.

It's starting to annoy me. I hope that he's not one of the

rec center aides. I don't know why my eating is good news to the driver. I let my attention stray to a large park that we're passing. A woman is pushing a stroller, and running ahead of her, is a yellow lab. Sometimes the center will bring in therapy dogs. It makes me think of Erin. She loves dogs and often throws a fit when they're taken out.

The dog stops and sniffs around a tree, then lifts its leg.

A jungle gym comes into view, and a bunch of kids are playing on it. With the amount of kids, I realize it must be a school holiday of some sort. I crane my neck as we drive past, trying to catch a better glimpse. A young boy, maybe about six, is swinging across the monkey bars.

Something at the edge of my vision moves inside the van, and I look behind me.

My heart nearly stops. A man is sitting on the back seat. It takes me a startled moment to realize that it's my brother. How did I not see him? He's wearing all black, and over his hair is a dark beanie.

"Charles," I whisper.

His eyes narrow, and he grips my shoulder.

"What are you doing here?"

He leans close, his breath like sour milk. "I'm taking you to a safe place."

I pull back from him and push his hand away. "I . . . I have a lawyer. He says that you . . . can't talk to me." My pulse is racing so fast, and I can't think, can't speak.

"Sorry, dear sister," Charles says. "I told you that I'm the only one who can take care of you." Then he's gripping my shoulder again, so hard that I know I'll bruise.

"Let me go," I say, looking over at the driver. "My brother isn't supposed to be in here," I tell him. It sounds lame when I say it, and the driver only speeds up the van. Now I feel the panic building inside of me.

"You aren't taking me to the new center, are you?" I ask.

"You're a smart girl," Charles says behind me, his voice a familiar sneer.

I have to get out of this van. I have to get away from my brother. He hasn't changed. He'll never change. He hates me enough to keep me in a place where I can't ever be free. He doesn't want me to remember what happened the night my parents died.

I twist to look at my brother. He's still gripping my shoulder with his left hand, and in his right hand, he holds a syringe.

Perspiration breaks out on my face and neck. "What's that for?" I ask, even though I know, but I can't quite believe my brother would be this cruel.

"It's to help you relax," he says, his voice low and hard. "It's for your own safety."

I want to throw up. I know the van doors are locked, but can I unlock them myself? How fast can I get the door open and jump out? We're in a neighborhood, so maybe I can run somewhere for help.

My brother's blue eyes are like ice. Cold. Hate filled.

He could overpower me in an instant if I try to fight him off. But that doesn't mean I shouldn't try.

"I remember," I say in a panic. I pull away from his grip, but he doesn't release me.

"What are you talking about?"

"You were there that night," I say, swallowing against the dryness of my throat. "You and Trevor were there."

He stares at me, and I realize I've shocked him.

I twist out of his grasp and dive toward the opposite door, away from him. I fumble with the lock and pull down on the handle.

But his shock doesn't last long enough, and he grabs my

arms, jerking me back before I can open the sliding door. I scream, though I know the driver must be under Charles's orders and won't help me. My brother's weight is on top of me, pinning me down, and I feel a sharp sting on the back of my shoulder.

He's jabbed me with the needle.

I try to reach for the needle before he can inject the drug, but his weight is diminishing my ability to breathe and sapping my strength. I claw for the door handle and manage to crack open the door. Air rushes in, and I gasp as Charles pulls my hand back, bending it at a sharp angle.

My shoulder is burning, and my head feels heavy, my mouth pasty.

I need to get away. I need to get away.

I need to shove Charles away, but I can't make my legs or arms fight him off. I can't even scream. My eyes are trying to close, and all I can see is the road through the crack in the door as we speed along.

I am still awake, I realize, but I can't move, and Charles's voice sounds far away. He's telling me to get up. To get out of the van. We've stopped. Another voice—that of the driver's, probably.

They are carrying me.

Away from the van and into darkness.

Chapter 21

Logan

IN MY PROFESSION, answering an unknown caller can be a risk. I'm not expecting a sales pitch on the other end of the line, but a patient who might be at the end of his rope—literally.

When the unknown call comes through an hour after Allen and I leave Jess, I answer, fully expecting it to be Charles. I'm sitting in Allen's office while he reviews Jess's former case.

"Dr. Mayer?" a woman says when I answer.

"Yes?" The voice is familiar, but I can't place it.

"This is Marlene from the psychiatric center," she says. "There's been a problem with your patient, Jessica Harper."

A psychiatrist can never fully brace himself for bad news—no matter how many times he's heard it or how often he's experienced it. But what Marlene says next is unexpected.

"Fifteen minutes ago, Jessica was picked by the driver," Marlene continues, her voice businesslike, yet I hear the tremor in it. "Ten minutes ago, another driver showed up, from the same place."

I'm not following.

"The first van was not an authorized driver, as it turns out." She pauses now.

As my mind starts to put together what she is telling me, I feel sick.

"We don't know who picked Jessica up, Dr. Mayer," Marlene continues, her voice plainly distressed now. "We believe that she's been abducted."

I can't respond for a moment. When I do speak, I'm still not sure I fully comprehend. "Did the center send two vehicles by mistake?"

Allen looks up at me from his side of the desk.

"No," Marlene says into the phone. "That's the first thing we tried to figure out. I thought maybe you might know—maybe she told you something, or planned something. Or maybe you and her brother know something."

Charles. It has to be Charles. My gaze connects with Allen.

"Did you notify the police?" I ask Marlene.

Allen's eyes widen as he listens.

"Not yet; I wanted to see if you knew something first," she says.

"Call the police," I say. "Thanks for letting me know so quickly." When I hang up with Marlene, I tell Allen what Marlene said, then I dial Gwen's number.

She doesn't answer, and I leave a quick message. Next, I text Sandra to send me Charles's address as soon as possible.

Allen stands, holding his cell phone. "Where are we going?"

"To Charles's house," I say, my mind reeling. "I hope the cops can get there in time."

"Do you think—" Allen doesn't finish; he doesn't have to.

"Can we take your car?" I ask.

"Of course," he says and leads the way out of his office. "Hold all my appointments," he tells his secretary without any other explanation.

By the time we're in Allen's car and Sandra has sent over the address, Gwen returns my call. She asks a couple of questions after I explain things, then says, "I'm on my way over there, and the SWAT team will be there soon. We've pinged his cell phone, and it's at his house, which leads us to believe he'd there too. Don't park near the house or try to enter. We don't want to force his hand."

"I agree," I say, thinking of the hostage situations that I've seen play out on the news.

"If they're not at his house, do you have any ideas where else he'd take her?" Gwen asks.

Allen speeds up his sports car, so we make it through a yellow light before it turns red.

I can't think. "I don't know," I say at last. "I need to look through everything he emailed me to see if there's a clue."

"Keep thinking," Gwen says. "If he's taken her to his house, then he's planning something big. I mean, it's the first place he'll expect the cops to come looking."

I don't like the insinuation of her words. "What do you mean by 'big'?"

"Murder-suicide," Gwen says, pulling no punches. "I know that's not what you want to hear right now."

My heart is already leaping out of my chest. As Allen follows the map directions on his phone, which keeps my phone free to use, I start to entertain more and more miserable ideas. I already know that Charles is a smart guy, a devious man, a controlling brother. What will he come up with to keep his sister silent . . . forever?

"We're almost there," I tell Gwen.

"Park a block away," she says. "The cops should be right behind you. Don't interfere with their work. We don't want any more complications than we already have."

I exhale. "All right. I wish I could do something, though."

"You're already doing a lot," Gwen says. Her voice is surprisingly calm. "I'm on my way and should be there in less than ten minutes. Pin your exact location and send it to me."

I nod, although she can't hear it. "I will."

Allen pulls to the side of a shaded curb and turns off the car.

"We've parked and will wait for the cops to get set up," I tell her.

"Good," Gwen says. "And if it makes you feel any better, the SWAT team is well prepared for this. They'll do everything possible to get Jessica out alive."

When I hang up with Gwen, my hands are shaking. I can't stop thinking about Jess and her helplessness around her brother, or anyone really. She hasn't been away from staff supervision for nine years. Just that alone must be messing with her psyche.

I picture her blue eyes, filled with gratitude when I told her I'd get into the Facebook account. Her blue eyes appraising Allen. The hope in her gaze. The trust she'd given me.

And now her brother has kidnapped her.

A black suburban passes along the street, moving slowly. The windows are too dark to see inside. I glance over at Allen, and he nods. We both get out of the car at the same time and begin to walk to the corner. Across from the corner of the street is where Charles's house sits. Another suburban drives past, going at a slow speed as well. The man in the passenger seat stares at us. He's wearing a dark beanie and black clothing.

They don't stop, and I exhale. I don't want to interfere, but I don't want to sit in Allen's car not knowing anything either.

When Charles's house comes into view, I don't know what I expected, but it's not a well-kept yard and trimmed rosebushes. The yard is immaculate, the narrow two-story house in good repair, even though the architecture is dated. The mailbox even has its flag up as if Charles is in the process of mailing out some bills. I guess I thought someone as decrepit as Charles would have let his lawn die and driveway crack.

Allen and I stop by a parked car a couple of houses down from the corner. One of the SUVs has parked right at the corner, partially blocking our view, and the other is currently out of sight.

The street is quiet, but the tension is palpable. A door shuts somewhere—a house door—and I flinch.

Both Allen and I look in the direction of the noise and watch as a blue Honda pulls out of a driveway.

The doors of the nearby Suburban open simultaneously, and several men climb out, clad in all black, wearing helmets and carrying weapons. They run across the street, toward Charles's house. From the right of us, more men come along the street—from the SUV we can't see.

The men disappear around the sides of Charles's house. Two men remain in front, but they've ducked down behind the rosebushes so that a casual glance outside the front window wouldn't reveal them.

"Wow," Allen whispers next to me. "This is really happening."

I nod, because I'm basically speechless.

The minutes seem to drag, and no one on the SWAT team moves their position—at least from our viewpoint.

My phone vibrates, and I look at it.

Gwen's text reads: *I'm here.*

I look around and see her walking toward us. She joins us by the car we're lurking behind, and I grasp her hand. She gives me a confident squeeze, then lets go. Her eyes are glued to the house down the street. "Anyone inside yet?" she says in a quiet voice.

"I don't think so," I whisper back.

She doesn't move, doesn't say anything else, just watches.

Nothing seems to be happening, yet I can't pull my gaze away from the manicured lawn and white shutters. There are blinds in the window, but none of them have moved or been parted.

A bird flies out of the tree above us, momentarily startling me with its sudden noise. I watch it fly away. Then I look back at the house. Does Charles have Jess upstairs? Or is there a basement? Is she awake? Drugged? Worse? *Wait for us,* I want to tell her. *We're right outside.*

Two SWAT team members suddenly rise from their positions and run to the side of the house, right behind each other.

"What's going on?" Allen asks in a hushed tone.

Gwen wraps her hand around my arm. "I think they've gained entrance from the side or back, but I don't know why they aren't keeping the front of the house covered."

I don't have answers either.

My heart pounds as the minutes pass without any sight of any of the SWAT team members. Then the side gate swings open, and several men come running through, crossing the front yard. They don't slow at the driveway but keep running toward the SUV within our sight range.

"Get down!" one of them shouts when he sees the three of us hovering behind a car.

I freeze while Gwen and Allen dive for a nearby bush.

I hear the explosion before I see it. Or maybe I see it before I hear it. I'm not sure. The top windows of the house explode, and flames dart out. And then a larger explosion rips apart the larger front window on the main level. The SWAT team men continue to exit the yard, streaming out like an army of ants while the house is sending glass and flames and debris everywhere.

Somehow in the middle of the explosion I hear Gwen scream my name, and my body finally unfreezes, and I turn toward her. I dive toward the ground, landing in a flower bed. The world about me numbs, and I instinctively cover my head.

I don't think the debris could reach us, but the sounds make my ears ring. My face is full of dirt, and I'm surprised I can still breathe. It's as if my heart has stopped, then restarted, over and over again.

I move to my knees and wipe dirt from my face, then I turn, looking for Gwen and Allen.

They're starting to disentangle themselves from the bushes, and I reach for Gwen to help her up.

"Are you okay?" I ask her. Her hair is messed, and her clothing stained, but she doesn't look injured.

"Yeah, you?" she says.

"Fine."

"What the hell happened?" Allen says, rubbing the side of his face.

We all look over at the SUV. The SWAT team hasn't gotten inside yet. A couple of them are on phones, and other members are warning off neighbors who've come out of their houses.

Sirens sound in the distance—the fire trucks, I assume.

The house is fully engulfed now, and I start to walk toward it. I can't leave Jess inside that house.

Gwen grabs my hand. "Don't get any closer, Logan."

"What if . . . What if she's inside?"

"Let's talk to the SWAT team," Gwen says. "Find out what they saw before the explosion."

I know she's only trying to pacify me. She keeps a firm

grip on my hand as we walk toward the SUV. Most of the men are still wearing their helmets. A giant of a man greets Gwen. "This your case?"

"Yeah," Gwen says. "How many people were inside?"

The man focuses on me. "Who's this guy?"

"The woman's doctor," Gwen answers for me.

He smirks. "You're too late, doc."

Gwen releases my hand and folds her arms. "Cut to the chase."

"We didn't see anyone inside," he says, his eyes darting from me to Gwen. "But that doesn't mean there aren't casualties. As soon as we can get the fire doused, we'll search for bodies."

CHAPTER 22

Nine Years Earlier

"CHARLES IS BACK," Trevor whispers after something thumps against Charles's bedroom window. After we narrowly escaped my mom's discovering Trevor in my room, I'm jumping at every noise.

"Really?"

"Yes," Trevor says, but there's hesitation in his voice. "He's back from camp."

I want to ask Trevor how he knows Charles is back. My brother is supposed to be at scout camp and shouldn't be returning until Saturday. Do my parents know about his return? And why is my brother back early? He's like the top scouter in our city. He has every merit badge possible and has probably come up with some of his own.

Is Trevor friends with Charles now? Have they been texting each other?

"Wait here," Trevor whispers. "I need to go talk to him before . . ."

When he doesn't finish, I say, "Before what?"

"Shh!" he hisses. He moves to the bedroom door that he's left open. Above us someone is walking across the floor.

Is my mom still awake? My dad? Or is Charles in the house?

After a minute, the footsteps fade, and no one comes downstairs. Trevor remains by the bedroom door, listening. Charles's room has changed since the last time I was in here a year ago. He has a lot more computer equipment for one thing. For a kid who doesn't have a job, he seems to have plenty of spending money. And I know that his allowance isn't much more than mine—or at least more than mine used to be.

"Why's Charles home?" I whisper.

Trevor holds up his hand, then turns his head to look at me. "Get in the closet."

"No," I say, shaking my head. My stomach roils at the thought of the last time I saw Charles's closet and all those porn pictures.

Something clicks against the window.

"He's coming," Trevor says in a harsh whisper. "Get in the closet now! He'll kill you if he sees you here."

I don't need to be told again. I'm closer to the closet than the bedroom door. The window starts to scrape open, and my pulse leaps. I hurry into the closet and pull the door mostly closed. My fingers perspire as I grip the doorknob.

The window scrapes again and closes. I'm assuming Charles is now inside.

A light flashes. A cell phone light? I grip the doorknob tighter, wishing I had shut the door all the way. I don't want to chance Charles seeing me. I have so many questions. Why are Charles and Trevor meeting like this? Why is Charles back so early?

"Did you bring the money?" Charles asks.

I flinch at the sound of his voice. *Money for what?*

"Of course, and in small bills," Trevor says.

My mind reels as I try to understand what they're talking about.

"Good," Charles says. "It's clean. Want to try it?"

"Not really," Trevor says. "It might trip me out."

Charles laughs, in a low chuckle that sends a shiver along my skin. My brother never laughs about anything innocent. "That's the point, bro."

"Yeah, well, I'll try the next batch."

I've smelled marijuana on my brother a few times but not on Trevor. Besides, this doesn't sound like they're talking about weed.

"Whatever," Charles says.

I hear a zipper and the rustling of fabric.

"Take good care of it," Charles says. "Remember, don't get screwed over on the price."

"I won't," Trevor says. "Here's the down payment."

I imagine the guys exchanging money . . . and I wonder what the money is for. Weed? Coke? Something stronger?

The window scrapes open again, and I cringe.

"How'd you get here?" Trevor asks.

"I can't tell you everything," Charles replies with a scoff. "I don't want you to rat me out to my sister or parents."

"Your sister wouldn't say anything," Trevor says.

Charles seems to pause, and I wish that Trevor hadn't defended me, even though it's nice to hear it.

"You think you know her—but you don't," Charles says. "She'd do anything to get me in trouble."

Trevor gives a soft laugh of his own. "That's what she says about you."

"Really?" Charles's tone hardens.

My stomach tightens. I know that tone of voice.

"Calm down, dude," Trevor says. "You know she's my girlfriend. She's cool."

I don't relax because I know this won't appease my brother.

"She's never been cool," Charles says. "I know what you want her for."

Trevor laughs—and I know it's a nervous laugh.

"Believe me," Charles continued. "If Jessie knew I was working for a dealer, she'd be the first one to call the cops."

My mouth is dry, my pulse drumming.

"Seriously, man," Trevor says. "She wouldn't. Especially if I tell her not to."

I want to yell at Trevor to tell him to shut up. The best approach with Charles is to stop talking.

"Why would you have to tell her not to?" Charles says much louder than his former whisper. "Did you tell her?"

"Not exactly," Trevor says, and I imagine him raising his hands in innocence. It's still the wrong thing to say.

"Not *exactly*?" Charles's voice rises another octave. "Damn you, Trevor. You're a freaking narc."

"I'm not—" Trevor starts to say, but a dull thud cuts off his words, followed by a thump and a groan.

I imagine the worst. Charles has hit Trevor. Trevor has fallen.

I inch open the door, hardly daring to breathe. I'm right. Trevor is lying on the side, holding his head and groaning.

Before I can stop myself, I burst out of the closet. "What did you do to him?" I screech.

Charles doesn't move as I crouch over Trevor. At least Trevor's still breathing. It's too dark to see how injured he is.

"You idiot," Charles spits out.

"Trevor, talk to me," I say, tears burning my eyes. "Are you all right?"

"Of course he's all right," Charles says, grabbing my hair and yanking my head back.

I cry out at the sharp pain.

"Shut the hell up," Charles hisses. "If you wake up Mom and Dad, you're seriously going to pay for it."

I stagger away from Charles and lean against the wall, pressing my hand against the side of my head where the pain is starting to ebb.

Trevor starts to sit up. "Jess, you need to get out of here."

I want to leave because Charles is being a jerk, but I can't leave Trevor.

"Come with me," I tell Trevor.

He's on his knees now, and with a moan, he stands and rubs the side of his face. "What did you hit me for?" he says to Charles.

"Because you suck," Charles says. "Give me the dope. I'm taking you out of the loop."

This is good, I think, but Trevor grasps my hand and moves toward the door. "I'm not giving up my cut. Come on, Jess."

"This isn't funny," Charles says.

"It's not supposed to be," Trevor says, yanking the bedroom door open.

"If you leave, I'll turn you in."

Trevor releases my hand and whirls on Charles. Simultaneously, they plow into each other. I stare as they crash onto the bed together. One of them hits his head on the wall, and fists are flying, but I can't tell who has the advantage.

"Stop," I say, my voice choking on a sob. "Stop, Charles!" I'm crying now, and I'm sure that my parents would have to be dead to the world to not hear the thumping on the wall.

I pull on Trevor's leg but only get kicked away. He's got Charles in a headlock, but then Charles elbows Trevor, and the two roll off the bed. Trevor's nose is bleeding. They're going to kill each other, I know it.

"Get off him!" I scream.

Charles is sitting on top of Trevor now, pinning him to the ground, choking him. Trevor is gasping for air.

"I'm getting Mom and Dad!" My sobs come in great gasps, and I can't breathe. I open the door and run for the stairs.

I must get help. I trip on the first step and fall forward, banging my knees.

I scramble to my feet, half running, half crawling up the stairs.

Then a hand wraps around my ankle, and I trip again. I reach out and brace myself with my hands so that I don't hit my chin.

"You bitch!" Charles growls.

I don't know where Trevor is, and I can only hope he's okay. Charles yanks on my ankle, and I slide down a step. I twist around, kicking him with my other foot. He's much stronger than me. If he can pin Trevor, he can overpower me.

Charles continues dragging me down the stairs, and I open my mouth and scream.

His hand clamps over my mouth and nose, cutting me off.

I twist and squirm to get free, but I can't escape his strength. I gasp for air but get very little. The night-light at the base of the stairs shows that Charles's eyes are dark with anger and his face red with rage. His strength gives me no chance.

My air is cut off. I can't breathe, and darkness soon closes around me. My last vision is my brother watching me die.

Chapter 23

Logan

I'M SITTING ON the curb, my head in my hands because I can't bear to watch anymore. The cops, investigators, and dogs have been going through the charred remains of the house for over two hours. Gwen reported back that no bodies were found on the upper level. But Charles's melted cell phone is recovered. He wanted us to come here.

After they finished the upper level, they brought in equipment to move the heavier stuff around so they could enter the basement.

Ash floats in the air, and I've drunk more than one cup of coffee, provided by a kindly neighbor. The cops cautioned me from chatting with anyone, and so I've kept mostly to myself. Allen already went back to his office since he has court appearances this afternoon.

Finally, I stand, anxious to stretch my legs and work off some of the agitation that won't go away. I walk around the block a couple of times. I nod to the neighbors hanging out on their lawns to watch the unfolding events, but I keep walking past everyone.

The knot in my stomach has formed a noose. I've discussed everything with Gwen, then with Allen, then with Gwen again. We haven't left one idea unexplored.

Charles kidnapped his sister, then blew up his house.

Who are we dealing with here?

I'm questioning everything that I thought I knew about Charles and everything that he told me.

Were the blackouts all a setup in order to start meeting with a therapist? Was I chosen randomly? Or specifically?

Was Charles always planning on abducting his sister—or was it a reaction to her returning memories?

I round the corner again, where I have a view of the burned house at the end of the cross street. Whatever happened to Charles, he deserved his fate. But what about Jess?

I can't get her blue eyes out of my mind. Her blonde hair. Her elegant neck. Her thin arms. What did she think when she realized she'd been kidnapped? What did she think when they arrived at this house? What were her last thoughts? If I hadn't insisted on her getting a lawyer and changing locations, would she still be alive?

There are several cops and investigators standing together in front of the house, talking. This is different than what was happening before when everyone was spread out, doing various tasks.

I increase my pace, feeling like I'm walking through a dream, where things don't feel quite real. My stomach feels like it's a hollow concave. I stop and hover a few paces away from the crime scene tape.

Gwen stands in the group, and I'm relieved because at least I know I'll get a straight story. The conversation seems intense, but I finally catch Gwen's eye. She nods in acknowledgment but doesn't motion me to come over.

Still, I wait. I look over at the ambulance. The paramedics are leaning against the truck and talking, not seeming in any hurry to go and fetch anyone. This doesn't give me any comfort, though.

The minutes drag by, and I start to pace.

Finally, Gwen breaks away from the group and jogs over. "We need you."

This surprises me. She lifts the crime scene tape, and I duck under. As we stride back to the others, she says, "No bodies have been found in the house."

"Not even in the basement?" I ask, daring to hope. Does this mean Jess could still be alive?

"Not in the basement either," Gwen says, placing a hand on my arm. "She could still be alive."

I nod. This is my hope too. Wherever Jess is or whatever her brother has done to her, if she's alive, I'll do whatever it takes to help find her.

"Hey, everyone," Gwen says as we reach the group.

The conversation cuts off, and everyone turns to look at me.

"This is Dr. Logan Mayer," she says. "Some of you know that he's Jessica Harper's psychiatrist. He also brought in the attorney this morning, who Jessica signed with."

The pairs of eyes staring back at me are critical, wary, curious, and even distrustful.

"Dr. Mayer will give you his predictions of where Jessica and Charles might be now," Gwen continues.

I raise my brows. *My predictions?* With everyone waiting, I have to think fast. Not that I haven't been mulling over other possibilities all morning. Yet, until about two minutes ago, I believed she could be dead in the burned house a few yards away. "Charles works only about five miles from here," I say. "There's also the cemetery where their parents are buried." I look to Gwen for approval. She nods her encouragement.

"Trevor Mills, Jessica's ex-boyfriend and a possible accomplice, lives north of here." I take a deep breath. "He has a sailboat that's docked at the Glorietta Bay Marina."

A couple of the cops and one of the investigators are taking notes.

As I speak, other ideas pop into my mind. "The high school that all three attended might be another location to check out. Also, Charles's grandparents used to own a cabin in Palomar Mountain."

"That's over an hour drive from here," Gwen muses.

"Which means they'd be there by now," one of the cops adds.

Gwen folds her arms. "What's our strategy, chief?" She's looking at a big burly guy with short salt-and-pepper hair.

"I have someone going over to the bank with a warrant to look into Charles Harper's recent finances to see if he's purchased an RV or something like a trailer. While that information is being gathered, we need to split up and check out all of those places," he says, looking at me.

I appreciate that he's taking my suggestions to heart. As the investigators put together their plan, Gwen pulls me aside. "I'm thinking the cabin—what about you?"

The thought of it sends a chill through me. "Agreed."

"My car?" Gwen asks, attempting a little humor.

I exhale. "Of course. Hungry?"

She smiles. "Starving."

After she talks to Chief Bergholm again and a couple more people, we're on our way. I've never been so glad to leave a place in my life. The smoldering ruin of Charles's house has been gut wrenching to stare at. So many unanswered questions are still sifting through my mind, but at least we can rule out one location and hope we aren't too late to salvage the situation.

Gwen's car is fast, and we hit the freeway before rush hour. I've got the map app open on my phone, and it says ninety minutes until we arrive at Palomar Mountain.

When we're cruising above the speed limit, Gwen looks over at me. "Are you all right?"

"I will be when we find Jess," I say.

She nods, then reaches her hand out. I link our fingers. I suppose in her line of work, she deals with emotional turmoil a lot. I'm in an emotionally charged industry as well, but this cat and mouse game with Charles is hard to stomach.

Gwen's phone rings, and she releases my hand and clicks over to her Bluetooth. "Yeah?" She pauses, glancing at me.

I'm all ears.

"Already?" Her voice holds a note of surprise. "Good to know. We're on our way now."

When she hangs up, she says, "They've culled Charles's bank statements and found some recent large purchases."

I can hardly stand the suspense. "Such as?"

"Well, the passenger van for one," she says.

"What he picked her up in," I muse. "What else?"

"You're not going to believe this," she says.

I'm staring at her, preparing myself for the worst.

"He bought his grandparents' cabin about three months ago," Gwen says. "It was on the market by the new owners."

I blow out a breath. "Was I set up? Were we all set up?"

"I don't know," Gwen says. "But we already have a head start. Let's hope we're not too late."

I look down at the app on my phone. One hour and twenty minutes. It feels like forever.

As if she's reading my mind, Gwen speeds up and passes a car.

My cell rings. It's Sandra, and I answer.

"Oh my heck, did you see the news?"

"Are you talking about Charles Harper's house?" I ask. "I've been there all morning."

"You have? Did they find the bodies yet?"

"No bodies," I say. "I'm not sure if that's public knowledge yet." I glance at Gwen, but she doesn't give me any warning to stay quiet.

"That poor, poor woman," Sandra continues. "I can't believe Charles is such a creep. I shook his hand and everything. Where did he take her then?"

"We don't know yet," I say. I don't want to tell Sandra anything that might be classified. "If he tries to call the office, let me know right away, okay?"

"I will," Sandra says with a sigh. "It's hard to believe. He told me his sister killed his parents. I guess you know that. I don't like to gossip about our patients, so I didn't ever ask you about it."

I appreciate that about Sandra, but now I'm wondering if he ever said anything to her that might help us out now. "Yeah, it's tragic. Although," I hedge, "the sister might not be entirely guilty."

"What do you mean?" Her voice is definitely alert.

"I mean that we don't know if she acted alone," I say. "I can't give out more details than that."

"I know, I know," she says. "Patient confidentiality and all that. But wow! This is really crazy. Did you ever suspect Charles would go off the deep end like this?"

"No," I can honestly say. "Not to this extreme."

"If there are no bodies in the house, that's a good thing, right?" Sandra presses.

"We hope it's a good thing."

"I'll be so relieved if she's found alive," she says. "Even if she's been through hell—she needs to get away from her brother once and for all."

My throat is tight when I swallow. Am I partially responsible for this mess? If I hadn't insisted she cut off communication with her brother, would she be safe in the psychiatric center now?

"Like I said, let me know if Charles contacts you," I say.

"Will do, boss."

Finally we hang up. The conversation with Sandra only makes me feel worse.

"You know none of this is your fault, right?" Gwen says in a soft voice.

"I know." Then why do I feel so rotten?

By the time we reach Palomar Mountain State Park, we're joined by three cop cruisers who've caught up with us. They must have used sirens on the freeway.

Gwen waves as they pass, and we follow them, turning on to a dirt road that winds past cabins set back from the main street. The setting is picturesque as the afternoon sun and leafy shade compete against each other. The sight of towering pine trees makes me feel like we're a lot farther north than San Diego County.

The cruisers pull off the road and park.

"We're here already?" I ask, looking at the map on my phone.

"We don't want him to hear the cars," Gwen explains.

"Got it," I say.

She meets my gaze, and the trepidation I see in her eyes is no comfort. She knows the drill, she has the intuition, and if she's worried, we might be walking into another crime scene.

"If you don't want to wait inside the car, you need to stay back a ways," she says.

I know this, and there's no way I'm staying in the car. I pop open the passenger door, and we both climb out. Gwen strides toward the cops who are speaking together in low tones, and I keep to the background.

When they start to walk down the road, keeping to the tree-lined edge of the road, I follow. My phone buzzes with a text, and I quickly silence it without checking the text. I don't want to compromise our approach in any way. It's not long before the cabin comes into view. There's no sign of the van. My first impression of the cabin is that it looks quaint, as if an older couple owns it, not one of those trendy power couples who like to spend weekends drinking with friends.

The flower pots that line the dark-wood porch are filled with faded plastic flowers. A wind chime rattles in the faint breeze. The windows appear black, indicating that the dark drapes are shut. Dirt and leaves have built up on the stairs leading to the porch.

Please be here. Please be safe, I plead in my mind.

I stay in a copse of trees while Gwen and the cops fan out, weapons drawn, as they search the grounds. Two cops walk around the back of the cabin, and another two move toward the front. I watch the windows intently, looking for any shift of the drapes or sign of other movement.

Moments pass in which I'm holding my breath. I want to be side by side with the cops, checking things out. But I also want to stay alive should any firepower be exchanged.

The two cops who'd gone behind the cabin return. They shake their heads, indicating they didn't find anything of note. Now four cops are on the front porch. Gwen and the remaining two cops are still at the perimeter.

One of the cops tries the door. Locked. Seconds later he busts it open, and the other cops stream into the cabin.

I can't breathe as I wait and listen.

I can hear them calling to each other, footsteps pounding, and still the time passes, and I'm frozen in place.

Minutes pass, or maybe only seconds, and one of the cops comes out. "Empty."

The single word makes me sag with relief. But the feeling is only temporary. If they aren't here, where are they?

The cops spend another ten minutes going through the cabin, taking pictures—maybe for future reference in case Charles ends up showing his face here. I stand in one place, staring at the cabin for several moments, until Gwen joins me.

"Any word on the other locations?" I ask.

"Nothing at the high school," she says. "Let's get back on the road."

I can't agree more. We walk back to her car, both of us lost in our own thoughts. My hopes have risen and been dashed more than once today. The feeling of helplessness is overwhelming.

As Gwen drives us out of the area and back toward the freeway, I stare out the window. Where would Charles take his sister—a woman he's afraid will remember too much? Jess isn't much of a physical match against her brother, especially if he has something to drug her with. Or maybe he won't bother with giving her anything but will go straight to killing her.

I'm sick at the thought.

Gwen's phone buzzes, and she answers it on her Bluetooth. She talks to the chief and updates him—though I'm sure he's already been informed by the other officers.

It's then I remember the text that came in that I never checked. I pull my phone out of my pocket. The text is from Sandra. *Call me. I've remembered something.*

When Gwen's phone call with Chief Bergholm ends a couple of minutes later, I tell her about the text from Sandra.

Sandra answers on the first ring, sounding breathless.

"What happened at the cabin?" she asks.

"It was empty," I say, glancing at Gwen. "What did you remember?"

Sandra takes a deep breath. "At a couple of the appointments, Charles talked to me while he waited. I never really liked him, you know. I thought he was pretentious, and he acted like he was superior to everyone. You know that type."

"Yes," I say, impatient.

"He asked me what I like to do on the weekends," Sandra continues. "I was really put off by it, and I didn't mention it to you because he never really *invited* me anywhere. So I don't think he was trying to ask me out or anything."

"What did he say?" I ask, trying to stay polite.

"He said that his favorite thing to do was to take his friend's sailboat out for the afternoon," Sandra says. "I said that he's lucky to have a friend who lets him borrow his boat. Charles said that his friend owed him from some stuff a long time ago."

"Trevor," I say.

"Who?"

"I've got to go, Sandra," I tell her. "Thanks so much."

Gwen glances over at me as I hang up.

"We need to get to Trevor Mills's boat as soon as possible," I say.

CHAPTER 24

Nine Years Earlier

I'M LYING ON the basement stairs, and my throat feels raw from screaming ... crying? I remember that Charles was trying to choke me. I must have passed out, but what stopped Charles?

Then I hear it. Arguing. Between Charles and Trevor again. This time it doesn't come from the basement. They're on the main level. What about my parents? Surely they're awake by now.

I push myself up, moaning at the throbbing in my neck. Once I'm on my feet, I use the handrail to help me walk up the steps.

Everything is dark, and I move stiffly through the kitchen toward the hallway that leads to my parents' bedroom.

The arguing is coming from that direction. I'm feeling relieved because if Trevor and Charles are down the hall, then my parents must be intervening. I hope that Charles won't lie to them. I wouldn't be surprised if my parents believe *him*. They believe everything he tells them.

The voices fall silent again, and someone steps into the hallway. I can't make out the shadowed form right away.

"Get out of here!" he whispers.

"Trevor, what's going on?"

"Jess, get out of here *now*," he says again, his tone furious.

Fear jolts through me at his vehemence. He hasn't spoken like this to me before. I haven't seen him fight either. Tonight is a series of firsts for Trevor.

A door opens. My parents' bedroom door.

Charles steps out—I know it's him purely by instinct. What are my parents doing, and why aren't they coming out? Dim light comes from the bedroom, indicating that a lamp is on.

I can't see my brother's face because the light is coming behind him, but I can feel the hatred in his gaze. I'm not going to let him get away with lying this time. I'm not going to let Charles blame me or Trevor for his actions.

I push past Trevor as he tries to stop me by grabbing my arm, but I'm full of adrenaline and determination and shake him off.

Charles is next. "Stop, Jess," he growls, and his hand clamps on my arm and twists.

I pull away from him with a sudden movement. Pain shoots up my arm. But my brother doesn't release me. "Let me go," I say as I try to jerk out of his grip again. I reach forward and shove my parents' bedroom door.

The door swings open. There's a single lamp on in the room, and my parents are both in bed.

Sleeping.

How could they be sleeping with all this commotion and arguing? Wasn't Charles just in their room?

And then I see the blood.

Their necks have been sliced. They aren't moving, and

their eyes are closed, their mouths open. My mom's blonde hair is matted with blood.

I freeze in place, even though Charles is still gripping my arm and shouting threats at me to get out of the room. I can't stop staring at the horrific scene before me.

It can't be real. I'm dreaming. I'm in the middle of a terrible nightmare.

How can my parents be dead?

I can't breathe, and I start to gasp for air. My legs give out, and I crumple to the ground as my stomach clenches. "What happened?" I ask, although I might be screaming the words.

"You *killed* them, Jess," Charles says. "Let's get out of here."

He's dragging me from the room by my arm. The pain of his fingers gripping me is nothing compared to the pain in my heart.

"Call the ambulance," I say through my gasps. "Maybe it's not too late." My chest heaves with each word. I know it's too late, but my mind can't accept it.

I'm in the dark hallway now, still on my knees, and Charles towers over me.

"We'll call the cops, all right," he says, then he leans down and presses something cold and wet against my face. It reeks.

Whatever chemical is on the cloth makes it impossible to breathe. I claw at Charles's hands to push the cloth away, but for the second time that night, everything blacks out around me.

When I awake, I'm alone in the dark hallway. At first, I'm disoriented. My stomach hurts, and my head is spinning—like a hangover—or at least what I've heard a hangover is like.

I've tried alcohol only once in my life, and that was last year. Trevor told me his uncle died of an overdose and that he'd vowed to stay away from drugs and alcohol.

And I believed him.

Why then, is he helping Charles deal drugs?

Then I remember my parents. Their bedroom door is open, and the lamp light filters into the hallway.

Was what I saw real? Are they really dead? I stay on the floor a minute longer, listening for sounds of my brother, for anyone. The house is quiet. Only the faint ticking of a clock comes from the kitchen. Despite all the electronics in our house, my mom still keeps a ticking clock above the kitchen sink.

The thought of it makes my eyes water.

Here I am, lying on the floor, while the night ticks away, and my parents are . . .

I force myself to my hands and knees. My stomach feels like it's been turned inside out. But I have to check. I have to see if what I dreamed is real.

I crawl into their bedroom. My mom's hand hangs off the bed, utterly still and unmoving. I get to my feet, keeping my hands on my knees for support. My mom still hasn't moved. The blood is dark now, nearly black.

She looks as if she's been frozen in a nightmare.

I can't even look at my dad. The sight of his motionless body in my peripheral vision is confirmation enough.

I am not dreaming. This is all real.

Turning, I stagger and catch myself on the nightstand. I need to get out of this room. Away from the sight of blood and stench of death. I need to call for help.

With every bit of willpower I have, I pick up the cordless phone that my mom keeps on the nightstand. The landline only rings with solicitors, and she usually keeps the ringer off.

I pick up the phone and look at the numbers. Then I dial 911.

The operator answers on the second ring, and for a

moment I can't speak. When she tells me to take a deep breath and tell me what happened, I start to sob. Over the next few minutes, I manage to tell her my address and that my parents are both dead.

The operator's voice is soothing, strong, calm . . . the opposite of all the things that I feel.

"Are you the only one in the house?" she asks after telling me that the ambulance is on its way.

I don't know. I don't know where Trevor or Charles went, but I sense that they've left.

I close my eyes. "I'm the only one here."

When I hear the sirens, I'm still on the phone with the operator. I'm now sitting on the floor of my parents' bedroom, their bodies only a few feet away from me. I start to hyperventilate when the paramedics burst into the bedroom. One of them tries to help me to my feet.

I can't support my own weight, and I can't breathe or talk. One of the paramedics injects something into my arm, and for the third time that night, my world goes black.

CHAPTER 25

LOGAN

THE GLORIETTA BAY Marina could be a postcard. With the setting sun casting orange and gold over the Pacific Ocean, complementing the violet shadows of the docked sailboats, it's a photographer's dreamscape.

I see the cop cars up ahead as Gwen slows her car. We drive as close as we can, then park and hop out.

We haven't spoken for about twenty minutes, although I know we are both thinking, and dreading, the same thing.

Jess is on a boat. And the chances of her being alive are slim.

After I talked to Sandra and relayed the information to Gwen, she called the chief back right away. In the course of their conversation, they discussed the chance Jess had of being alive. Both believe that the chance is very small since Charles hasn't made any ransom demands.

He wants his little sister out of the way. He can't risk her memories returning. Whatever happened the night of their parents' deaths, Charles is afraid of the truth. His desperation now is proving that theory.

There are no sirens, no rushing about, and no one is calling to each other in a panic.

Things at the marina are calm and quiet. This calmness sends an eerie chill up my back.

We've arrived only a short time after the cops arrived, and so as we hurry around the yellow tape, we watch everything play out in real time.

There are several cops and investigators standing on the dock near a sailboat that's called *Little Miss*. The boat is in good condition, but there's definitely wear and tear.

Gwen leaves my side and joins the investigators who are boarding the boat. I want to be there, searching among them. I also don't want to be here at all. My phone buzzes, and I look down to see a text from Sandra. She's done some digging of her own and has screenshotted a picture of Trevor's Facebook page where he's standing on his boat, waving at the person behind the camera.

I zoom in on the picture. Sure enough, the sailboat is called *Little Miss*, the very one I'm standing before now. On the other side of the sailboat is another boat that's not currently in its slip. I can't make out the name of the other sailboat, but it doesn't matter.

Sandra's text only confirms the connection between Trevor and *Little Miss*, and of course, Charles.

I pocket my phone and look up at the sailboat again. Gwen disappears with a couple of the investigators below deck. I exhale. What is she seeing right now? Is Charles standing there, with a gun, Jess tied up behind him? Is she still alive? Or has she been killed by her brother?

Moments pass, slow and arduous, but I know it's been only about thirty seconds when suddenly Gwen appears above deck. She motions for me to come closer, and I see the panic in her eyes.

My stomach does a somersault as I hurry to the side of the boat.

She leans over the side.

"They were here," she says. "Inside the cabin. At least I'm almost sure they were. They're examining and cataloging everything now. But they've recently left."

"Is . . . do you think Jess is still alive?"

Gwen blows out a breath. "It's impossible to know." She straightens and scans the marina, as if she can find the answer by looking at the other boats.

"Do you think they're close?" I ask. "Maybe they heard the sirens and relocated?"

Her eyes snap back to mine. "There were no sirens."

"It's been all over the news," I say. "At least the house fire. Charles could see it on his phone."

"You're right," Gwen says. She climbs down from the sailboat, and I extend my hand to help her. When she's standing next to me, she says, "If you were Charles and you were panicking, what would you do?"

I blink. I need to think like Charles. Now. "If my plan was to take Jess out on a boat . . . and get rid of her body." My throat burns with acid. "And I knew the cops might be able to trace me to Trevor's sailboat . . . I'd . . ." I look around. The empty slip on the other side of *Little Miss* catches my eye.

My gaze connects with Gwen's. Her mouth lifts in a grim smile as if she's following my thoughts.

"I'd take another sailboat," I finish.

Gwen nods, her eyes widening. She turns and without a word, we both walk past *Little Miss* and stop in front of the abandoned slip.

Our gazes both stray to the horizon—golden and vast and . . . empty.

"Which direction do you think he's gone?"

Gwen looks up at me. "That's easy. Mexico." She shakes her head and looks back to the horizon. "Dump the body and keep sailing. He might even know some Spanish already."

"Yeah," I say, mostly to myself. I pull the phone out of my pocket and open the text that Sandra sent over. Rotating the phone so that Gwen can see the image, I say, "This is from Trevor's Facebook page."

Gwen's eyes widen. She takes the phone and zooms in, just like I did moments before. After a few seconds, she hands it back. "Text that picture to me. We've got some phone calls to make, including one to the coast guard."

I text Sandra back. *Thx for the pic. This is going to help big time.*

Seconds later she texts back a prayer emoji.

Amen, I think.

I don't know if I can hope that Jess is still alive. Whatever her state is, I want Charles behind bars. If only to taste a little of what he's put his sister through. She'll never be fully avenged. But prison would at least be a start.

I turn to see that Gwen is already talking to the investigators, showing them the picture I texted to her phone. Soon, the police chief is also on the scene, and it's not long before the US Coast Guard arrives, pulling up to the dock.

I see Gwen climb on, and I'm green with envy. Although I don't know how my stomach would fare on such a choppy ride. Someone hands Gwen a life jacket, and she gives me a brief wave before she turns to one of the crew members.

"Coming?" someone says next to me.

I turn to see Chief Bergholm. "We're going to drive south and try to keep tabs on the patrol boat."

He doesn't need to ask me twice.

Not five minutes later, I'm riding in an undercover police SUV. Two other officers are with us, and I listen as they discuss the various leads.

"Thanks for your help, Dr. Mayer," the chief says, cutting through the conversation. "Gwen says that your observations have been invaluable."

"I wish I could do more," I say. "No one deserves a brother like Charles."

"Even a woman who murdered her parents?" one of the cops asks.

The chief hushes him. "There's a reason Gwen reopened the case. Our job right now is to stop another tragedy from happening."

The radio squawks to life, and the three cops listen intently. It sounds like a dispatcher reporting in on one of the other searches—which I already know produced nothing.

As we drive, I watch the darkening ocean from Route 75, and I wonder how far we are behind the patrol boat. And how much of a head start does Charles have?

Overhead, a helicopter roars, and I crane my neck to see out the window. It's a search and rescue helicopter.

"It's about time," one of the cops says.

I suppose that in this line of work, irony gets everyone through the day.

The lights of San Diego to the east of us are coming on in full force, like a thousand stars against the deepening night. We connect with I-5 without any sighting of the coast guard or a sailboat that might be Charles.

As the Mexican border comes into view, I find myself wondering if the San Diego Police Department will continue its pursuit. But it seems the border station is already fully apprised of the search, and we drive across the border with only a nod from border security.

The chief takes a call on his Bluetooth, but his words are so cryptic that I'm not sure what's happening. When he ends the call, he says, "We're headed to Rosarito Beach."

Over an hour drive, but the chief puts on his siren, and we blast down the Mexico 1D route.

I text Gwen: *Any service out there? Any news?*

There's no response. The hour drive is reduced to forty minutes, and by the time we turn into the beach town, it's completely dark. The streets are a mix of bright lights and tourist-flavored music. Crowds mill about, currently oblivious to the drama that's about to erupt.

The chief has taken two more calls on the drive, but he hasn't shared anything new with us. As we catch a full view of the ocean from the road, I see that there are several patrol boats out on the water.

"The Mexican police have been waiting for the sailboat," Bergholm says. "No sighting of him yet."

Just as he speaks, one of the boats turns on a bright spotlight that floods the dark waters with brilliant white.

"I take that back." Bergholm parks next to a car that reads *Policía Federal* on the side of it. A Mexican police car.

We're out of the SUV in an instant, and although my muscles are cramped from sitting in such a tense position for the past couple of hours, I keep pace with the cops.

People are starting to congregate on the beach behind a barricade that the Mexican police have set up. I'm stopped as soon as they spot my civilian clothing, although the American cops make it through fine. Chief Bergholm seems to have forgotten about me temporarily, and so he should. The action on the ocean is much more important than worrying about a psychiatrist who picked the wrong clients.

I move among the crowd until I have a clearer view of the boats on the water. Three of them are Mexican, and then I spot the US Coast Guard boat that Gwen is traveling on. My heart rate ratchets up several notches as I worry about her safety.

And then the massive spotlight lands on a sailboat. My pulse skyrockets.

It has to be the one Charles stole. It better be.

The patrol boats are moving closer to the sailboat, and I realize that it's surrounded now. Four against one.

A man in the crowd behind me shouts something in Spanish, and an argument breaks out. They sound like a bunch of drunks looking for a show.

I get bumped from behind, rather aggressively, but instead of confronting whoever pushed into me, I move farther down the beach. The crowd is sparser here.

The boats are getting closer, and the spotlight keeps its focus. I can hear distant commands being shouted over one of the boat's loudspeakers. And although I can't decipher the words, I know they're in English.

Please be alive, please be alive, I chant inside my head.

I can only watch the action, and the minutes crawl. I barely notice the wind picking up and the sand stirring about my feet and legs. I've sand in my shoes, no doubt, and my throat is dry as the Mexican desert around us.

My phone buzzes in my pocket, and the only reason I take it out is because I'm hoping that it's Gwen.

It is.

He's threatening to blow up the boat. We're gonna get the bastard.

I type back a short text. *Good. I'm on the beach, watching.*

I don't ask the question I want to ask—has she seen any sign of Jess?

So I wait.

The spotlight sweeps up into the sky, but I keep my gaze on the sailboat. Something flashes, and I'm not sure if I'm seeing right. It looks like gunfire is being exchanged.

The crowd is getting rowdy with speculation. More fights break out. Damn drunks.

The spotlight moves back to the sailboat, and I can tell

something is different. I don't know enough about boats to decipher it. But an ambulance that's parked on the beach suddenly lights up.

The US boat pulls right alongside the sailboat, and the dark forms of the coast guard board the sailboat.

They've caught Charles. He might even be dead.

When they carry off two bodies from the sailboat, I can't move.

Jess.

CHAPTER 26

JESS

THEY SAY THAT heaven is white. Angels are white. Even God is white, by most religious accounts. But when I die, all I see is the darkness. Whatever my brother injected me with in the van sends me into an endless, spinning void so that I feel like I'm in a half-dream state.

When my heart stops, I wait for the tunnel and the light at the end to appear. I can't move, though; I can't even see the light, let alone walk toward it. Also, I can still feel air, damp air, move in and out of my lungs. I can't move, but I am somehow breathing?

I didn't know that dead people can breathe.

My mouth feels swollen, and I can taste salt. Most likely blood, but it's stronger than any blood I've encountered. The bitterness makes my stomach roil.

I try to move again, to find the tunnel, to find the light. It's as if my dead soul is heavier than a boulder. Maybe whatever creates a soul isn't something that moves on to heaven but rots in a decaying body.

Maybe my soul will remain trapped in darkness until the end of the world. A world where the sound of beeping plagues my mind, making me feel as if I've arrived in the bowels of insanity.

Or hell.

I realize I've been listening to the same beeping sound for hours, or maybe even days. Is time measured after you're dead? I want the noise to stop. But it's better than my brother screaming at me.

My stomach finally stops churning and grows still. This begs the question of whether or not dead people can feel pain or illness, or hear beeps.

And then the voices start up again. I realize that I've heard them . . . before . . . before what, I'm not sure. Before I died? Before my brother killed me?

The darkness shifts and changes. The black morphs into a deep violet, and then a blue.

"Jess," someone says.

Death is strange.

"Jess, can you hear us?" the voice again. It's familiar. Low. Male.

Something brushes my skin, so light that it could be a puff of wind or maybe a feather. Or a hand closing over my fingers.

I am being touched. Is this death? No, I don't think it can be death.

"Jess, it's time to wake up," the male voice says.

Wake up? I recognize the voice.

Dr. Mayer is speaking to me. Does this mean he's dead too?

Did my brother hurt him?

The memories surround me now, and I remember everything with clarity. It's like the last nine years of fog have been lifted and I've been plunged into the light. The memories are there—all at once. They don't play out like a scene in a book, but they are suddenly all fully formed, all complete.

My parents were already dead when I reached their bedroom that night.

Charles had been inside. Trevor too. He tried to stop me from entering. But I forced my way past Trevor, past Charles. When I saw my parents in their bed, they were already gone . . . at the hand of my brother.

He abandoned me there, in the hallway. Charles and Trevor both left me alone in that house to face the paramedics, the police, and all the questions. But my mind couldn't absorb the horrific event, so it cocooned itself in order to protect my young mind.

The brother I should have loved, but hated, had murdered my parents. There was no one to trust, no one to turn to, no one to believe me, so my memories went dormant.

Air rushes through my lungs. In and out.

I am alive.

The thought wriggles its way into my mind.

I am alive.

I need to open my eyes.

Although I know that once I do, the memories will become a part of my new life. I will have to face my brother. I will have to live with knowing that I've been kept silent for nine years in order to save him.

"Jess."

Slowly, deliberately, I focus on lifting my eyelids.

The darkness shifts from gray to a dull yellow. To brown. The warm brown of Dr. Mayer's eyes.

They crinkle at the corner as if he's smiling.

"Welcome back, Jess," he says in a soft voice.

The beeping continues, but it's faded now. "Where . . ." The single word is a huge effort.

"You're at the hospital," Dr. Mayer says.

I close my eyes, then open them again. Dr. Mayer is still

there. His dark hair falls over his forehead as he leans toward me. His brown eyes and their flecks of gold are focused solely on me. He watches me as if he's afraid I'll disappear again.

"My brother . . . ?" I whisper.

"He's in another hospital," Dr. Mayer says. "I don't know how much you remember, but he was . . . injured . . . in our attempt to rescue you."

Charles is alive. What has he said about me? What lies has he told?

Dr. Mayer, always astute, must see the emotional battle playing out in my expressions.

"We know the truth, Jess," he says. His touch is light on my hand. His touch makes me feel safe. "We know that you didn't kill your parents. You're innocent."

The word *innocent* is something I haven't even dared to dream about. Now, when I hear it, in application to me, my eyes burn with tears.

Dr. Mayer leans closer. "Your brother confessed last night. Ironically, he's pleading insanity."

I wait for the shock, the anger, the disbelief to set in. But only my tears continue, and I feel their warm wetness trail down the sides of my face. The room shifts and blurs, and I try to blink away the tears.

Dr. Mayer uses a tissue to wipe them away, although they keep coming.

"Am I dreaming?" I ask.

"You're not dreaming, Jess," Dr. Mayer says, his voice cracking. "You're a free woman."

I don't know if I can fully comprehend what he's telling me.

"Charles asked me to be his court psychiatrist," he says.

I stare at Dr. Mayer. "Are you?"

His laugh is soft. "No. The only thing I'll do in court is testify for the prosecutor. I don't think the defense wants me."

I am relieved because Charles doesn't deserve Dr. Mayer.

"What about . . . me?" I ask. "I don't know how to be free. It's been so long."

"I'm here for you, Jess." He leans closer and presses a kiss on my forehead. "As long as you need me."

CHAPTER 27

LOGAN

WHEN CHIEF BERGHOLM asks if I want to watch Charles give his official statement, I don't even have to think about my answer. It seems that any invitation from the cops in regard to this case has my full interest.

Jess will remain in the hospital for a few more days, so I don't feel any trepidation about her well-being. With her brother in custody, I'm even more confident that she can begin the process of returning to a normal life. Well, I should clarify. Jess will never have a "normal" life, but I believe she can have a happy and fulfilled life.

I've already been witness to her strength of character and purity of soul.

"Logan?" Gwen says as I approach the police station.

She's standing outside, speaking to another officer.

Since the night of the rescue, we, surprisingly, haven't talked much. I gave her a huge hug when I first saw her come off that US Coast Guard boat. But we've been pulled in different directions, and things between us have . . . cooled.

Perhaps a life-and-death experience will do that to someone. Rearrange priorities. Alter outlooks.

I'm more determined than ever to protect my patients

and to help them navigate the murky waters of their personal hells.

If needed, I'll face any censure for my involvement in this case. But I'll take comfort in the old adage, all's well that ends well.

Charles behind bars and Jess living free is the best conclusion I could have ever come up with.

Trevor Mills has also been charged with accomplice to murder, although he's currently out on bail. I've already caught wind of the high-powered lawyer he's retained. Trevor will, unfortunately, get off easier than he should. Prison time, certainly, but it won't be enough for what I consider nine years of lies.

Nine years of subjecting an innocent woman to emotional, mental, and physical torture through medication and institutionalism.

"Hi, Gwen," I say, approaching and nodding to the officer. "Chief Bergholm invited me."

"Great," she says, her smile a bit too wide.

Then I take a closer look at the officer. He's tall, young, has that intense gaze that so many officers do . . . and he's definitely interested in Gwen. Have I interrupted them . . . flirting?

I smile back at Gwen. "I can't wait."

"Me neither," Gwen replies. "I'll meet you in there in a couple of minutes."

"Sounds good." I shove my hands into my pockets and move toward the entrance. As I walk away, I hear Gwen explain to the officer who I am.

My thoughts don't take long to move from Gwen and her flirting with an officer to the woman in a hospital bed only a few miles away. Jess is eating regular food now, and when I visited her this morning, I felt gratified to see her eyes light up at the sight of me.

I didn't take it as any sort of compliment, though. I took it as a sign of progress. A sign that Jess might yet find joy in living life after nine years of enduring what no one ever should.

In the getaway van, Charles had injected his sister with a strong sedative. Jess had been lucky. Because she'd cut back on her other medications on her own in the psychiatric center, the reaction to the sedative was not as dramatic as it could have been.

Charles had tied her up at some point, because when the coast guard found her on the floor of the cabin, she was bound and gagged. She was also barely breathing.

Her bruises are minor compared to what could have been, and my own theory is that Charles was planning on pitching her overboard as soon as he crossed into Mexican waters.

But the Mexican police already had their patrol boats ready.

Sometimes I wonder what might have happened if Sandra hadn't sent me that text with the picture of Trevor's sailboat. I'm sure that Gwen and the other investigators would have figured things out eventually. But how long would that have taken? Ten minutes? Thirty? An hour or two?

By then, Charles could have made it across the border and disappeared forever.

I enter the police station, and after checking in and putting on a visitor badge, I'm shown to an observation room. Two other officers greet me, and I recognize them both as the ones who rode with us to Mexico.

I take a seat on a hard chair, and moments later Charles is led into the interrogation room. The one-way glass lets us observe him without being seen.

But Charles knows we're here and probably assumes that

I'm here as well. His piercing blue eyes focus on the window, and I have the uncanny feeling that he can see me, although I know it's impossible.

"This is a one-way window, right?" I ask anyway.

The officers chortle. "You'll get used to it, doc," one of them says. "Don't worry, it's been tested."

Despite their assurance, I'm still tense because Charles's gaze is unwavering. His hands might be cuffed together, as well as his ankles, and his blue jumpsuit marks him as a prisoner, but he's still intimidating.

I know I'm looking into the eyes of a man whose cruelty is beyond comprehension.

"Hi, everyone," Chief Bergholm says as he enters the observation room.

Gwen is right behind him. Her face is slightly flushed as if she spent too much time in the warm sun. She nods at me without a comment and takes a seat.

I stand to shake the chief's hand, and when we're all settled again, he says, "How's Jessica Harper doing?"

I appreciate that he remembers her by her first name. "She's eating normally and should be out of the hospital in a couple of days."

"Where's she going?" the chief asks.

It's a good question. Gwen seems interested in the answer as well.

"I've arranged a foster situation," I say. "Sort of a halfway house, but of course it's not a halfway house. She'll be staying with an older couple who's experienced in helping others transition from full-time residency to becoming more independent."

"Do you think she'll be able to live on her own?" the chief asks.

I glance at Gwen. "Eventually. I don't know how long it will take, though. Months, maybe."

The chief nods thoughtfully as two men enter the interrogation room. Everyone on our side of the glass goes quiet.

Both investigators sit across the table from Charles, but we still have a good view of him, for better or for worse.

One of the investigators, clearly in charge, begins by asking some routine questions, such as his name, place of residence, occupation, his education background.

I know all of this, yet I am fascinated as I listen. Fascinated because it's hard to fathom how coldhearted and calculated another human being can be.

Charles has waived his right to legal counsel, stating that he'll represent himself and that he wants to enter in an official confession. It seems that he's resigned himself to a life of incarceration.

For some reason, I'm suspicious of Charles's intentions. But how can I be suspicious of them? He's already in prison and will remain there indefinitely, accused of a double homicide, also kidnapping and maybe attempted murder. He'll never have control over his sister again. Yet his insistence on entering in a confession has me feeling uncomfortable. I should be relieved, ecstatic.

I glance over at Gwen, and she, too, is hyperfocused on Charles. I can't guess what's going through her mind, but she seems more acclimated than me.

"Let's start with the day of the incident, Mr. Harper," the investigator says. "Tell us about what happened when you woke up that morning."

Charles smiles. Actually *smiles*. It officially creeps me out.

"I woke up to a text from my friend, Trevor," he says. "Well, he was Jessie's boyfriend, but that wasn't about to last very long. He'd told her some story about never doing drugs or drinking, or whatever, but he was doing stuff behind her back that she didn't know about."

"What was the text about?" the investigator asks.

"I'll get to that," Charles snaps. "Can I talk without all the questions? You'll get your confession—if anything, I always keep my word."

The statement is in no way comforting. He doesn't say he tells the truth, just that he keeps his word, which sounds sinister enough.

Gwen raises her brows and glances at me. I meet her gaze. I'm assuming this is an unusual request from a prisoner.

"I was at scout camp, as you all probably know," Charles continues, and the investigator nods.

I'm certain that every officer on both sides of the glass has familiarized themselves on the Harper murder case.

"I wasn't supposed to have electronics with me, but I had important business going on, so I had to keep my phone on me." Charles rubs his nose as if he has an itch, and his cuffs clatter. "Trevor tells me he has a buyer, and so I make plans to leave camp for a few hours. I know that Trevor won't be able to pick me up, so I have to use public transportation. I called an Uber to pick me up down the road from the scout camp around eleven p.m."

He reaches to pick up the Styrofoam cup of water that's been sitting on the table the entire time. After taking a drink, he says, "Everything goes well with the drug pickup, and so I just have to do the hand off to Trevor. I get home around midnight, but there's a light on in my parents' bedroom. So I have to wait until it goes off since I know the house is locked up. I've already decided to go in through my window, or even Jessie's if I have to.

"Trevor's car is parked down the road. He's such a schmuck, thinking he's so sneaky. At least it tells me that he's at my house already—with Jessie, of course. It pisses me off, and I decide to blow his cover. That night seems like a good enough time to do it."

I shake my head and don't even realize I'm doing it until Gwen sends me a commiserating look.

Charles continues. "I go in through my bedroom window, and Trevor only has half of the money when I explicitly told him to have all of it. But I can be a flexible guy." His face reddens. "Jess was hiding in my closet listening. That little bitch. She's always been out to get me in trouble. Sneaking in my room. Telling lies to my parents. Telling the girls at school to stay away from me. Trevor and I had an agreement, and now she was about to screw everything up."

My hands tighten into fists. How can the investigators sit there and listen? They're even better than me, and I'm the psychiatrist who's paid to listen to other people.

Charles takes another drink from his water cup. "Jessie freaked out of course. She went ballistic. I knew she'd wake up my parents, so I had to be proactive. I mean, people were counting on me. You might think that people who take drugs are the bad guys, but they're really trying to function on a normal level like the rest of us. They need some help, and there's nothing wrong with a little help."

My throat feels dry, but I don't have water with me. I should have planned ahead.

Charles finishes his water and starts to methodically pick apart the Styrofoam. The investigators do nothing to stop his nervous habit.

We're all waiting for him to talk about what happened with his parents.

"I hurried upstairs before Jessie could tell my parents and ruin everything," he says. "My mom was just coming down the hall from her bedroom, and I told her that something serious had happened and I needed to talk to her privately."

He shrugs. "We talk in the kitchen, and I knew we had only a few minutes before Jessie . . . woke up."

Woke up? What had happened to her?

Charles's eyes shift from the investigators to the window that separates us. It's as if he's staring at me again. "I was sure grateful that I'd thought to keep a bottle of chloroform in the bottom kitchen cupboard. I knew my parents wouldn't notice it, and that night it came in handy. While Trevor stuttered out our fake story about why I was home from camp early, I grabbed a dish towel and the chloroform. It worked like a charm on my mom."

I shudder at the robotic way that Charles is speaking right now. Or maybe it's his intense gaze that isn't wavering from the window.

"We carried her back into the bedroom. Tucked her in." He smirks. "My father slept through the whole thing. So I used the chloroform on him too." He's finished with ripping apart the Styrofoam cup now, and the tiny pieces litter the table. No one makes a move to clean it up.

"At first when I heard Jessie coming up the stairs, I was furious," he says. "It would be her word against mine, and I couldn't rely on the bumbling, stuttering Trevor." He stops talking for a moment and looks down at his hands that are now clasped on the table.

When he lifts his head again, I swear his eyes are darker.

"You know those moments when you have one decision to make," he says, "and you have to do it right away in order to save other people?"

No one answers.

"I had to kill my parents then and there," he says. "I had to put a stop to everything they'd try to do to me. I couldn't let them turn me into the cops. I couldn't let Jessie tell them about what I was doing, because I was *helping* a lot of people. And I couldn't let Trevor make everything worse."

He spreads his hands on the table as if he's doing a clean

inspection. "I always keep my pocketknife sharpened, like every good Boy Scout."

His words hang in the air. I don't think any of us are breathing.

Charles scoffs, and I flinch at the sound. "Don't look so glum, my friends. I mean, I gave you the golden ticket. You can print that, you know. 'Eagle Scout uses knife to cut his parents' throats in a clean kill.'"

One of the investigators shifts in his chair, but he doesn't say anything.

He lifts his hands. "Yep, that's right. In case you're wondering, after my sister was sent to the looney bin, I finished up my Eagle Scout project. There's even an article about it in the newspaper, and the Boy Scouts themselves sent me a certification commemorating my difficult circumstances."

Charles looks from the investigators to the window, then back at the men sitting across from him. "My sister was in the right place at the right time, so she became the suspect. It was really all her fault anyway. But now here I am." He lifts his wrists. "With these on. I guess the bitch gets the last laugh after all."

I wonder if the one-way glass is breakable. I wonder if I slam my shoulder against it, if it will crack or if I'll merely bounce off.

I don't realize I'm standing until Chief Bergholm grasps my arm. "Sit down, son. As tough as this is to listen to, it's the best thing we can hope for. With every word, he condemns himself further. Just focus on that."

Forcing myself to retake my seat, I deliberately swallow. Then I sit on my trembling hands.

Gwen leaves her seat and sits in the empty one by me. She places a hand on my shoulder. I appreciate the gesture, but I don't feel any better. How does she do this for a job?

"Well, that's pretty much it," Charles says. "I guess you can ask me questions now. But I'm warning you, I've gotta piss, so be quick about it."

I guess that the questions and answers continue for almost another hour, but I am numb to the passage of time. I'm barely aware of the others sitting around me. All I can do is try to contain the rage that won't go away. Every word that drips from Charles's mouth is disgusting to me. And I hope to all that's holy that Jess never reads his statement or hears a word of it.

When the prisoner is finally led out of the interrogation room, Gwen turns to me and whispers, "Are you okay?"

"Not right now," I say. I rise from my chair and make the barest of conversations with the chief, and then I'm walking through the station until I step out of the doors.

It's started to rain, which is fitting. I'm in no condition to ride my motorcycle right now, and I don't know how long I stand on the steps of the police station, letting the drizzle fall around me.

CHAPTER 28

JESS

MR. AND MRS. Jackson insist that I call them by their first names, so even though they're well into their seventies, I call them Bruce and Patty.

"Come see your room, dear," Patty says, linking her arm with mine. Her paisley skirt and light-pink blouse are a throwback to the eighties grandmas I watched on TV.

I walk, arm and arm, with Patty along the narrow hallway. Their house decorations are quite dated, but comfortable. I fully expect to see a crocheted doily on the bedside table. And I'm right.

We enter the room together, with Bruce carrying my sack of meager belongings. He sets the sack on the bed and places his hands on his hips while he catches his breath.

I really hate feeling like I'm putting this sweet couple out, but Dr. Mayer says that this place is what is called a transition home. And if there's anyone who needs to learn how to live in normal society, it's me.

"What do you think?" Bruce asks in his gravelly voice.

"It's wonderful," I say, because it truly is. The window is

partway open, and the San Diego breeze wafts through, stirring the yellow checked curtains. The bedspread is a yellow-and-white quilt.

"Are those flowers real?" I ask, crossing to the nightstand where a doily is spread out beneath a vase of yellow daisies.

"They are," Patty says. "We thought it would cheer you up."

I touch one of the petals. "I love them, thank you."

"Dr. Mayer says you like to garden," Patty continues.

I look over my shoulder at her. "I love to garden. At the . . . center . . . I was given free reign over the plants most of the time."

"Great," Patty says, clapping her hands together and throwing a smile in her husband's direction, who smiles right back. "We've something to show you."

I want to stay in this room for a while longer. To lie on the bed and watch the curtains sift in the breeze. But I say, "I'd like that."

We make the trek down the hall again, and then through the kitchen and out the back door. One advantage of an older house, I'm soon to learn, is that the foliage and trees are all mature. And the soil of the garden plot is dark and rich.

Nearly the entire back section of their yard is a garden plot. Row upon row of greens have poked through the soil. Tomato vines climb wire cones, and the cornstalks are nearly two feet high.

I swallow against the growing lump in my throat. I'm going to love this place. Not for the first time, I wonder how I can be so lucky to be free, to be starting over.

My brother will be facing the judge in a few days—the cold case has been officially reopened and expedited. He's in a prison cell, and I'm here, in a beautiful backyard. I cross the lawn with Bruce and Patty. The cool shade gives me goosebumps, but I don't mind. I can already smell the soil and the growing plants.

I spot a couple of weeds and practically pounce on them. They pull up easily, and Patty smiles as she watches me.

"You'll do fine here, Jessica," Patty says.

I smile back at her. It's nice, this smiling thing. It's also nice that it's Tuesday and I won't see my brother.

"When you're ready, we need to do some shopping today," Patty continues. "Get you a couple of outfits to wear."

I like my mismatched and ill-fitted clothing. They were the only things that I could choose for myself at the psychiatric center. Perhaps it's time to move forward and not have so many reminders of the last nine years.

"All right," I say, straightening and brushing the dirt from my hands. It feels good to see some dirt beneath my nails. "I'll wash my hands."

Patty does a quick glance at my clothing. I'm wearing cutoff red sweatpants and a stretchy gray T-shirt. The T-shirt does nothing to conceal the fading bruises on my arms, both from my brother's handling and from the IV at the hospital.

The three of us walk back into the house, and I go into my bedroom. The adjoining bathroom is well stocked. There's even a razor. I haven't been allowed to shave in a long time, but at the hospital, they gave me a razor.

I gaze at my reflection for a few moments. My ponytail is firmly in place. My skin is pink from the short time outdoors. It won't be hard to get a tan if I spend time in the garden. I analyze my eyes—the color I used to think was so much like my brother's.

But Charles's eye color is darker, almost gray. Mine are definitely a clear blue. I look down at my hands and decide to scrub them in the sink. I don't mind the dirt, but I don't want to be a bother to Patty. So I wash and dry my hands, then join

Patty and Bruce in the living room where Patty is waiting with her purse.

Her eyes brighten as she sees me. "Ready?"

I nod, and she continues, "Bruce will stay here. He's not a very affable shopper." She laughs. "And it will be nice to have some girl time."

Something inside me twinges. I remember my mom saying that to me when I was young. Somewhere along the way, we stopped doing things together. We always fought when we were in the same room. If she had lived, I wonder if we would have ever become buddies again.

I follow Patty to her car, a small blue sedan. As we drive, I roll down the window to feel the rush of wind against my face. When Patty parks in a shopping complex lot, I'm having second thoughts about going into a store.

"We can wait as long as you need to," Patty says in a gentle voice, patting my hand.

I exhale. "I'm ready, or at least I'm willing to be ready."

"That's a great attitude." She gets out of the car.

I pop open my door and step out onto the pavement. I can feel the heat radiating from the asphalt. A few yards away, a woman ushers two children in front of her as they head for one of the stores. I watch the young children. I was once like them. Innocent in everything.

I look over at Patty. She's waiting patiently, and for that, I'm grateful.

"Let's head to the shoe store first," she says. "Maybe you can wear whatever we buy for the rest of our errands. And if you get burned out, let me know, and we can come back another day."

I take a deep breath and start toward her. Together we enter the shoe store, and the bright colors stand out to me first. The store is mostly orange and white, and the fluorescent lighting makes everything glow. A store clerk greets us, and Patty replies.

A couple of people mill about the store, and Patty leads me to a wall with a display of ladies' tennis shoes. I'm not even sure of my size. So I try on a couple of different sizes that the clerk brings until I land on size 7.5. It fits well enough.

The clerk doesn't seem to notice me much. He's polite and speaks mostly to Patty—because she's asking all the questions. Less than twenty minutes later, we're out of the store, with our purchases of tennis shoes and sandals.

We load them in the car, and I want to get in the car and drive back to Patty's house.

"How about we get you something other than sweats to wear?" Patty says in a kind voice.

"Okay," I say. *Just walk. Patty will help you.*

I walk with Patty across the parking lot again while I focus on my breathing. The clothing store seems jam packed with clothing racks. I used to love to browse with my friends, but walking around the store only makes me feel uncomfortable. The clothes are so clean, so new, and so expensive.

I stop in front of a rounder of sundresses. They all have straps, bright colors, flowy fabric.

"This would look nice on you," Patty says, coming to stand by me and holding up a peach-and-white floral dress.

"It's short," I say.

She lifts the dress from the rounder and holds it against me. The fabric billows against my skin. It's so soft. "It will cover your knees."

"All right," I say, although my heart is thumping. "But I'll need a bigger size."

Patty lifts her brows. "You're quite thin, Jessica. I think this is your size. Do you want to try it on in the dressing room?"

I glance over at the row of dressing rooms. They look small and narrow. "No, I guess we could return it if it doesn't fit?"

"Of course," Patty says. "Does anything else catch your eye?"

When I don't answer right away, she says, "How about this blue shirt? It will bring out your eye color."

The shirt looks harmless enough. The pale-blue shirt is cut into a V at the neck, and it has short sleeves. My bruises will definitely show. They can't last forever, though. "Sure," I say.

We leave the store with four shirts, two sundresses, and three pairs of capri pants.

I am done.

Patty senses it. So we go back to the car, load the bags, and I climb into the passenger seat. My head is hurting. I close my eyes as we drive back to my new home.

CHAPTER 29

LOGAN

CHARLES IS SENTENCED to life in prison two days before Jess comes to my office for the first time. She's with Patty, although Patty stays in the lobby while Jess meets with me. We've shared a few phone calls, but it's been weeks since I've seen her in person. I can hardly believe the transformation.

She's wearing a peach-and-white sundress and strappy white sandals. Her hair has been cut to her shoulders, and it sways softly as she enters my office. She's carrying a small purse, and if I didn't know better, I'd think she was a normal, pretty woman. I'm on my feet in an instant, and I reach out to shake her hand.

Somehow, I end up hugging Jess without planning to. She smells nice, like lemon and fresh flowers. She also feels nice, but I don't dwell on that. My mind strays to Gwen and how we're definitely finished once and for all. I didn't realize how much the Harper case weighed me down until the sentencing was finished and Gwen asked if I wanted to meet for dinner.

I told her no, and she didn't seem surprised. I wasn't even tempted to spend more time with her. Our communication won't completely cut off because we can't help but cross paths once in a while. This morning, Gwen texted me that a trial date has been set for Trevor Mills. I don't really care what happens to him, since I know he was more of a bystander. Although he also kept Charles's secret all of this time.

For now, I'll focus on ways I can help Jess. She's perhaps my most fragile client, and all I want is for her to have a happy and as-normal-as-possible life.

When she smiles at me after I release her from our hug, I think my heart has momentarily stopped. My eyes feel misty with tears. I couldn't have planned or expected a better outcome.

"You look great, Jess," I say, and I'm rewarded with a faint blush to her cheeks.

"I'm wearing clothes that fit me," she says in a soft voice.

It's more than that—much, much more. Although the dress is a nice touch too. We settle into our respective chairs, and I make sure I keep my gaze on her face and don't let it wander.

"How has your day been?" I ask. Our last phone call was about five days ago, and I always start out with this question. Talking about the present for a few minutes is a good way to ease into talking about the past or the worries about the future.

"Today I've been nervous," she admits, touching the ends of her hair as if she's not sure if she likes her new haircut.

"Nervous about what?" I prompt.

She lifts a shoulder. "About seeing you again."

I swallow. "I'm the same as always."

"I know," she says. "But you're the one person in my life right now who saw me before . . ." She motions to her dress and hair. "Before all of this. I mean, you *know* me. You know what I've been through. Even Patty and Bruce don't know everything."

"You can tell them anything you want," I say. "They can

be trusted. And as for me, do you think I'm judging you or something?"

Her laugh is faint.

I'll admit I love hearing her laugh. It's like the sun breaking through dark clouds.

"I think you have to judge all of your clients," she says. "I mean, it's sort of your job, right?"

"Right," I say. "I'm not judging you in the way you might think. I like to call it 'evaluating' so that I best know how to help you."

She folds her hands together in her lap and looks down. She hasn't completely changed, I see. And I don't want her to, I realize.

"You were a big help in the psych center, Dr. Mayer," she says. "I mean, if it weren't for you, I might still be there . . . taking meds, doing puzzles, sneaking on to Facebook." She looks up at me.

I smile. "Do you have a Facebook account yet?"

"No." Her voice is breathy. "Patty and I talked about it, and she suggests I wait at least a year."

I am so glad Patty is in Jess's life. "Wise advice."

"In fact, she reminds me a lot of you—since you've told me waiting a year for a lot of things will be best."

"You don't have to wait a year on everything, you know," I say. "You might be ready for some things sooner."

She nods, and I realize this is what she wants to talk to me about. She opens the purse on her lap and pulls out a small notebook.

This reminds me. "Are you still keeping a journal?"

"Mostly," she says. "I write in it every few days, though, and not when I'm feeling depressed." She shrugs and opens the notebook. "When I'm having a bad day, or a bad few hours, my perception is skewed anyway. I forget the journal and go out in the garden. Or sometimes I'll take a walk with Patty. I use this notebook to write down goals, or my bucket list, whatever you want to call it."

I'm pleased. This is definitely progress. Not only is she learning to recognize signs of depression, but she's actively staying busy when the last thing she wants to do is get out of bed.

I lean forward. "Well, let's hear your goals."

Her smile is hesitant, and I guess she's nervous. Even though she's right, and I probably know her more than anyone, I understand that sharing something personal is still hard.

"I want to walk the beach at twilight . . . by myself. I don't want to be afraid of walking by myself." She turns the page. Apparently she has written down one goal per page. "I want to take driver's ed classes and get my driver's license back."

"Those all sound great," I say.

She glances up at me, then back down and turns the page.

"I want to get a job," she says, then flips a page. "I want to have my own apartment." Another page. "Own a car—that might take a few years. Get a cell phone." She gives a small scoff.

I smile.

She turns another page and doesn't say anything for a moment. "I want to visit my parents' grave."

"I'll go with you if you want," I say. It's perhaps unorthodox, and I don't know why I offer, but I don't always stop what comes out of my mouth around Jess.

She gazes at me for a moment, and I wish I knew what was going through her mind. Then she looks back at her notebook and turns to the next page. "I want to . . . um . . . get married." Shaking her head, she says, "No children, though. I mean, I don't think I'll ever be normal enough to be trusted with a baby."

I don't let her get away with her self-criticism. "Why not?"

"Because"—she closes the notebook and puts it back in her purse—"because I can't even take care of myself right now."

Her voice is starting to tremble, and I say, "A year from now, you might feel differently."

She nods, but I don't think I've convinced her.

"You've already accomplished so much, Jess," I say in a quiet voice.

She blinks rapidly, and tears spill onto her cheeks.

"You've gone through more in a few weeks than most people do in a lifetime," I add. "You've been betrayed in the worst way possible, yet here you are, carrying around a list of life goals." I hand her a tissue, and she uses it to swipe at her cheeks.

"Have you heard the saying, take one day at a time?"

She nods and sniffles.

"That's what I want you to do this week," I say. "I'm glad you have your list—your goals are important—but this week, take one day at a time."

She takes a shuddering breath. "All right." When she looks up again, the tears are no longer coming. She rises to her feet. "There's one more thing on my bucket list."

I stand as well and shove my hands in my pockets. It would be too easy to hug her and offer her comfort. Not that I haven't before, and it's fine because I would never cross that line, but I'll admit I wasn't quite prepared for this new dolled-up Jess to walk into my office.

"I need to find a new psychiatrist," she says quickly, then turns to leave.

I'm speechless. I didn't expect this at all. My mind turns over, and before she can leave the office, I say, "Wait, Jess."

She pauses but doesn't look at me. "I don't have to tell you everything, Dr. Mayer."

No, she doesn't. But I can't help worry—has she been in communication with her brother? Letters and visits are allowed. Even though he's in prison, Jess could still find ways to talk to him. What if . . . what if he's still controlling her?

I cross to the door and put my hand over hers, which remains on the doorknob.

"What's going on?" I say it firmly, when in fact I feel like begging her not to change doctors. No one knows her like I do. No one has helped her like I have.

"It's . . . complicated." She withdraws her hand so that we're no longer touching, and she won't look me in the eyes.

"Jess, you can tell me," I say. "I won't be mad, but I'd like to at least talk about your decision."

She brings her crumpled tissue to her face again.

Now she's crying about *me?*

"You can read about my decision," she says, her voice shaky but sounding resolved as well. She pulls out the notebook and holds it out to me.

I hesitate. I'd rather her tell me, but I don't want her crying again. So I take the notebook and flip through the pages. I notice that below each listed goal, she's written "why" and "when." The "walk on the beach at twilight by myself" has the "why" of "so I won't be afraid to walk by myself outside in the dark" and the "when" is listed as "one to three months."

At the top of one of the middle pages, she's clearly written "find a new psychiatrist." My breath hitches when I read the "why": "when you fall in love with your doctor, you need to find a new one and forget about childish crushes."

I reread the words again, and again. I'm not sure if I can look at her because my heart is pounding so hard. Patients becoming attached to their doctors is no small thing, and it shouldn't be dismissed or laughed at or taken lightly. The patient's emotions are very real to him or her, even though the doctor knows that the confidential discussions taking place between doctor and patient can create a bond—especially from the patient's viewpoint.

"Oh, Jess, I don't think—"

She doesn't let me finish. She grabs the notebook, then yanks the door open and disappears through the lobby before I can even come up with anything to say that will convince her not to run out of the office. Especially in her distressed state.

Patty stands from where she's sitting in the waiting room.

I want to tell her what Jess wrote in the notebook, but I can't. Through the front windows, I see that Jess has climbed into Patty's car. So that's a good thing. I walk toward Patty and say, "The session went really well, but we had a hiccup at the end."

She nods, businesslike. "I'll keep an eye on her today."

"Thanks for everything," I tell Patty. "Please keep me posted—call, text, anything. You have my number."

Patty thanks *me,* which I find ironic. I shouldn't be thanked. I watch her walk out of my office and get into the car with Jess. She's looking down. Of course.

I turn to Sandra, who's heard my exchange with Patty. Sandra is wearing a peach-colored blouse, white slacks, and a peach-and-white necklace and earrings. The peach color reminds me of the dress that Jess was wearing.

"When's my next appointment?" I ask, even though I know, but it's giving me something to say to Sandra.

She blinks so that her eyes aren't quite so wide anymore. "Twenty minutes."

"Then what?"

She clicks on my schedule on her computer. "You have a scheduled lunch break."

I nod. "Tell my next appointment I'm running late. I can use my lunch break to keep the session."

"All right," Sandra says, typing something in.

I walk out the front door without saying anything more to Sandra and without allowing her time to ask me questions. I can't answer her questions right now; I can't even answer my own.

Patty's car is nowhere in sight, and I don't expect it to be. I shove my hands in my pockets and walk around the building to the beach access path. Not many people are on the beach this time of morning, especially when school's in session and the hubbub of a typical workday in full swing.

The day is partly cloudy, and the gulls congregate around the overflowing trash bins at the path's entrance. They peck at each other as they compete for the best morsels.

I walk past the seagulls, and a few of them scatter, but the others are too immune to the threat of a human's presence to be bothered by any potential danger.

The ocean churns a few dozen yards in front of me, and I slip off my shoes and socks, then walk through the warm sand toward the water's edge. Before I reach the wet sandbar, I drop my shoes and fold up the hem on my pants. The wind is good and stiff this close to the ocean, bringing with it the tang of salt.

I take more steps until the ocean water slaps against my feet and ankles, then draws away with a tug, leaving wet sand between my toes. The cold water is refreshing, and I close my eyes.

I can hear the water approaching but can't see it. With each undulation, I feel the cold sensation again, and again.

My thoughts can no longer be delayed, and I let them run free. Even if I were able to convince Jess that she doesn't have true feelings for me—which I believe is the case—her progress might be hindered by her embarrassment in confessing her attraction.

Keeping my eyes open and focused on the gray waves heading my direction, I can visualize her blonde, blunt-cut hair touching her shoulders, her blue eyes smiling at me, the smooth skin of her neck and how her sundress revealed her as a striking woman. One who was hard to keep my eyes off.

I groan.

Have I made her believe that our relationship is more than what it should be? Have I unintentionally given her signals that have raised her hopes?

I'm not flattered by any means. I'm not that great of a catch. All right. I'm flattered. Someday, Jess will have her life back in order, and someday, a man will be lucky to have her.

I've no doubt that she'll make a great mom too. Her children will be fortunate. I understand her fear and her reluctance, but in a few short weeks, she's made so much progress. Like she said, a year from now, she'll be ready for much, much more.

I feel envious at the thought. I won't be a part of the "more." In fact, I might not be a part of her next session at all.

She wants to find a new psychiatrist so that she can forget about me. I think of the words that I read in her notebook: "when you fall in love with your doctor, you need to find a new one and forget about childish crushes." The only thing that brings me comfort is that she thinks it's a childish crush.

That's a good thing.

Right?

Yes, it's the best thing, and the only right thing.

I just don't want to have to say goodbye to her.

I start to walk down the beach as the surf moves in and out, soaking my feet and ankles, then withdrawing quickly.

Most of all, I hate that she was crying about me. I hate

that I've been the cause of anything that would distress her. She's had enough of that in her life.

For her sake, I need to honor her wish. I need to let her go.

CHAPTER 30

JESS

IT's FULLY DARK when Patty comes outside to find me in the backyard trimming the rosebushes. I'm not wearing gloves because the sharp pricks of pain from the thorns don't bother me. In fact, if I'm to be honest, the pain helps to distract me from what I confessed to Dr. Mayer today.

I hadn't planned on sharing my goal with him in such a way. But I suppose it's better to get rid of all the weight of my baggage sooner than later. And Dr. Mayer has become baggage on my heart.

It's a crush. A silly crush. I've had them before. In fact, I'd say that I still have a crush on Trevor after all those years in the psych center. Even pictures of his wife and kids on Facebook didn't deter that.

Maybe that's something I can work on with my new psychiatrist.

Meanwhile, I'll have to get over the gentle set-down from Dr. Mayer. I know he felt bad about it, which only makes me feel worse.

"Jessica, dear," Patty says. "At least come in and eat something. You can work out here all night if you want, but you need sustenance."

If I wasn't so tense, I might find this funny. I step back from the rosebush to see that it's perfectly pruned. Time to move on to the next one.

"A water bottle would be welcome," I say, glancing at her. I hate seeing the concern in her gaze. This woman is a literal angel for having me in her home and taking care of me.

Patty presses her lips together, then says, "All right. I'll be back in a minute."

While she's gone, I dump the clipped rose branches into the recycling container I've dragged across the lawn. The container is half-full from all the work I've been keeping myself busy doing.

Patty returns, carrying a cold water bottle and a ham sandwich on a tray. She sets the tray near where I'm working.

"Thanks," I say, feeling the emotion in my voice trying to push its way through. But I'm done with tears. The ones I shed in front of Dr. Mayer were mortifying enough.

"I'll be inside if you need anything," she says.

I nod and start to clip the next bush.

Alone again, I can't stop my traitorous thoughts from turning to Dr. Mayer. I should be laughing at myself. I don't even think of him as Logan, his first name. He's always been Dr. Mayer to me and always will be.

I love it when he leans forward to listen more intently. I love how he asks me questions as if he's truly interested. One part of me says that's his job; the other part of me says that he's asking, remembering, and caring—because he sees me as a person of value. And he'd be the first person to tell me that.

I love how his hair is always a bit out of place and how he rarely takes notes during our sessions. Yet he remembers what I tell him.

His eyes are my favorite feature. Their brown color is always warm, always receptive, always focused on me with kindness and understanding.

My throat tightens as I wonder if he feels sorry for me. If he pities me. I don't want to be that girl—the one who's sad and pathetic and has a tragic story. There's no way around it.

A thorn pricks my finger, deeper than any of the others. I gasp and suck on my finger, trying to ease the sting. Maybe I can think of Dr. Mayer as one of the roses of my life. He's beautiful, but there are too many thorns surrounding him.

I open the water bottle and take a long swallow, then I realize that I'm starving. So I sit on the ground and eat the ham sandwich Patty brought. By the time I finish, I'm feeling the ache in my muscles. Leaving the clippers behind, I take the tray and water bottle back into the house.

Bruce is sitting in the living room, reading. He looks up when I enter.

"Going to bed?" he asks.

I'm sure that Patty commissioned him to the task of waiting up for me.

"Yes," I say. "Your rosebushes look good."

He chuckles. "Thank you. Our neighbors are already envious of all the work you've done in the yard." He stands and crosses to me, still holding his book. Placing a hand on my shoulder, he says, "I'm proud of you, Jessica. You're a blessing in our home."

He turns and walks to the front door to double-check the locks before I can formulate a reply.

Finally I simply tell him goodnight and make my way back to my room. I burrow into the covers and am surprised that I'm dry eyed. Perhaps Bruce's kind words have erased my humiliation of the day.

Tomorrow, I tell myself, *tomorrow can only be better.* Perhaps I can start working on getting my driver's license.

With that thought, I finally drift to sleep, but my dreams are the stuff of nightmares.

Charles is released on some contingent, some overlooked flaw in the case, and he knocks on Patty and Bruce's door. They aren't home for some reason, so I answer the door without looking through the peephole. This is because every nightmare seems to pattern itself after an eighties horror film.

Seeing Charles on the front porch shoots so much adrenaline through me that I wake up in a panic. First, I realize it was a dream, second, I realize that I'm on the floor of my bedroom, which means that I actually got out of the bed to answer the door.

Then I hear a knock. Coming from the front door.

My pulse spikes. Someone is really knocking on the front door, and it's pitch dark outside. My half-awake blurred gaze focuses on the digital clock. It's 1:15 a.m.

Another knock sounds. Am I hearing things? Is there a windstorm? Am I still in my dream? A dream within a dream?

I can't move as I listen to the knocking. It won't stop, and I don't hear Patty or Bruce stirring. Then a horrible thought crosses my mind.

What if Charles came to the house and killed them?

I can't breathe. I barely make it to my bedroom door, where I lock it and then crumple on the floor next to the door. I cover my ears to block out the sound.

Hours later, I startle awake.

"Jess?" Patty calls through my door. My room is filled with sunlight.

Patty knocks on my door, and the sound jolts through me. Then I remember the knocking from last night.

My next thought is that Patty is alive.

I scoot away from the door and crack it open.

"Oh, you're awake," she says, smiling, although the worry in her eyes is plain. "Sorry, I didn't mean to wake you up. It's just that it's almost lunchtime."

I look over to the clock to see that it's 11:30 a.m.

"I had a long night," I say, brushing my hair back from my face. "Did you hear the knocking last night? Someone was at the door."

She lifts her brows. "No . . . Bruce might have heard it, but he didn't say anything to me."

I am going crazy. I finally got out of the psych ward, and here I am becoming schizophrenic, a diagnosis I've witnessed firsthand with Erin.

"I need to get ready, then I'll come for lunch," I say.

Patty smiles and bustles away. I'm not fooled by her cheerfulness, though. I know that she keeps in touch with Dr. Mayer separately from me, and I'm sure she's been giving him updates, especially after what happened yesterday in his office and my late-night gardening stint.

At the lunch table, I ask Bruce about the door knocking last night. His brows pull together as he thinks. "No," he says at last. "But I see you left the recycling container in the yard, and the lid was open. It could have been banging against the side if any sort of wind stirred up."

I nod, feeling relieved. I hope, truly hope, that was the case. I, for one, will never leave the lid open on the recycling container again.

I'm feeling better after sleeping, after food, after learning that no one was knocking on the door in the middle of the night.

The sound of a motorcycle passes the house, then it sounds as if it's stopping on the road in front.

A few moments later, someone knocks on the door. I jump.

"I'll get it," Patty says, rising from the table. I listen as she walks to the door and opens it, then says, "Well, hello, Dr. Mayer."

Dr. Mayer? I glance at Bruce, who looks as surprised as I feel.

I can't understand what he says to Patty, but I can hear the deep rumble of his voice. I get up from the table and leave the kitchen to escape to my bedroom. I'm not ready to see him yet. In fact, I had planned on never seeing him again. I don't need a picture or video to remind me of him. It's all in my head.

But moments after I shut myself in my bedroom, Patty knocks. "Jessica, dear, Dr. Mayer is here to speak with you."

I don't say anything for a moment.

"Jessica?"

"I'll be there in a minute." I rush to the bathroom and flip on the light. I brush through my now-shorter hair and pull it back into a clip. I don't have as much to work with as I used to, but I'm not about to take time with a straightening iron either.

Next, I brush my teeth, then dress in my V-neck blue shirt and a pair of tan capris. That will have to be good enough. I leave my bedroom before I can get any ideas about putting on makeup. Patty bought me a kit, but I have yet to experiment with the new stuff.

Dr. Mayer is waiting in the living room, and Patty and Bruce are nowhere to be seen. All right, then.

He's standing in front of the window, looking out at the front yard and street. He turns when I enter, and I know that I won't be able to forget him. No matter how hard I try, he will always have this effect on me. He's not wearing his usual button-down shirt and slacks. Instead he has on a gray T-shirt and jeans that, well, look really good.

And it doesn't help matters that his hair looks slightly damp as if he's fresh out of the shower.

The warmth in his brown eyes both makes me sad and

happy. I'm almost a 100 percent sure he's coming to say good-bye and give me a referral to another psychiatrist. Still, for a moment, I wish he was a regular guy, and I was a regular girl, and he's stopping by to say hi. Or even take me out on a date.

"Hi, Jess," he says.

I can't help how the timbre of his voice washes over me, moving through my body to the ends of my toes.

It's then that I notice that he's holding a gift bag of some sort in his hand. Great, a going-away gift? My heart and stomach plummet.

"I'm glad I caught you at home," he continues, staying on his side of the room while I stay on my side.

I realize that I haven't said a thing yet. "Yeah, not much going on today."

"Gardening?"

"Oh yeah," I say, feeling the urge to laugh. "Gardening" is an understatement. More like landscaping.

"So . . . ," he says, hedging.

It's unlike him to be indirect, but I'm not going to call him out on it.

"I've been thinking about what you said yesterday," he says, using his free hand to scrub through his hair.

Which only makes him look more appealing.

"I'm sorry," I burst out. "I was stupid to show you the notebook. I didn't want to put you on the defensive. But . . . I wanted to be honest about why I need to change psychiatrists."

"First of all, you're not stupid," he says.

Of course he would say that. I nod numbly.

"And, second, I'm glad you were honest," he says, stepping toward me. "The most important part of a relationship is honesty. Without that, what else is there, really?"

I can't look away from his eyes now. I'm completely

caught up in them. Honesty would have prevented me from living in a psych center for nine years. Honesty would have put my brother behind bars a long time ago. Honesty would have meant that Trevor wouldn't have let me fall for my brother's crime. And if I dig even deeper, honesty would have saved my parents' lives.

If my brother had been honest in his dealings, he wouldn't have gotten into drugs, and whatever else, and there wouldn't have been anything to hide from our parents.

Dr. Mayer has reached me by now. "Jess," he says in a hesitant voice. I don't think I've ever seen him hesitant. That's my department.

"I hope . . . I hope that one day you'll be able to see yourself as who you really are," he says.

This is why I don't want to let this man go. But I must.

"You are amazing," he says, his voice dropping low. "I don't know anyone who could do what you do and keep doing so much on a daily basis."

I look down. I could argue with him, but it's nice to hear, and nice that he's standing so close to me. I can smell his clean shower scent, and my stomach flips.

"I've got you lined up with a colleague of mine," he continues.

And there it is.

"His office is only a few blocks from mine, so you won't have to travel too far."

My eyes burn, betraying my determination to remain calm and collected.

When I say nothing, he says, "Jess?"

Finally, I look at him. "What?" I whisper.

He stares at me, and I feel my face warm, along with the rest of my body. I don't understand what's happening. He's leaning toward me with that intense gaze of his. One hand lifts, and he cups my cheek. "You'll be fine. I promise. If we were in another time or place or situation, believe me . . . I would love to take you on a date."

My breath rushes out of me. I'm not sure if I've heard him right.

"I'll miss you," he whispers, and then he does close the distance and kisses me on the cheek.

I want it to be more, and my cracking heart echoes my sentiment. I want him to pull me into a hug.

His hand falls away, and the warmth of his touch is gone all too soon. "I brought you something. I think you'll like it." He holds up that infernal gift bag.

I'm not quite sure what happened, what he'd just said, but I take the bag, if only to still my trembling hands. I pull out a rectangular box. I know immediately what it is.

"A cell phone?" I ask, looking up at him.

He smiles, although it's a bit wistful. "Yeah, I thought I could at least check off one thing on your bucket list."

I open the box and pull out a gold-colored phone. "Thank you," I say, keeping it simple, although I have questions to ask him. I refuse to bother him with anything more.

He taps on the home button. "You'll have to set everything up, but it's activated, and I've already put in my number."

I can't look at him for a moment.

"Jess, if you need anything, anytime, call or text me."

I still can't look at him.

"Okay?" he prompts.

"Okay," I finally say. My eyes are burning again.

"I know that you'll have a new psychiatrist and that I won't see you much anymore, but you're still important to me."

I nod. The tears have escaped now, and I blink rapidly.

He squeezes my hand, then takes a couple of steps back.

"I'd love to hear about your progress with your bucket list."

I swipe at my cheeks. He's moving away. He's leaving. And there's nothing I can do to stop it. "Goodbye, Dr. Mayer," I say.

He gives me a half smile. "Logan."

"Okay, Logan."

He lifts a hand in a half wave and opens the front door.

I lift my hand as well.

Seconds later, he's out the door.

Chapter 31

Logan

I'VE TAKEN UP running again. As I pound the pavement in the early mornings, and sometimes in the evenings, I realize that I've let my exercising routine slacken off quite a bit since I was dating Gwen. When we were going out, I must have felt more motivated.

And now? There's no new girlfriend on the horizon, but the physical exertion keeps me on the path of not calling Jess if only to see how she's doing. It would be completely unprofessional. I have, a time or two, or three, called her new psychiatrist Dr. Ferre for an update.

His reports have been very general but positive so far. I should be happy, pleased, yet . . . I still run. Sometimes twice a day.

Calling Jess would not be fair, not to her, not to me. Besides, I wouldn't be surprised if she's been dating. I have no idea because I couldn't very well ask Dr. Ferre about that.

Today, I'm running in the evening just as the sun sets. I don't think it's a coincidence that I'm near the beach down the road from Bruce and Patty's home. It would be a coincidence if Jess decided to walk that beach at the twilight hour.

She's nowhere in sight, and I don't have to worry about crossing any lines. I'm sort of proud of myself for that.

When my phone buzzes with a text, I ignore it. I'm not one of those gifted people who can walk/run and text at the same time. I'd miss a step or bump into a signpost.

So I don't check my phone until I reach my motorcycle sitting in the beach parking lot.

My heart rate spikes when I see it's from Jess.

Do you still want to go to the cemetery with me?

I think a full thirty seconds passes before I breathe again. My first instinct is to text back and say *yes*. Then, I start to rethink my response. If I say yes, then what will that look like? I pick her up? She rides on the back of my motorcycle, her arms wrapped around my waist?

Or will I meet her at the cemetery? Will she be with Patty and Bruce? How can I text her to ask about them? It will make her feel like I'm trying to back out. And if I tell her no, then she'll think I was all talk and no action when I promised that she could call or text me anytime.

It's been three weeks and four days since I gave her the cell phone. I've made so much progress in separating myself from her and thoughts of her, and worrying about her, mostly, that I'm not sure if seeing her again—at least so soon—is a good idea.

I look at the text again, and I type: *Sure, anytime.*

That "anytime" ends up being Saturday. She texts back that she doesn't want to interfere with my busy schedule, and I want to tell her that I'd rearrange things if needed. But I don't tell her that. I agree on Saturday.

Which can't come fast enough, or slow enough, depending on the moment that I'm thinking about it. We've agreed to meet at the cemetery, so I assume that Patty or Bruce will be driving her. Maybe both. This should fill me with relief, but

I also would love to be alone with her, even at a cemetery. Which is probably morbid to consider, especially since this visit will be a huge step in Jess's grieving process for her parents.

In the nine years since their murder, she's never visited their gravesite. She wasn't even allowed to attend the funeral.

I know that this event will be an epic step in Jess's life, and I hope I don't screw it up in any way.

Friday night, I don't sleep much. I feel as if I'm awake more than asleep, so it's with some relief that I see the sun start to rise. I can legitimately start my day. I pull on my socks and running shoes and go run for an hour. The rising sun in a clear sky proves that the day will be warm and bright.

I'm meeting Jess at ten a.m., which means the next few hours crawl by. I arrive at the cemetery twenty minutes early. As I walk among the headstones of the Holy Cross Cemetery, I see a burial ceremony taking place in the far corner of the lot. I steer clear of the mourners and stop in front of a few headstones to read their inscriptions.

I'm carrying a bunch of daisies that I hope will be okay to put on the Harper grave.

I don't hear a car pull up, but I sense that Jess has arrived all the same. I turn to see her walking out of the office building carrying a piece of paper, which I assume is the map. In her other hand, she's carrying what looks to be a dozen red roses.

I glance around but don't see any sign of either Patty or Bruce. Maybe one of them is inside the building or parking the car.

Jess hasn't seen me yet, which gives me a chance to observe her mannerisms. I don't profess that I can gauge her emotions from this distance, but I'm impressed with the confident way that she's walking. She's wearing a dress again. This one is pale green with short sleeves, with the skirt portion longer than her sundress.

She has sunglasses on—something I've never seen her wear. And her hair has some wavy curls in it, which makes it look shorter than I remember.

As I watch her walk toward me without noticing me, I know I've done the right thing by letting her go. She's becoming her own beautiful person. She'll learn how to be independently strong and enjoy a rich and full life. She doesn't need me to help her anymore.

This visit to the cemetery will be our last encounter, of that I'm sure.

Suddenly she looks up from the paper, and she slows. She's seen me. I lift a hand in a half wave and start toward her. She walks in my direction, and we meet by a massive grave marker with a stone angel on top of it.

"Am I late?" she asks, peering up at me.

I can't see her eyes because of her sunglasses, but I can tell she's wearing lip gloss.

"No, I was early," I say. "How are you?"

"Fine, how are you?" There's humor in her voice.

I smile. We don't hug, and that's okay. It's probably best. "Great. Are you here with Patty or Bruce?" I look past her, as if one of them might appear at any moment.

"Patty dropped me off," Jess says. "She'll pick me up later, when I text her I'm finished."

"Ah, so you're becoming a texting fanatic?"

She laughs. I love her laugh. I love that she's laughing. I love that I'm standing with her in this beautiful place on a beautiful day.

"I don't have a lot of people to text . . . yet," she says. "But at least I got a cell phone checked off my bucket list, thanks to you."

My throat tightens for some reason. "It was my pleasure. And I'm glad you reached out to me." I look about us, toward the mourners, then back to Jess. "I haven't been to this cemetery before—it's really peaceful."

Jess nods. The mourners have caught her eye. She looks down at her map and points to a number. "They're in this plot."

On the opposite side from the funeral service. This is good. "Shall we?" I ask.

She nods again, and we both start to walk slowly among the headstones. Once in a while Jess stops to read something, and I'm not sure if she's really interested in the inscriptions or if she's delaying our arrival at her parents' site.

We stand before a headstone that touts the attributes of someone's beloved wife. I read the dates and see that the woman has been gone for about twenty years. There's a jar of fresh flowers at the foot of the headstone. That in and of itself is a testament to those she left behind.

We start walking again. The breeze picks up and stirs the fragrances of the flower offerings to life. It's like we're walking in a garden.

The mourners on the other side of the cemetery start to break up, some of them moving back to their parked cars. Others linger, talking to each other. It seems their service is over.

We pass grave after grave, and then I know we're close because Jess slows down even more. I see the curved headstone first with the name *Harper* written in all caps on the upper portion.

Jess takes a couple more steps, then stops completely. She's still about five or six feet from the grave. I stand next to her and read the names and dates.

Richard Bertram Harper
Lisa Smith Harper

The dates are the same day and month as today. It's the

anniversary of their death. I should have known. Surely Jess knows, and this is why we're here—today of all days.

Jess isn't moving, and a glance at her doesn't give me a sense of what she's feeling since she's wearing her sunglasses. The sun is warm upon my head and shoulders, but not too hot.

More mourners on the other side of the cemetery leave, and it seems that only a handful of family members remain.

Every child deserves to attend her parents' funerals and to mourn and be comforted by loved ones. Jess missed out on that. Not only were her parents taken too early, but her brother broke apart their family forever.

I take a few steps forward and place the daisies I brought in front of the headstone. Then I move away, and soon Jess moves forward too. She sets her roses down. The grave really does look better with flowers in front of it, and I wonder if Charles ever came here to put flowers down. Or if what little conscience he has prevented him from doing even that.

Jess remains right in front of the grave, staring down at the flowers as the breeze stirs her hair. After a couple of minutes, she moves the sunglasses to the top of her head and wipes at her eyes.

I don't know if she wants to talk, so I wait for her to speak first.

But then her shoulders start to shake, and I realize her emotions have built up. I move to her side and settle my arm around her shoulders. She turns toward me instantly and wraps both of her arms about my waist. She cries quietly, and I close my eyes and keep holding her.

I don't know how long we stand there while she cries into my shirt, but when she finally straightens, all the mourners from the other service are gone.

Jess wipes at her face, then releases a sigh. "Sorry about your shirt."

I look down at my wrinkled and slightly damp shirt. "No problem." I give her a half smile.

Her blue eyes gaze back at me. Her cheeks are still tear stained, and her lip trembles when she nods. I link my fingers with hers, and she squeezes my hand. It's the best I can do, the best way I can stop myself from pulling her into my arms again. I need to let her do this her own way.

"Tell me about your parents," I say. It's something we've discussed before, of course, but never here, in front of their graves.

Her hand tightens around mine.

"My dad loved to make pancakes on the weekends when I was little," she says, her voice sounding nostalgic. But she's no longer crying, and that's good enough for me.

"I love pancakes," I say, encouraging her.

"I used to eat three of them, even though I'd get so stuffed, my stomach would hurt for hours afterward." She exhales. "His homemade syrup was the best."

"I'm starting to get hungry now."

She looks up at me again and lifts her eyebrows. "Remember, you can't take me on a date."

"I remember." And I need to keep remembering that. "Did your mom cook?" I ask, trying to refocus the conversation.

Jess blinks those beautiful blue eyes. "Yeah, when I was a kid she cooked a lot; not so much when I was a teen, though. She got a job at the library, which kept her pretty busy. It also kept her in the loop of hearing every terrible thing a teenager could possibly do, which she projected onto me."

Yes, I'd heard about her parents' strict parenting style.

She looks back at the headstone. "I know that I changed as a teenager—I mean everyone does. Hormones are crazy, bodies change, life becomes more intense . . . but she changed as a parent too. She stopped trusting me. She'd rather that I cut myself off from every normal high school experience and live in my room. Ironically, she would have been totally against homeschooling."

I let her rant about her mom. I didn't mean for this to happen, but I'm not going to try and steer the conversation. This is Jess's day, and I'm no longer her doctor.

"My mom and dad used to argue over me—my dad was the more lenient one." Jess shrugs. "I think he got tired of fighting with my mom, so he let her basically make all the decisions regarding me. And of course, Charles didn't help."

We haven't talked about Charles this whole time in the cemetery.

"I went to visit him, you know," she says.

I snap my head toward her. "What? In prison?"

She nods. "I got as far as the parking lot, then told Patty to take me back home."

"I'm impressed you got as far as the parking lot," I say, shaking my head. "You are amazing, Jess. Have I told you that?"

She moves closer to me, still holding my hand. "You have told me that, and I appreciate it."

"Can I *ask* you why you went to visit Charles?" I ask because I'm having a hard time comprehending her motivation. In truth, I worry that she's still bonded with him in some dysfunctional way. I know that's not a very accurate medical term, but my mind is reeling here.

"It's on my bucket list," she says matter-of-factly, as if visiting a brother like she has is something that she can set a goal for.

"Okay . . . why is it on your bucket list?" I prompt.

"So that I'm not afraid of the worst thing that could have happened to me," she says. "It was tough being in a psych center, but prison would have been much worse. If I can bring myself to visit my brother in prison and see him there, then I can feel like I've finally been avenged."

"That's very astute," I tell her. It makes sense. I had worried that she was going to say she had forgiveness on her bucket list or something. Of course, standing here in a cemetery, surrounded by statues of angels and deity, forgiveness is practically promoted at every turn.

"Thanks." She's looking at me again, and I like it. Too much.

"I wanted to ask you something, Logan," she says.

I think it's the first time she's called me Logan without me asking her to.

"I know that I sort of freaked you out when I shared my bucket list with you," she says.

"I don't think psychiatrists are allowed to get freaked out," I say in a teasing tone. "It's like a rule."

Her smile is faint, but her eyes are still focused on me. "I want you to be my first date." Before I can answer, she rushes on. "Not because I'm going to declare I have a crush on you, but because you're a man, and I want to go on a practice date."

"A practice date?"

"You know, to get the first one over with," she says, her blue eyes sparkling up at me. "So when I go on a real date, I'll have the awkwardness already conquered."

I stare down at her. I'm thinking about it, I'm really thinking about it, and I shouldn't be. I know what my answer must be, even though it will kill me to say it. "I'm sorry, Jess. I'd love to be your date, practice or not practice. But I don't think it's a good idea."

"Okay," she says in a soft voice.

I hate that she agrees with me.

She doesn't look defeated, though, and that makes me

like her even more. The Jess of only a few weeks ago might have reacted differently. This newer Jess is already much stronger, and she understands where I'm coming from. And points go to her for even trying. This fact alone makes my heart ache.

She releases my hand and bends to brush away some leaves near the gravestone. When she stands again, we are separate. This distance feels more final, permanent. It's not how I want things, but it's how they need to be.

When it's time for me to leave, I say, "Thank you for inviting me today."

Her eyes meet mine, and the depth of emotion in them twists at my heart. "You're the only person I wanted to be here with me."

I can't speak for a moment because the emotion is cutting off the words. Finally, I nod, and I think she understands. As I walk away, I want to turn around. I want to take her in my arms. But I continue to walk until I reach my motorcycle. But I can't leave, not yet.

So I wait until she's picked up by Patty. Jess smiles at Patty when she climbs into the car, and this makes me smile to myself. But as the car leaves the parking lot, it's as if a part of me has left with her.

CHAPTER 32

One Year Later

TODAY IS THE anniversary of my parents' deaths. This is my first thought that comes when I open my eyes in the bedroom of my new apartment—well, new to me. I stare up at the lavender ceiling that I painted myself. Patty told me that it's not typical to paint the ceiling a color, but I told her I wanted to look at a color when I first woke up. White walls and white ceilings remind me of the psychiatric center.

Also on the ceiling, I've affixed glow-in-the-dark stars and planets. They're the last thing that I see before I fall asleep at night.

I've awakened before my alarm, so I stay in bed for a few more minutes. Today, I'll visit the cemetery. I've gone several times since that first time with Logan. It's a surreal thought to think that my parents have been gone for eleven years. The passage of time is a strange thing. It's been a year since I've seen or talked to Logan too.

Yes, I've started to think of him as Logan. It's easier somehow. Since I know him so well as Dr. Mayer, if I think of him as Logan, then he just seems like a man who's part of my past. Not a man who dominates my present thoughts with the potential to dominate my future thoughts as well.

It's also the anniversary of the last text I've had from Logan. After that day in the cemetery together, and after I told him I'd like him to be my practice date, I thought he'd be pretty much finished with me. But later that night, he texted me.

One year. Give it one year, Jess.

I read that text over and over, and I've saved it all this time.

I didn't dare reply. I didn't know exactly what he meant. So I waited. Then I got tired of waiting. I almost texted him, but I didn't. Patty and Bruce set me up on a handful of dates, and I've decided that I hate blind dates. Patty and Bruce have strict instructions to never set me up again.

The soft patter of steps crosses my room, and my cat jumps on my bed.

I have a cat. I have an apartment. I have a car. I have a job.

Working four days a week at the corner bakery barely covers my expenses, but I don't need much. The car was a gift from Patty and Bruce. The cat, a stray. And someone prepaid my cell phone bill for three years—I know who that is.

"Hello, Juno," I tell the striped tabby on my bed. She starts to purr, but I'm not fooled. She doesn't want to snuggle; she's hungry. Besides, she's not allowed on my bed or in my bedroom, so she's purposely trying to get my attention.

"All right, I'm up," I say, pushing back the covers and climbing out of bed.

I've gotten rid of every stitch of clothing from the psychiatric center, and everything I now own was purchased by Patty or myself. Although lately I've taken to browsing at Goodwill. I'm careful to buy only what I absolutely need, though.

I walk into the kitchen and get out a scoop of cat food for Juno, then replenish her water bowl. She settles down to eat, and I scratch the top of her head for a couple of minutes.

Patty offered to go with me to the cemetery, but this is something I want to do on my own. Logan was right. I needed to give myself a year, to not rush or push things, to be patient with myself.

My bucket list is only halfway finished. But that's okay. Dr. Ferre has taught me that learning new things and having new experiences step by step is better than trying to jump in all at once.

I check out the window of my apartment. The weather looks temperamental, but it should stay warm at least. I cross to the fridge and pull out cream cheese, then I pop a sliced bagel into the toaster.

Just over a year ago, I wouldn't have been able to imagine this scenario at all. Living by myself feels like an accomplishment. And I don't feel lonely like I thought I might. That could also be due to the fact that Patty and Bruce come over a couple of times a week, and on my days off I volunteer at the local retirement home.

Spending time with people who've lived their lives, and lived them well, teaches me more than any self-help book ever could. I love to sit and do puzzles and play games. Erin would be proud.

Erin is mostly a good memory, but when I start to dwell on the more negative aspects of my earlier life, Dr. Ferre has counseled me to have three go-to's. Sometimes my go-to's change, but right now they're music, calling Patty or Bruce, and gardening. I think gardening will always be on my list.

I turn on the radio over the kitchen counter. The news is on, but I don't mind. It keeps me company, even though I don't pay much attention to what the DJs are talking about. I eat my bagel while nudging Juno away with my foot. She has an affinity for cream cheese, but I don't care for cat hairs in my food.

In the end, I leave a small morsel for Juno after all, and she gobbles it up.

Once I'm showered and dressed, I make the drive to the cemetery, which I've pulled up on the maps app on my cell phone. I can't help but think of Logan every time I use the phone, but I no longer cringe about the memories of asking him on a date and him turning me down.

He was right to do it. Even if I did fantasize that he might like me—his patient—I needed to become me.

I see the cemetery and turn into the parking lot. The breeze has become stiff, and the clouds have turned a deep gray. There's no funeral service, so I feel like I'm practically the only one on the grounds.

I know there's at least someone in the office building by the sight of another car in the parking lot. I grab my jacket, pull it on, then pick up the roses I've set on the passenger seat. Next I grab a water bottle and scrub brush I've also brought along, and I make my way across the now-familiar cemetery.

I don't stop to read any of the headstones. I take my time walking through and appreciating the peaceful beauty of the flowers, grass, and stones.

My parents' headstone is well taken care of, since I've made it part of my duty. I'm the only one who visits regularly. When I reach their grave, I proceed to pour the water I brought over the headstone, then use the scrub brush to gently clean away the dirt and the occasional bird refuse.

Moments later, the headstone glistens a darker color. Then I set the roses in front. I sit cross legged and pick at some of the grass. I don't say anything; I don't need to.

I don't know how much time has passed when I pull out

my notebook. Leafing through the pages, I turn down the corners of the goals that I've completed. Some of them might seem silly—but each one has been a milestone for me. "Visit a carnival and go on every single ride." Check. "Take a yoga class." Check. I made it through three sessions, then decided to do them at home from YouTube videos.

I look at the ones I have yet to accomplish. "Visit the psychiatric center." I have mixed feelings about seeing the patients again, but I'd like to see Patrick and Marlene.

"Write Charles a letter." I've decided not to visit him or to see him in any way. But one day I want to write him a letter detailing my feelings from the time things between us were sour—which is as long as I can remember. I don't know if he'll ever read it, but that doesn't matter to me. I need to write it.

"Write Trevor a letter." Trevor served nine months and is currently on a five-year probation. I don't plan to see him either. But I'm going to write him a letter too. Someday.

"First kiss." That one might take a while. I've decided that my "firsts" will be things I do since I've been free. What happened to the old Jess doesn't count for the goals in my notebook.

I add another goal in my notebook. "Find out what Logan meant when he said to 'give it a year.'" It's been a year exactly, and he might not even want to hear from me. A lot can change in a year. I'm a testament of that.

I rise to my feet and brush off my worn jeans that I bought at the thrift store. I'm much better at picking out clothing that fits me now. The sound of a motorcycle starts up, and I look toward the cemetery parking lot. The row of trees blocks me from seeing anyone, though. I don't remember seeing a motorcycle when I first arrived.

I turn back to my parents' grave and pick up the empty water bottle and scrub brush. Then I make my way to the car and drive to my apartment.

Juno greets me at the door, only to run outside and into the bushes. My apartment suddenly feels very empty, and I don't work again until tomorrow, so I decide to visit Patty and Bruce. I'm not good with cloudy afternoons and nothing to stay focused on.

I lock my apartment door and get back in the car.

Driving myself gives me a sense of independence, and it's a heady feeling to know that I can drive anywhere. I can even keep driving until I end up someplace completely new. But I'm not ready for that. Maybe I'll add it to my bucket list.

As I pass the beach near Patty's house, I notice a motorcycle in the parking lot. Logan drives one. A lot of people do. I don't know enough about motorcycles to recognize Logan's. Then I remember that I heard one at the cemetery.

I slow down and turn into the beach parking lot. No one's at the beach—the day is too dismal for that, it seems. I wonder who the motorcycle belongs to, while at the same time I don't know why I even care.

Climbing out of my car, I zip up my jacket and walk toward the sand. Then I see a man down the beach, standing near the surf, watching the churning waves.

I know it's him. *Logan.*

It has to be. I start walking toward him, and he doesn't see me for a while. I don't know what he's doing here, and I'm not exactly sure what he's been doing over the past year. All I know is that my feet have a mind of their own.

When I'm about ten yards away, Logan looks over his shoulder and sees me.

There's surprise on his face, and . . . recognition. He stares at me for a moment, and I'm not sure how to read his expression. Is he happy to see me?

Then he smiles, and my entire body feels warm despite the cool breeze.

He starts to move toward me, and I realize that I'm

smiling too. When we reach each other, he doesn't even hesitate to pull me into a tight hug.

I wrap my arms about his neck and hang on. I am stunned. Logan is on this beach, and he's hugging me. His neck is warm and smells of sea air and spice. The edges of his hair brush against my cheek with the wind, and I can feel his heart pounding against my own chest.

When we draw away from each other, I'm breathless.

"You're here," Logan says, his eyes that warm brown I could never forget.

"*You're* here," I say with a laugh.

He laughs too. And then we're hugging again, and it's different this time. Slow. Serious. He buries his face against my neck as if he wants to breathe me in.

When he draws away, he tucks a blowing strand of my hair behind my ear. His hand lingers on my cheek, then he finally drops it. My heart is racing like mad with all this touching.

He steps back, shoving his hands in his pockets. The wind tugs at his fitted T-shirt and jeans. He's barefoot, and I can't help but notice that he's seems even leaner and fitter than I remember. Maybe it's been a long time.

"I was at the cemetery," he says in a low voice, his gaze searching mine, as if he's worried I won't approve. "I wanted to talk to you there, but when I saw you, I changed my mind . . . I didn't want to intrude."

"I thought I heard a motorcycle."

His smile is faint, but he's still gazing at me, quite intensely. "That was me."

"How have you been?" I ask.

I expect him to give the generic answer of "fine," but instead he says, "Wondering how *you're* doing."

I spread my arms to tease him. "You tell me, Dr. Mayer. How do I look like I'm doing?"

He shakes his head, still smiling. "You're amazing, Jess."

Raising my brows, I say, "Yeah, I've heard that before."

"And you're beautiful," he continues.

My heart misses a beat.

"Stunning, really," he says, and I don't know if I can process any more compliments from him. "You seem to shine from the inside out. It's like you're a beacon or something. An angel."

"I'm hardly an angel." I fold my arms and tilt my head. His words sound wistful, as if he's sad about something. I never thought our roles would be reversed and that I'd be questioning him about his emotions. "Are you all right? You seem a little . . . tense."

"Yeah," he says, rubbing the back of his neck. "I feel a little tense."

I move closer, and I want to hug him, or take his hand, or do something to comfort him. But we're well past the greeting stage.

"Do you want to talk about it?" I ask, still feeling strange with this role reversal.

"If you really want to hear it."

"Definitely." This time I do reach for his hand. His fingers link through mine easily, naturally.

Of course, there's nothing easy about my pounding pulse.

"I can't stop thinking about you," he says. "I haven't since the first time we met. For a while, I thought I was just intrigued by your memory loss and your tragic story. I mean, I was treading into uncharted psychological territory, and it was fascinating. But I soon learned my interest in you went much deeper than what should be a doctor's interest in a patient."

His face is flushed, and I don't know if I should find this appealing or not, but I do.

He's talking so fast that I'm not sure if I'm catching all of his meaning. It's like he's memorized stage lines and is racing through them.

"Although I refused to admit that I might . . . care about you more than I should," Logan continues. "But . . . that last day in my office something changed. I know that you left in a hurry and our conversation was cut short. Yet, from then on I started to wonder if there was ever a possibility for us to ever . . ."

"To ever go on a date?" I say. I've decided that Dr. Logan Mayer is a master at beating around the bush.

"That's one way to put it." He takes my other hand so that he's holding both of my hands now. He faces me as the ocean breeze pushes around us. "I've had a year to think of my mistakes with you."

"Mistakes?" I'm not expecting this.

"I shouldn't have made you feel like I was pushing you away." He's standing close to me now. "Because that's the last thing I wanted to do. It took me a while to *allow* myself to think of you as someone other than a patient."

I don't look away from him. The old Jess might have, but the new Jess isn't going to let this man get away again. "I'm not your patient anymore."

"I realize that." His lips quirk. His gaze seems to soak me in, and I'm the one flushing now. "I miss seeing you on a regular basis." He pauses. "Do you think we could change that?"

"You want to be my doctor again?" I don't really believe this, but I have to ask.

"No," he says, leaning down. "I want to take you on a *real* date, and not a practice date."

I lift my eyebrows. "I've already been dating."

He seems to falter, but he says in a false cheerful tone, "That's really great."

"You don't seem too excited for me," I say, goading him.

"I'm . . ." He releases my hands. "I'm glad. It's what you should be doing. I hope you can have a good relationship with someone you trust."

"You're sort of dense for being such a great psychiatrist." I step closer this time and run my hands up his chest. I know I'm being forward. And I can thank Dr. Ferre for telling me that if I don't take charge of my life, then it will take charge of me. So I smile up at Logan. "I'd love to go on a date with you."

He stares at me for a second, then breaks out into a smile. "Great. What are you doing now?"

I blink. "Now? Um . . ."

"We could go grab something to eat if you're hungry."

It's all happening so fast that I can hardly think. "All right. Do you want to park your motorcycle at my apartment, and we can take my car? I should probably grab a jacket too."

"Your apartment?"

"I've been there only a few weeks," I say. "It's not much, but I'm paying for it myself with my job at a bakery. I even have a cat."

He chuckles. "I'd love to meet your cat."

We walk to the parking lot, and I point to the lone car, as if he couldn't guess. "Here it is." The only other vehicle is his motorcycle.

He turns to look at me. "I'm proud of you, Jess."

My eyes sting with the praise. "Thanks, I'm sort of proud of me too."

"You should be," he says, crossing to his motorcycle and picking up his helmet.

I open the door to my car. "Follow me."

He laughs. "Lead the way."

CHAPTER 33

JESS LIVES IN a quaint neighborhood that's complete with a newspaper shop, bakery, and a small grocery store. When I stopped at the beach, I of course had her on my mind and was even tempted to visit her at Patty's. Now that I know she has her own place, I'm glad I didn't knock on Patty's door.

I'm not sure if Patty and Bruce would approve of my interest in Jess. But I've spent over a year trying to tamp it down, telling myself that I probably just feel a sense of protection over her.

Now the year has passed, and I didn't forget her. In fact, more and more things would remind me of her. A commercial for gardening tools, a blonde woman walking in front of me, Sandra wearing the same color blue as Jess's eyes, an emailed update from Gwen on either Trevor Mills or Charles Harper.

Jess pulls into the parking lot of a two-story apartment building. It's an older building, but the landscaping is kept up, and the parking lot is in decent shape. I park my motorcycle by the outer curb and take off my helmet.

A short distance away, Jess climbs out of her car, and I'm so pleased to see her doing such an ordinary act. She's truly an independent woman. I love seeing her this way.

Jess motions for me to follow her, and I cross the side-walk. The wind is quite fierce now, pushing the dark clouds across the sky in a race. It looks like we're in for a deluge.

The first drops land as we reach her door. She fumbles with the keys for a second, then gets the door open. A cat comes out of nowhere and darts through my legs and into the apartment.

"Oh, there you are, Juno," Jess says to the cat. She picks up the creature and cuddles it, crooning, "You're so cold, you poor thing."

I shut the front door. "I don't think cats get cold with all that fur on them."

She looks up at me, her brows lifted.

I see that I do have competition after all. Not from other "dates" but from a striped cat.

"Juno, this is Logan," Jess says, turning the cat's head toward me. The cat surveys me with bored green eyes. "Logan, this is Juno. She might take a while to warm up to you, but she's a sweetheart."

I shrug. "Well, I have plenty of time."

Jess smirks at me. Another thing I love about this "new Jess"—she teases me, and I can tease her back.

The rain starts in earnest outside.

She sets down the cat, who takes off down the hall. "What do you think?" she asks, spreading her arms wide. "Pretty great, huh?"

I glance about me. The kitchen table has two chairs, and there's a love seat and an armchair in the small adjoining living room. No TV, just a bookshelf and a coffee table. And several houseplants. Of course. The place is simple but cozy. "It *is* great." Then I spy a whole row of herb plants on her kitchen counter. I'm not surprised in the least. "It looks like you brought your garden inside."

She laughs. "I wish I had a garden. The landlord said I can build up the patch on the side of the building, but I won't be able to grow plants that require a lot of sun since that area is in the shade most of the time."

I love that her apartment feels so normal, and I love seeing her excited about something. "I'm sure that you'll do wonders with that patch of dirt." I can't stop watching her, and she isn't looking away from me.

"There's a café on the corner that has great soup and salads. Do you want to try it?"

"I'd love to," I say honestly.

She fetches a jacket and umbrella from the hall closet, then turns to me and smiles expectantly.

It's a moment I know I'll never forget: A vision of confident and beautiful Jess. Happy Jess.

I open the door, and we step out into the rain. She holds on to my arm as we walk down the wet sidewalk, and I hold the umbrella above both of us. The wind and rain patter against my pants legs, but I don't mind. When we reach the café, I'm immediately charmed. The smell of good food, baking bread, and herbs greets us. We order, then take our seats in a cozy corner. We're practically alone in the café; no one else has braved the weather.

As I look across the table at Jess as she talks, I am fascinated. I hang on her every word. I am lost in everything that she is.

The server brings our food, and Jess thanks him with a smile. The young man smiles back, and I see she's charmed more than just me—Jess has found her way into the world.

It seems that we've been sitting and eating for only a few minutes when my phone buzzes. I check to see a calendar reminder for a phone call session with a client. Time has flown, but I don't want to call it an evening. I don't want to say goodbye.

"Do you need to call someone?" Jess asks, eyeing my phone.

"It's an appointment reminder," I say. "I have to call a client in an hour." I clear my throat. "What are you doing tomorrow night?"

Her hesitation makes me stiffen. This is the first time since we ran into each other at the beach that her eyes hold anything but joy. My heart sinks, and I hope that I haven't been too forward.

"I'm going to a book club," Jess says in an apologetic voice.

"That's great," I say, but why the apology? We can go out another night. But before I can make the suggestion, she cuts me off.

"Logan, I need to tell you something important," she says in a rush as if she's been waiting to say this for a while. "I didn't write it on my bucket list because I didn't want it to be something to check off."

When she looks down at her clasped hands resting on the table, I begin to worry. Has she been having nightmares? Has she been experiencing new anxieties? The human brain is remarkable, but PTSD is a serious condition.

Her gaze connects with mine again, and there are tears in her eyes. "I love you, Logan. I have loved you for a long time. You rescued me from a literal hell. But to you I will always be a patient."

My stomach hurts. "No, Jess—"

She grabs my hand. "There are some things I need to put in the past—forever—if I'm ever going to completely live in the future. You are part of all that happened to me—a blessed part—but still a reminder of the pain. What makes this so hard is that I thought I'd fallen out of love with you, but I haven't. Yet I know that *we* will never work. When we're together, you'll always be the doctor, the rescuer, and I'll always be the lost and frightened girl. You and I together will never allow me to completely be free."

I can't breathe. I can't move. "Jess . . ." Tears burn in my own eyes because as I hold her gaze, I know she's right. Right now, *she* is the psychiatrist with all the answers.

I wipe at my face, and her lip trembles as tears fall from her eyes. Finally, I release a shaky breath and stand. Then I hold out my hand, and she takes it. Together, we walk out of the café. The rain has stopped, leaving behind the fragrance of fresh earth and blooming flowers.

We don't speak as we walk back to her apartment. At her doorstep, she releases my hand and turns to face me.

"Goodbye, Logan," she whispers.

I stare at her for what I know will be the last time. I won't be crossing her threshold again. I will never forget her blue eyes, her many expressions, the touch of her skin. Slowly, I lean down and press a kiss on her cool cheek. She doesn't move. When I straighten, my throat is tight. "I love you too, Jess."

She holds my gaze for a few seconds, and then she nods and moves away. She unlocks her door and disappears inside.

I don't know how long I stare at her closed door, but finally the sound of returning rain urges me off her doorstep and into the dark night. I strap on my helmet and start up the motorcycle. The familiar humming vibration of the engine is like an echo of my weeping heart.

As I drive along the roads toward home, I think of a remarkable woman who was a slip of a girl a year ago. I think of the changes she's made and continues to make. I think of the woman she is now and how she is the strongest and most amazing person I've ever known. I will miss her.

As I drive through the streets of La Jolla, I don't feel the cold or the rain, because everything inside me is warm.

Jess has won.

And Jess is free.

H.B. Moore is a four-time *USA Today* bestselling author. She writes historical thrillers under the pen name H.B. Moore; her latest thrillers include *Slave Queen* and *The Killing Curse*. Under the name Heather B. Moore, she writes romance and women's fiction, and her newest releases include the historical novel *Condemn Me Not: Accused of Witchcraft*. She's also the coauthor of the *USA Today* bestselling series: A Timeless Romance Anthology. Heather is represented by Dystel, Goderich, and Bourret Literary Agency.

For book updates, sign up for Heather's email list: hbmoore.com/contact
Website: HBMoore.com
Facebook: Fans of H. B. Moore
Blog: MyWritersLair.blogspot.com
Instagram: @authorhbmoore
Twitter: @HeatherBMoore

ACKNOWLEDGMENTS

Many thanks to:

Susan Aylworth, who read more than one version of this story and gave me much-needed advice.

And many thanks to the following readers who read this manuscript under a very tight deadline and gave me valuable feedback: Autumn Needs, Laura Char, Kathleen Brebes, Tabitha Valencic, Katie Larson, and Jessica Cottam.

A final thanks to Jane Dystel, Lauren Abramo, and Ann Leslie Tuttle.